MW00473587

The
BILLIONAIRE'S
Desire

The BILLIONAIRE'S Desire

CASSIE CROSS

Cover design by Mayhem Cover Creations
Interior formatted by

E.M.
TIPPETTS
BOOK DESIGNS

emtippettsbookdesigns.com

For the latest news on upcoming releases, please visit
CassieCross.com

CHAPTER
One

*A*nyone with half a brain would probably tell you that falling in love with your boss is the worst possible thing you could do in the business world. But they don't know what Abby Waters does: it's not the love that gets you in trouble, it's the lust. That insatiable, hormone-driven gateway drug that gives you a taste of the thing you fantasize about the most and leaves you wanting more and more. It's an unpredictable disease; simmering one minute, burning out of control the next.

That morning, she was simmering. The object of her desire, Cole Kerrigan, had just left the office for a late-morning meeting, and her best-friend-slash roommate, Becca, was waiting for Abby to join her for an early lunch at her favorite diner.

It was a gorgeous day outside; the first one since

1

November that Abby hadn't needed a coat, and she was giddy at the prospect of pulling her spring wardrobe out of storage. When she opened the diner's door, she immediately spotted Becca in the far corner, her blonde curls spilling down her back.

Like a true angel, Becca had already ordered for Abby, knowing how pressed for time she was and how rare it was for her to be able to go out to lunch. She was usually chained to her desk. Abby thanked Becca and she grinned, wearing a shade of lip gloss that Abby was certain she'd bought for herself last week. She was in too good of a mood though, so she decided not to call Becca out for being a thief.

"We come to the best diner in the city and you order a salad?" Abby asked, lifting a spoonful of the heartiest, most delicious chili the island of Manhattan had to offer to her lips.

Becca glared at her and tossed a few strands of hair over her shoulder. "You don't get to comment on my rabbit food, Abby. Especially since you use me as a guinea pig for all that godforsaken chocolate you insist on making every day."

Abby rolled her eyes. "No one makes you eat it. How am I supposed to eventually become New York's premier candy maker if I don't get some practice?"

Becca sighed, pushing a grape tomato around her plate. "Practice on the people you work with and leave my hips alone."

"The people I work with consider themselves obese if they can't fit into sample sizes, Beck. They wouldn't know good chocolate if they rolled around naked in it." Becca was tall, curvy in all the right places, and had absolutely no issues with her hips. Of course, no one could tell her that. To hear her talk about herself, you would think she was hideous.

"Besides," Abby said. "You love me."

"Eh." Becca shrugged, giving Abby an impassive look. After taking another bite of her salad, she reached into her huge tote bag and pulled out her copy of The City Whisper, Manhattan's own celebrity gossip paper, delivered to Abby and Becca's mailbox every morning.

"Really?" Abby asked, shaking her head. "During lunch?"

"I'm an addict, I can't help myself." Becca placed the paper on the table and thumbed through the first few pages, completely uninterested in the ads and desperate to get to the gossip. Her impatience was one of the things Abby loved most about her. "I like to see how the other half lives."

"They don't eat at hole-in-the wall diners, that's for sure." Abby leaned over, trying to read the headline Becca was fixated on. "And they don't read at the table, it's uncouth."

"Unless it's the Wall Street Journal." Becca quirked her brow, grinning.

"Or their trust fund statements."

"Probably." She flipped the page. "It's just, have you seen the slobs that ask us out? Stained t-shirt wearing fools who live in a one-bedroom apartment with their five roommates. Couldn't find your clit with two maps and a turn-by-turn navigation system."

Abby clapped her hand to her mouth to stifle her laugh and stop herself from spitting out her drink.

Becca held up the paper and pointed to a picture of a

hot-bodied man in soaking-wet swim trunks. "You can't tell me this guy wouldn't know what to do with you. Look at those abs, my god. And the shoulders, Abby. His shoulders! That muscle definition. I bet he could pick a girl up while he fucked her."

"Okay!" Abby flicked a few drops of ice water at Becca's face, trying to cool her down. "I get the picture."

"I don't think you do. Look at this man." She turned the paper so that Abby could get a better look. "Cole Kerrigan, I would let you do such dirty things to me."

Cole Kerrigan? Abby thought, her heart beating faster.

"What did you say?" Just the mention of his name made Abby forget her manners, and she grabbed the paper from Becca and examined it closer than she probably should have. It *was* him. Most of the country knew him as a 29-year-old billionaire and the city's most eligible bachelor. And even though he was those things, Abby couldn't help but see him as a little something more: the object of her out-of-control lust and a Grade A pain in her ass.

You see, Cole Kerrigan was her boss.

She had been working as his assistant at Kerrigan Corp. for six months, and had wanted him ever since she walked through the door for her interview. Cole made it difficult for her to like him most of the time, but it was never difficult to think about what he would look like half-naked. Thanks to Becca's obsession with gossip and the photographers at The City Whisper, Abby didn't have to imagine anymore.

Paparazzi, blessed be thy name.

Looking at his picture made him seem more unattainable

than ever. If the size of his bank account didn't make his life completely unfair already, he had to be gorgeous, too. Rich and gorgeous men didn't usually go for women like Abby. At least not according to her. She wasn't ugly, that's for sure. She was pretty in that plain, girl-next-door kind of way. With wavy brown hair, hazel eyes, and a fairly average body, she thought she was the kind of girl that a guy hit on in high school while he was lifeguarding for the summer, then quickly forgot about once he went off to college and realized that there was a whole world full of blondes and redheads to be had.

Cole had perfectly tanned skin and chestnut hair that Abby dreamed about running her fingers through. Clear, bluish-green eyes, like the water on an island shore. Most of the female population of the Eastern seaboard had a thing for him, and Abby certainly couldn't blame them, although she might've been able to put an end to those crushes by arranging for those lovelorn women to spend one day doing her job. She dealt with constant pressure, work that was never good enough, and nightly phone calls regarding all kinds of "emergencies" that just had to be tended to when all Abby really wanted to do was get some damn sleep. Sleep during which Abby would inevitably dream about Cole doing all the things to her that Becca just described.

Abby had only seen Cole shirtless once, and that vision fueled all the aforementioned dreaming. That day, she walked into his office to have him sign a few contracts, and he was changing into his gym clothes. Abby stood there, mouth agape, and Cole said nothing. He just looked at her with humor in his eyes and his lips quirked up into a smile because he knew she was appreciating the view.

He was correct.

"See, you know what I mean now, don't you?" Becca shoved a forkful of lettuce into her mouth. Truth be told, Abby had completely forgotten that Becca was even sitting there while she was dreaming about Cole's half-nakedness. At that point, Abby was kind of wishing she was alone.

Fortunately she had signed a non-disclosure agreement when she started working for Kerrigan Corp. No one in Abby's life knew that she worked for Cole, not even Becca. *Especially* not Becca.

"Yeah, yeah," Abby replied, examining the picture.

Cole had just climbed out of a pool, dripping wet, dark swim trunks clinging to his muscular thighs. Beads of water glistened on his chest and in the shallow valleys of his perfectly shaped abs. His hair was flung haphazardly across his forehead, like he'd shaken his head when he stepped out of the water. He was smiling in the photo, something he rarely did at work, and Abby would've given anything to know who he was smiling at. She was jealous of that woman already. Given Cole's reputation, Abby was certain that it was a woman.

The smile lit up his eyes and carved out a cute dimple in his cheek. Abby never had the chance to really look at Cole without worrying that he'd catch her staring. She was so fixated on him that it took her a while to realize that there was someone else in the corner of the picture. The someone Cole was smiling at, who was conveniently not named in the caption.

"Who is this?" Abby turned the paper toward Becca and pointed at the woman with the long blonde hair in the skimpy white bikini. She looked like she was having a blast, and never in her entire life had Abby been so irrationally jealous of another human being.

Cole's level of beauty usually attracted the same level of beauty. Models, actresses, people you only saw in magazines. Girls like Abby—short ones with unruly hair and a need for concealer—were usually the ones Cole asked to arrange romantic weekend getaways in Paris, not the ones he asked to go with him.

"I think that's a model. Her name is Kalia or something," Becca replied, sounding half as interested as she did earlier. She had an incredibly short attention span.

"Kalia what?"

"I don't know, she just goes by one name."

"Can you imagine the kind of confidence you have to have to go by one name?"

Becca shrugged. "If you looked like that, you'd have confidence too."

"Maybe she just has a horrible last name. Like… Funderbunk."

Becca looked at Abby, her brown eyes full of sympathy as she reached over and patted Abby's hand. "If that makes you feel better, sweetie."

For a moment, it did.

CHAPTER
Two

*C*ole Kerrigan stepped out of his limo onto the bustling Manhattan sidewalk, adjusting his Ray-Bans to shield his eyes from the blaring sun. As usual, the crowd seemed to slow down for him, clearing a path between the car and the front door of his office building. Women around him openly stared, while the men at least tried to not be so obvious about it.

The very second he took the first step toward the building, he saw her. Abigail must've had some sort of beacon implanted in her body that alerted him whenever she was around. Her presence stirred something inside of him that simultaneously made him uneasy and pumped him full of desire. She definitely made him hard.

"Abigail," he said as he walked toward her, nodding in her direction. She preferred to be called Abby, but he couldn't allow himself that small bit of familiarity. Every night she stayed late he had to force himself not to kiss her soft, full lips. It took every ounce of self-control he had not to ravage her. He'd never been as turned on by a woman as he was by her; she was so effortlessly beautiful, but had no idea. A lethal combination.

They walked together to the elevator lobby, the thrumming crowd giving them a wide berth. Cole pressed the 'up' button on the wall of the elevator bank, then turned to look at Abigail.

He could tell that she'd hurried back from lunch, because a few tendrils fell from the haphazard twist of hair piled up on the crown of her head, and her cheeks were flushed. He loved that look on her, and often thought about the things he could do to her that would make her cheeks flush even more. She was wearing a flattering button-down blouse that accentuated her curves, and her black skirt hugged her hips just so. He often thought about what it would feel like to grip those hips as Abigail rode him, her hair spilling over her perfect breasts.

It was an odd thing, Cole thought, that he could have his pick of gorgeous, scantily-clad women, but he always fixated on the curves of a woman whom he could not, and *should* not have.

Remembering the wool coat that he'd been carrying since he left his apartment this morning, he handed it to her, hoping its length would hide those flawless curves.

"You realize it's sixty-five degrees out, right?" she asked.

Above everything else, Cole enjoyed Abigail's smart

mouth, and counted their verbal sparring sessions among one of his favorite pastimes. Occasionally he'd rile her up just to hear whatever biting remark would roll off her tongue.

"When I left my apartment at five-thirty this morning, it most definitely was not sixty-five degrees outside." Cole fiddled with his gold cufflinks, hoping to distract himself. He didn't want her to think he was some pervert, incapable of not ogling her. But his eyes went to the floor, then to her shoes, then her calves…

"So it's okay with you if I put 'Human Coat Rack' as one of my duties on my next self-assessment?" Abigail shifted the coat to her other arm when the elevator door finally opened and the two of them stepped inside.

Cole reached forward and pressed the button for the 40th floor. "You can do what you like, Abigail, but that doesn't come with a pay raise." He stifled a smile as he heard her huff. He imagined she was probably rolling her eyes at him.

"I almost forgot," Abigail said, holding a bag out to Cole.

"What is this?" He raised his brow, surprised at her offering.

"It's your lunch. A sandwich."

"A sandwich," he repeated dumbly.

"Yes, a sandwich," she replied slowly. "Deli meat and cheese between two slices of bread, usually paired with a pickle. Common lunch staple, popular among the working class."

God, he loved that mouth. Cole wanted to press the emergency stop, so he could pull her close to him and feel those tight curves against his body.

"I thought you might be hungry, so I brought something in case you didn't have time to grab a bite to eat after your meeting. If you don't want it, I'll put it in the fridge and have it for dinner." As if on cue, he felt his stomach rumble, so he reached out and took the bag.

"I didn't have time to eat," he replied, smiling. "This was very thoughtful of you."

"You're welcome," she said under her breath, even though he hadn't thanked her.

The elevator doors opened, and Cole stepped out into the lobby, walking toward his office with long, sure strides. He wanted to see more of that fire in her; he was beginning to need it as much as he needed air. And he had a plan. So he looked straight ahead when he said the following words.

"Cancel your plans for this evening. You need to finish the monthly sales report before you can leave."

Behind him, he could feel her eyes boring through his back, a white-hot fire-filled stare.

He grinned.

CHAPTER
Three

I hate numbers.
     I hate monthly sales reports.
I hate this job.

Abby had been working on this data for the better part of four hours, and since it was nearly eight o'clock and she hadn't eaten since lunch, her stomach was growling. She had been fussing with the figures, but there was one that wasn't adding up and she couldn't figure out where the mistake was. She knew Cole would be able to find it, but she wanted to beat him to the punch.

He hadn't stepped foot outside of his office since three, and in her hunger-induced delirium, Abby briefly wondered if he wanted something to eat as badly as she did.

Probably not, he's a freak that way, she thought. She wished she'd kept the sandwich that she gave him for herself.

She was just about to go over the figures again when a chat window popped up on her computer screen.

Are you almost finished?

Even in print, Cole was impatient. Abby took a few moments to respond, trying to figure out exactly what to type. She really didn't want to tell him that there was a mistake she couldn't find. In the end, she kept it simple.

I'm just double-checking the numbers.

She had barely hit the return key before Cole replied.

In my office immediately. Bring the report.

The report was up on Kerrigan's intranet site in Cole's network folder. Abby wouldn't have been surprised if he had been watching her work the entire time and had already taken a look at the report. In fact, she figured he'd probably already located the mistake and was tired of waiting for her to find it herself. That meant she was in for a real treat when she walked into his office.

Abby took a deep breath to calm her temper and steady her nerves. She was so tired, hungry and frustrated that she was worried that if he started harping on her, she was going to lose it.

Abby stood and made her way to Cole's office, gripping the report in her fingers. Her heart was thumping in time with her footsteps. The oversized mahogany door creaked as she pushed it open, making it sound like she was in a horror movie, which didn't help at all. And, when she thought her heart couldn't beat any faster, it proved her wrong when she looked up and saw Cole sitting behind his desk.

The task lighting cast a soft glow on his face, creating shadows that accentuated his bone structure. His tie was loosened a bit, his sleeves were rolled up to the middle of his forearms, and he looked so sexy that Abby had to bite her lip to keep herself from sighing dreamily. Seeing him look like that might make the reaming she was about to get worthwhile. All of a sudden, her nervousness and dread calmed immediately and melted into that damned lust she was always trying to fend off. She couldn't escape it, and it was all Becca's fault for revving it into high gear by showing her Cole's half-naked picture this afternoon at lunch.

"You wanted to see me?" Abby's shaky voice stated the obvious. All she wanted was for him to look up at her with his piercing eyes, but he insisted on staring down at the papers in front of him.

"Turn to page thirteen." The coldness in his voice prompted her to hurry to the seat on the opposite side of his desk.

The mistake was on page thirteen, and Abby knew that Cole was dying to show it to her. She flipped through the pages, her fingers shaking from all the adrenaline coursing through her veins. She used to be so calm and collected around him, and now she was starting to come apart at the seams.

Like a true shark, Cole sensed Abby's vulnerability and zeroed in on it. He stood and slowly walked over, giving her time to think over what was about to happen. He placed his hand next to hers on the desk, and leaned over her so closely that she could feel his tie brush her back. So closely she could smell him; that blend of starch and detergent that was so incredibly him, and made her want to bury her face in his neck because she couldn't get enough of it.

Think, Abby. Think, she reminded herself. *Now is not the time to let him distract you.*

Abby scanned the numbers on page thirteen, hoping to find her mistake, but she couldn't focus on anything other than Cole and his smell and how much she wanted him to pull her down onto the floor and fuck her into oblivion.

Cole reached over her shoulder and slid his finger down the paper until it came to rest beneath a row of data about halfway down the page. Nothing looked out of the ordinary to Abby, but then again, this report had thousands of rows of financials, and, unlike him, she hadn't committed them all to memory.

Abby's heart was pounding and at that moment, her stomach growled. She was certain Cole heard it, because she felt the air on her cheek as he let out an almost imperceptible laugh under his breath. Nervous and hungry, this slow reveal was about to push Abby over the edge. Little by little, second by second, all that lust was being swept away by a buzzing annoyance and low-level anger that she was beginning to feel down deep in her bones. She needed Cole to stop teasing her and just get this over with.

"Do you see this?" He tapped his finger beneath an eight-figure number in the totals column.

Of course I see it, she thought. *It's right in front of my face.* She wanted to speak the words aloud, but didn't.

"What am I paying you for if you can't catch the simplest mistake? This particular group has shown a steady increase in sales over the past two quarters. How is it that this number is thirty-five percent less than it was last month?"

Abby wracked her brain trying to come up with an answer, but she couldn't think straight. It was her fault and she should've taken responsibility, but the heat of the moment made her say something else.

"This isn't my data," she replied. Technically, it was the truth. She just compiled the numbers, so she wasn't as familiar with them as she should've been. "I'll check with John-"

"I don't care whose data it is." His words were a low grumble, and Abby knew that she was making him angry. The spiteful part of her wanted to make him even angrier for making her stay so late and then yelling at her to boot. "It's your job to compile it, Abigail. It's your job to make sure it's correct before I waste my time looking at data that isn't right."

Abby wanted to mention to Cole that he wasn't exactly wasting his time if he could tell her that a number was wrong just by looking at it. "First of all," she said, sounding much louder than she should have, "I told you I was still double-checking the numbers. I never said that I was finished. And you're not wasting your time if you can pick that number out of a fifty-page report and tell me that it's incorrect. And, honestly, if I spent all of my time tracking down incorrect data that *your* employees sent me, I'd never be able to do anything else!" Abby could've run down a list of the rest of her workload, but Cole knew what it was. He was the one who gave it to her.

"And I'm sure you'd do it in the most efficient way possible," Cole said sarcastically, rolling his eyes as he threw her report into the recycle bin.

Abby could handle a lot of things, but she could not handle Cole poking fun at her work ethic or her efficiency. She took care of twice the workload of any of his previous assistants. He knew that, and must've said what he said to get under her skin.

Well, two can play at that game.

Abby stood. Cole was no more than a foot away from her, and her blood was still thrumming from having him in such proximity. She wanted her calm collectedness back, so she made sure to look Cole in the eyes when she said the following words.

"Alex and John aren't my employees, and they provided me with incorrect data. You should probably be reprimanding them, Cole." Cole's eyes widened when Abby said his name, and even though he was a foot taller than she was, she felt powerful in that moment. "I didn't make this mistake. They did. And if you want to lecture someone about efficiency, you should probably be lecturing one of them."

Cole stepped forward, closing the distance between himself and Abby. Abby reached down and smoothed her skirt; it gave her something to do to steady her hands.

Their faces were inches apart, and Cole's pale blue eyes were too intense. Abby wanted them looking at her, but not like this. Not in anger, or whatever it was he was feeling. Still, she wasn't going to back down.

"You did make this mistake, Abigail. Ultimately this is your responsibility." Cole thrived on moments like this, and Abby knew that he wanted her to fight back. She wasn't going to give him the satisfaction.

He stared her down, and she could see his breathing quicken. It was too much to look him in the eyes, so she focused on his mouth, those supple lips. Even though she was so incredibly heated, anger making her skin thrum all the way down to her fingertips, all Abby could think about was what would happen if she grabbed Cole's tie and pulled his lips to hers. She had never wanted anything so badly in her life.

As Cole stared at Abby and Abby stared at Cole's mouth, the air in the room changed. It shifted in such a palpable way that it was vibrating in the space between them.

Not wanting Cole to think that he had won, Abby gave him a hard look and narrowed his eyes. "I will fix it. *Sir.*"

She had meant the last word to get under his skin, but she didn't think it would have quite the effect on him that it did. It set off a fire in him, and the tide had shifted, she could feel it. Cole and Abby looked at each other for a long while before he broke her gaze to look down at her mouth.

The whole exchange had Abby practically bouncing, she was so turned on, but she couldn't find it within herself to believe that Cole was turned on, too. Even so, she knew she needed to get out of that room before she made a fool of herself.

She didn't even make it two steps before Cole clasped his hand around her wrist. She could practically feel the fire through his skin, and the warmth of his touch surprised her. She gasped as he pulled her to him, and in one swift move she was pinned to the desk. She had never experienced such opposite reactions to someone in her entire life. She wanted Cole to rip off her clothes, and she wanted to smack him at the same time.

Cole leaned in close and Abby closed her eyes as she breathed him in, unable to believe that this was really happening.

"You drive me crazy," he said in a gravely voice, his words so full of want that they made her heart skip a beat. Those words flipped a switch inside of her, and all of the doubt went away, replaced by desire. For months she'd wanted this to happen, and now it was all within her reach. "You've been driving me crazy since the first day you walked through this door."

"I can drive you crazier." Abby wrapped her fingers around Cole's tie like she'd wanted to do before, and his beautiful eyes searched her own. Abby wondered if he was as surprised as she was that this was happening. She didn't care about her job or her future in that moment, she just cared about what his lips tasted like. So she pushed herself up on her toes and kissed his beautiful mouth, opening up to him as his tongue swept across hers.

Cole grabbed Abby's hips, sliding her onto his desk, and she spread her legs to give him room to get closer. As they kissed, Abby slid her fingers through Cole's soft, perfect hair. He pressed his chest against hers and back she went, her elbows resting on the desk. She wrapped her legs around him, feeling his erection against the inside of her thigh. Cole was rich, powerful, and more handsome than anyone Abby had ever seen, and knowing she could make him that hard urged her on. She reached down and stroked his dick, and their kisses grew frantic. Cole cupped her breast through her shirt, gently squeezing Abby's nipples as she moaned in his mouth.

"You like that, don't you?"

Abby could feel Cole's smile as his mouth moved to her neck.

She nodded, she couldn't help it. "More," she said, grinding against his erection. She wanted Cole inside of her. Now.

Too impatient for buttons, Cole pulled at Abby's shirt, popping it open until just below her bra. He kissed his way down her neck, laving her skin, then slowly slid down the cups of her bra and traced his tongue around her left nipple, then her right. He looked up at her wearing a devilish grin as he took her nipple into his mouth, sucking a little before he gently pinched it between his teeth.

Abby gasped and lifted her hips to grind against Cole again, a move that left him breathless. Just that bit of friction made Abby impatient for more, so she reached down and unbuckled his belt, then pulled at the button on his pants.

After she finally had him unbuttoned and unzipped she pushed his boxers down, freeing his dick. Abby admired its beauty: thick, hard, and ready for her. She slid her hand down the shaft and he strained against her palm, kissing her harder than before as her fingers glided over his warm, throbbing skin.

Cole slid up her skirt and slowly pulled her panties down before he reached across the desk and pulled a condom out of his wallet.

Abby wrapped her arms around his neck as he rolled it on, all the while nibbling impatiently on his earlobe.

"Hurry up," she said.

Cole let out a mischievous laugh, his hands moving agonizingly slowly.

Abby huffed. "You can't just take your sweet time when you've got a girl all spread out on your desk, waiting for you to fuck her." She was surprised at the words that came out of her mouth, but they felt right in the moment.

"Wanna bet?" Cole pulled away and for the first time since this started, Abby got a really good look at him.

God, he's so beautiful. Abby couldn't believe this was happening, and she wasn't about to waste a single second of it.

Cole, however, was intent on punishing Abby for her impatience.

"I'll make you wait for as long as it pleases me, Abigail. Until you're begging me to make you come."

Abby wanted to beg him now, but there was a sadistic part of her that wanted to see what he was going to do to her

21

while he made her wait.

Cole reached behind her, cupping her ass, and pulled her almost to the edge of the desk. Then he spread her legs as far as they would go, until the sides of her knees were touching the wood. Slowly, he brought his fingers to his mouth and licked them.

The next sensation Abby felt was just a whisper of a touch between her thighs as Cole's fingertips teased the sides of her clit, never once touching her with the pressure she so desperately craved.

"You're so wet," he said. There was a hint of wonder in his voice that confused Abby, because she was certain that countless women before her had the same reaction to him.

Cole slipped two fingers inside of Abby, and she couldn't help herself, she wrapped her arms around his neck and their lips crashed together again and again, the two of them so full of desire as she moved her hips in quick thrusts against his hand, needing to feel some kind of satisfaction.

"Please," Abby begged. She couldn't wait any longer.

"Ask me again."

"Please." Abby was so breathless, her pleading almost sounded like a whine.

"What do you want?"

"I want you to make me come."

With Abby's ass still near the edge of Cole's desk, her legs still parted, he pulled her close to him so her head was cradled against his neck. She breathed deep, loving his smell. His talented fingers moved in a way that made Abby cry out; they created such a delicious pressure inside of her.

She rocked against the pad of his hand, faster and faster, and Cole held her up when she lost all strength in her arms.

"I should make you wait." Cole's mouth was pressed against Abby's ear, his voice husky and low, and he pulled his hand away quickly just to tease her. "I've been waiting for you for months."

He has? Abby couldn't even process that admission.

"Please, please, please." Abby repeated in a long, soft string of completely indistinguishable words. Cole resumed his ministrations, and Abby was desperately trying to stop herself from giving into the pleasure, wanting to savor this feeling a little while longer.

"If you think I'm talented with my hands, wait until you find out how good I can make you feel with my cock."

Abby couldn't wait for that and neither could her body, because his words made her explode, her muscles squeezing his fingers as she cried out.

Abby was still coming when Cole pressed his forehead against hers and splayed his palms out on his desk, his hands on either side of her hips as he pushed into her. Abby's skin was slick and her body weak, but she wanted more of him, and couldn't help but sigh as he slid inside. He made her feel so full; fuller than anyone ever had before.

"You feel so fucking perfect," Cole said, his voice strained. "I knew you would feel good, but this…" His voice trailed off as he focused on his first few deep thrusts, and Abby ground against him when he was so close, wanting to take advantage of her position.

"Harder," Abby said, gasping. "Fuck me harder. You're

not the only one who's been waiting." She gripped Cole's ass, desperate for him to be closer, desperate to get caught up in that wave of ecstasy again.

Cole kissed her, and when he pulled back, Abby looked into his hooded eyes. She thought they were perfect on a regular day, but a regular day had nothing on their beauty when he looked at her like this, all consumed with lust as he pounded inside of her. Cole began moving even faster as she wrapped her arms around him, holding on as tightly as she could. His thumb circled her clit, stirring a tide inside her that began in her belly, slowly heating the rest of her as waves of pleasure lapped out to the rest of her body.

"I'm gonna…I'm gonna," she breathed, unable to complete a coherent sentence. She'd never come twice in one go before.

"You gonna come?"

Abby nodded.

"I want to feel it." Cole's lips brushed the shell of Abby's ear, his hot breath spurring her on and his thumb pressed against her clit, winding her into a frenzy. "Make me feel it."

Seconds later Abby cried out, and Cole kept thrusting through her orgasm as her muscles squeezed him, pleasure reverberating from her center all the way to her fingertips. He slid his hands beneath her ass and picked her up, pulling her against him. His breath was heavy—ragged and strained—and she wrapped her legs around his waist to hold herself up and give herself leverage to grind against him, making sure that she took every drop of pleasure from him that she could.

"Your turn," Abby breathed as Cole's bright blue eyes

found hers. She wanted him to feel everything she just felt, so she rotated her hips twice before he came undone, holding her tighter as he twitched inside of her, his head falling to her neck where he kissed her skin until he was spent.

Cole placed Abby back down on the desk and she leaned back, resting her body against the cool wood. Cole hovered over her for a few moments, and Abby savored the last of this perfect feeling. She didn't want to turn away because she wanted this to last as long as it could. She'd never had anyone like him before, and no one had ever made her feel the way Cole just did. Besides, she wasn't sure what was going to happen when the reality of what they'd done sank in.

Reality could wait just a while longer.

When Cole finally did pull away, he and Abby looked at each other before Cole turned and went into the washroom. It wasn't until he walked away that Abby realized she'd never even bothered to unbutton his shirt. Hers was still on too, even though most of the buttons had been popped off.

Abby tried to gracefully slide her undies back on, but there was really nothing graceful about cleaning up after a quickie with your boss. She almost had to laugh at the thought of it. She managed to smooth her skirt and get her bra back on correctly, all the while remembering the feel of Cole's stubble on her skin.

When Cole exited the bathroom, Abby was trying to figure out how she was going to get home with her blouse being completely decimated, all the buttons above her midriff having been popped off mid-fling. Briefly she wondered if she had enough safety pins in her desk to make herself presentable for the train ride.

Cole walked over to the closet on the far side of his office. From the corner of her eye, Abby could see him glancing in her direction a few times, and she tried to think of something to say to break the silence. If she made a big deal about the sex, it certainly wouldn't happen again, and she couldn't just ask him about the weather. Work, she figured, was the common denominator.

"I'll come in early tomorrow and fix those figures."

Cole nodded, pulling a crisp white shirt off its hanger. "I'll have a talk with Alex and John about the inaccuracy in their reporting."

Abby couldn't hide her smile. Cole admitting that Alex and John had a part in her mistake was a victory. She'd have to send them a thank you gift, because if they'd reported their numbers correctly, tonight never would've happened. Still, those words weren't exactly the ones Abby imagined she'd hear after a night like this. She laughed, thinking of all the times she'd fantasized about it, and how the reality was nothing at all like she'd imagined.

"What's so funny?" Cole asked.

"It's just that in all the times I thought about this happening—and believe me, I've thought about it a lot—I never imagined that the first thing you would say to me after would be, 'I'll have a talk with Alex and John about the inaccuracy in their reporting.'"

"What did you imagine me saying to you?" Cole asked, grinning.

Abby's heart nearly stopped. What would she have

wanted to hear? A million things, but she did her best to put on a playful expression before answering Cole as lightheartedly as she could.

"Oh, I don't know. That I've ruined you for all other women, that I was the best you've ever had. The usual."

Cole walked towards Abby, his expression unreadable as his eyes met hers. Not knowing what he was about to do, her heartbeat went haywire, pounding an uneasy rhythm inside her chest. Without saying a word, Cole placed the clean shirt he was holding across the back of the chair beside the two of them, then slid his fingers down the plackets of Abby's blouse. His knuckles gently skimmed her breasts, and even though Abby only felt him through her bra, she still got goosebumps.

Cole curled his fingers around the plackets and pulled, ripping off the remaining buttons, then pushed the fabric over Abby's shoulders. She shivered as she shrugged out of the sleeves and let the blouse fall to the floor. He reached over and grabbed the spare shirt he'd pulled from his closet and held it out so Abby could slide her arms through. It was ten times too big for her; her hands didn't even clear the cuffs.

"What are you-"

"You can't go home wearing that," Cole said, gesturing to Abby's discarded shirt as he started buttoning the new one from the bottom up. Abby watched as he dressed her, focusing on the deft movements of his fingers and the flawlessness of his skin.

When every last button was secure, Cole rolled up each of the sleeves. His blue eyes met Abby's for one fleeting moment, and then he brushed the underside of her chin with his index finger.

"My car is downstairs," he said softly. "Jack will take you home."

"I take the train all the time. I'll be alright."

Cole shook his head, then gently pushed a strand of Abby's hair behind her ear. "Not tonight."

"But won't he wonder why I'm wearing your shirt?"

Cole smiled, and Abby wanted to lick the dimple on his cheek.

"I don't pay him to wonder why you're wearing my shirt, I pay him to drive whomever I want wherever I want. And tonight, I want him to drive you home. I thought you would know by now," Cole said, dragging his finger along Abby's collarbone. "All of my employees are incredibly discreet."

Their eyes met as he said those words, and Abby understood exactly what he meant.

She must be discreet.

Abby looked at the clock, surprised at the time. "You have a conference call with Tokyo in two minutes."

Cole sighed. "I know."

Before Abby left, Cole kissed her. Long and slow and perfect, enough to make her want more, enough to make it difficult for her to leave him. But she didn't have a choice because as soon as his lips left hers, his phone rang. Abby watched him as he walked away and returned to his chair, right where she'd found him. She could hear her pulse beating in her ears, and her fingers were shaking.

Oh, what that man can do to me. There are so many

possibilities, and I want them all.

Abby made her way to the door, and was about to close it behind her when she heard Cole speak.

"Goodnight, Abigail," he said softly.

"Goodnight." It was the first time she liked the sound of her full name falling from his lips.

Later, when Abby was in bed, still wearing Cole's shirt, she replayed the events of the night over and over in her head, wondering if she'd imagined them. Wondering what they would say to each other in the morning.

Should I pretend like it never happened?

She wanted it to happen again (and again, and again). But if it was just a one-time thing, a lapse in judgment, could she live with that? Could she look at Cole the same way and be the same assistant to him that she was before he'd made her want to melt out of her own skin from the sheer pleasure he gave her?

She could.

She had to.

CHAPTER
Four

*I*t was well after midnight and Cole was still at work, sunken into his chair, staring out the window. He had chosen this office because he loved the view, but tonight he couldn't even appreciate the scenery. During tonight's teleconference with his Tokyo office, Cole was tipped off that one of his employees was attempting to sell information about KC-23, the codename for one of the biggest and most secretive software projects that the company had undertaken.

Cole's mind was swimming.

This was an entirely new situation for him. Even though he demanded a lot from his employees, he had always treated them well. He'd never had anyone betray him. The traitor's name was Josh Hamilton. Cole hired him straight out of the MBA program at Yale, Cole's alma mater, based on a recommendation from one of the faculty advisors that

Cole frequently consulted when he was recruiting. Cole even knew Josh's father. What he didn't know was exactly what Josh was attempting to sell.

While this new software was innovative, Kerrigan Corp. was mired in issues with patent attorneys, so the work was currently unprotected. That's why he had the people he trusted most working on the project.

Cole had just gotten off the phone with the head of the Chicago office, where Josh worked. They had agreed to start sending Josh false specs to limit the damage done until they could figure out exactly what he was up to, and, most importantly, if he was working alone. Then, Cole would fire Josh's ass and pursue whatever legal options were available to him.

Cole turned his chair back toward his desk to check his email. He was waiting for an email from the IT department in Chicago, detailing all of Josh's outgoing phone calls and chat conversations. Still nothing.

His gaze drifted to the edge of his desk, where he'd had Abigail only hours earlier. Cole should've been singularly focused on saving his company, but he couldn't stop thinking about Abigail. The sweet strawberry smell of her hair, the way her lips tasted, the warmth of her body when he slid into her. All the times he'd imagined fucking her (and he had imagined that a lot), he never dreamed she'd feel so exquisite. He never dreamed he could make her bloom with just one touch of his hand.

Hell, just thinking about her made him hard.

Abigail.

What was he going to do? He hadn't intended tonight to go the way that it did, although he couldn't say he was sorry for the outcome. He was going to have to navigate this carefully; he'd never had sex with an employee before. It was strictly against his rules. He'd written it into the company Code of Conduct, for Christ's sake. But Abigail, she was worth breaking rules for. Cole knew he couldn't settle for having her once. Hell, he wanted to have her again, just thinking about the way the brush of her hair across his wrist set his skin aflame.

Cole reached into his pants pocket and fished out his Blackberry, then pressed his Contacts button. Hers was the first name listed. His cock ached for her. He slid his hand down between his legs and allowed himself one stroke for relief. Cole refused to beat off to the memory of a woman he could have in his bed with the press of a button.

In fact, his thumb hovered over that button. He could call her and have his driver pick her up. She would come as soon as he asked, he knew that much. He could have her in his bed, fall asleep to the smell of her on his sheets. He could have her in this very chair, and watch her perfect tits bounce as she rode him.

Just as he was about to call her, someone called him. He pressed the button for the speaker phone.

"Hello?"

"Yes, sir. This is Clark from IT. I've just emailed you transcripts of Josh Hamilton's chat conversations and phone records. "

"Thank you, Clark." Cole went to end the call.

"Sir?"

"Yes," Cole replied, sounding exasperated.

"I happened to notice that there was one number he's been calling frequently over the past few days. It's a number in your office."

Cole could feel the adrenaline surging through his veins. "In my office?"

"Yes. It belongs to an Abigail Waters."

Cole's heart sank into his stomach. "Abigail Waters? You're sure?" He didn't want to believe it. He *couldn't* believe it.

"Positive. You'll see it when you open the call listing."

"Will you get me a call listing from Abigail's work phone, please?"

"Absolutely. I'll send it over as soon as I can."

"And I want to see his emails too."

"No problem."

"Thanks," Cole said, then ended the call.

Cole didn't like spying on his employees, but he wouldn't have any employees left to spy on if he allowed them to steal from him. Still, whatever it was that he had with Abigail was only going to be complicated by this. Cole repeatedly clicked on the Send/Receive button in his email client, waiting for Clark's message to appear.

A minute later, it did. The file was huge, no wonder it had taken so long.

There were two attachments. One with Josh's phone log in it, the other with the chat transcripts. Cole opted to open the phone log first.

He scanned the list of numbers, all of which appeared to be business related, and most of which were Abigail's direct line. The call log went back three months. At first, the calls to Abigail were sporadic, and lasted no longer than five minutes. Those, Cole figured, were probably work-related. At that point in time, Josh was still finishing up another project and only beginning to transition over to KC-23. The call frequency increased over the past three weeks, but each call lasted less than a minute; not long enough for any meaningful conversation. If Abigail was conspiring with Josh, Cole thought it would've been wise for Josh to use her personal cell to talk to her. If he had her personal cell, he wouldn't have called her work numbers every day.

Cole took a deep breath as a calm spread over him like a warm blanket. He was confident Abigail wasn't involved. Still, he wanted to check the chat transcripts to be sure. He clicked on that file.

Cole scrolled through work-related conversation after work-related conversation, only paying close attention to the ones Josh texted to Abigail, afraid of what he might find. There was some fairly lighthearted (for Abigail, at least) grumbling about workload, but what caught Cole's attention was the flirting. A wave of possessiveness came over Cole, and he had to fight off the urge to fly to Chicago to kick Josh's ass. He didn't stop to think about what it meant that he was as angry about the flirting as he was about Josh's attempted theft.

What is he doing?

Cole looked back over the messages—a task that made

his stomach turn—and realized that the flirting was mostly one-sided on Josh's end. That only brought him a small sense of satisfaction, because he still didn't understand why he was so persistent when Abigail clearly wasn't interested.

Then, it hit him.

Josh was trying to use Abigail to get to him.

Cole felt a fierce spark of protectiveness for Abigail deep within him. It was then that he realized that he was going to have to keep Josh Hamilton close, and Abigail even closer.

CHAPTER
Five

*A*bby arrived at work early the next morning, despite the fact that she spent an extra twenty minutes on her hair and makeup. She didn't know who she thought she was fooling. Cole was the most observant person she'd ever met, and he would know that something was up when he saw her putting in more effort than she normally did. Not that she went into the office looking like a slob, but she was usually a little more understated. Eyeliner, mascara, some lip gloss. Today Abby was wearing eye shadow too, and a rose-colored lipstick she'd lifted from Becca's makeup drawer.

She hadn't slept very well last night. She tossed and turned, trying to reconcile things in her mind. What did what happened with Cole mean, if it meant anything at all? Abby knew the smart thing for her to do would be to go on about her life and her work as if last night had never happened, because the minute she started having expectations, she was inevitably going to be disappointed."

It wasn't like she and Cole were going to get married, and he couldn't start stepping out with his assistant at social gatherings. Hook-ups like theirs had to be hidden in shadows and behind closed doors. There wasn't much future in a beginning like that.

Abby reasoned with herself for hours, and just when she decided that a one-time thing would be for the best, she'd close her eyes and remember the feel of his stubble along the curve of her shoulder, or the sugary-sweet taste of his tongue, and she knew that one time would never be enough for her.

True to her word, Abby did clean up the figures on the sales report like she said she would, and she emailed the finished file to Cole right away. He had an appointment early this morning, and wouldn't be in until after nine, so Abby started working on a few proposals that she knew he would be asking her for at some point during the day. She was interrupted by a phone call from Josh, a co-worker in Kerrigan's Chicago office. She and Josh shared a work-appropriate flirtation that Abby always looked forward to, even though there was something about Josh that was a little smarmy and disingenuous. Still, their flirtation was a harmless kind of fun, since the miles between them meant that nothing serious would ever come of it.

"Hey," Abby said, cradling the phone. She was smiling, and she knew he could hear it in her voice.

"How's my favorite New Yorker?"

"Eh, I can't complain."

"You can always complain," Josh replied. "It's just that most people won't care."

Abby laughed, twirling the phone cord around her index finger. "What can I do for you this morning?"

"Not much. I was just calling to see how you were doing. It's been forever since I talked to you."

"I saw that you called a few times, but I haven't had time to call you back. Work, work, sleep, eat. Work. Then more work," Abby told him. "The usual."

"Kerrigan's still got you overloaded, huh?"

Josh wasn't Cole's biggest fan. He and Abby used to joke about him a lot during their conversations, but now it felt wrong. She didn't want to tip off Josh that there was anything out of the ordinary, so she tried to pick her words carefully.

"You know he is," Abby replied, sighing.

"Listen, I need to-"

Abby's phone beeped to let her know there was a call on the other line. When she saw Cole's cell number on the display, her heart skipped a beat.

"Josh, I've gotta go."

"I wanted to talk to you about something, Abby."

"We can talk later, I've gotta go."

"Okay," he said, sounding reluctant. "I'll call you later."

Abby clicked over to the other line and took a deep breath, hoping that she'd sound casual. But Cole didn't even wait for her to answer before he started talking.

"I'm going to need the Brighton and Pyncorp proposals by eleven." He sounded as bossy as he usually did, and relief smoothed the edges of Abby's frazzled nerves. No awkwardness, just business as usual. She guessed that was a good sign.

"They're almost finished. I'll have them ready when you get in. Anything else?"

If she didn't know any better, she'd bet he was surprised that she was already a step ahead of him.

"Ten copies each for the stakeholders."

"Ten copies. Got it."

Abby could hear the hum of the limo in the background, and for a split second she wondered if Cole had forgotten to hang up the phone. "Goodbye, Abigail."

"Goodbye."

And then the line went dead.

Once Abby had put the finishing touches on the proposals and packaged them for the clients the way Cole liked, she headed to the office kitchen for some coffee. She was dragging and needed some caffeine.

Two other assistants were leaning against the counter, speaking in whispers and giggling. Paulette, who worked for one of the area directors, and Marley, who worked for the head of product development, Keith McCall.

"Ladies," Abby said, approaching slowly, not wanting to disturb their gossip session. *It's a pity Becca doesn't work here*, Abby thought. *She'd fit right in*. Abby opened the cupboard over the coffee maker and grabbed a cup. "How are you this morning?"

Marley, a pretty brunette who was the office's leading shit-stirrer, leaned toward Abby and said, "Fraternization is against the rules here, isn't it?"

Abby's breath caught in her throat. *How could they possibly know already?* Her face was hot, and she had to put the cup down in order to wring her hands together, just to stop them from shaking. *Don't panic, Abby. Whatever you do, don't panic.*

Abby cleared her throat. "I'm not really sure," she said, her voice shaky. "You should probably check with someone in HR." Trying to look as innocent as possible, Abby's gaze moved from Marley to Paulette. "Why, what happened?"

They grinned at each other, trying to stifle a laugh, and for the love of god Abby just wanted them to get on with it.

"Brianne got drunk at happy hour last night and had sex with Tom at the bar," Marley said, her eyes practically bulging out of her head with excitement. Abby breathed a long sigh of relief, thankful that there weren't any rumors about her. Marley was the last person in this office Abby would ever want to have anything to hang over her head.

"Tom." Abby searched her memory for a face to put with that name, when suddenly it hit her. "The guy from the mail room?"

They both nodded enthusiastically, trying not to laugh.

"You two shouldn't be spreading something like that around." *Poor Brianne, having to look at herself in the mirror this morning.* "She's probably embarrassed enough as it is."

"Hey, Abby," said a male voice from the other side of the room. Abby turned to see Jake Neal, one of the senior associates.

"Hey, what can I do for you?" she asked.

"Cole wants to see you in his office."

Immediately Abby felt a tremble inside of her, like all of her vital organs were trying to figure out the fastest route to escape from her body. She kept telling herself not to panic as she followed Jake out the door and walked in a quick clip toward her desk. *Surely Cole wouldn't have sent one of his associates to find me if we were going to have The Talk, right?*

Abby hurried to her desk and opened the top left drawer, frantically searching for a compact. She checked her hair and blotted some powder on her nose, then shoved the compact back in the drawer, grabbed her pen and paper, and headed for the door. It wasn't lost on her that the last time she walked in here was right before she and Cole had the best sex of her life.

Abby hesitated for only a second before she turned the doorknob and walked in.

She didn't know whether she was expecting him to look at her longingly or to smile at her like they shared a little secret, but he did neither of those things. In the past Cole would usually greet her with a steely gaze, but today he looked unsure, and that was more jarring than any other expression Abby could've seen on his face.

She stood in front of his desk. "Jake said you wanted to see me."

"I just wanted to make sure that the presentations I asked

you for are ready."

"They are. Ten copies each, like you asked."

An awkward silence. Abby got the feeling that Cole was expecting her to leave.

"Should I go?" she asked, feeling slightly stupid.

Cole regarded her for a moment, looking amused. "Were you expecting something more?"

Abby's cheeks grew hot and she looked down at her shoes. "I don't know, I just thought…" She wasn't quite sure how to finish that sentence.

Cole stood and Abby's eyes met his. He was definitely amused now. "You wanted me to fuck you again," he said mischievously as he rounded the desk and walked behind her.

Just the sound of his voice, all seductive and low, made Abby wet. She shifted her weight, trying to relieve the growing ache between her legs.

"Answer me, Abigail." His chest was pressed against her back, his breath on her cheek as he twirled a strand of her hair around his finger.

"Yes."

Abby could feel Cole's smile against her cheek. "When you came in here, you wanted me to run my hand up your leg."

"Yes," she replied breathily. She wanted him to do whatever he wanted to her.

Cole reached down and slid his fingers up the back of Abby's thigh and instinctively she bent at the waist and splayed her hands out on the desk. "You wanted me to touch you here," he said. After pushing her panties to the side, his fingers slid up and down her slit; her wetness the evidence of her desire.

"Yes."

Cole leaned down and said, "You wanted me to make you come." He pulled his hand away, and Abby missed the feel of it immediately.

She couldn't help but sound disappointed as she replied. "Yes."

"Soon, Abigail. Very soon. I do have a business to run, and I can't let my cock start making all of my decisions for me. Although I can't deny that I thought about you this morning. How tight you were, how good it felt to be inside you. Tell me, if I make you wait, do you think that will make you want me more or less?"

"More," Abby said, her voice breathy.

"I guess we'll see."

Frustrated, she huffed. "You really get off on delayed gratification, don't you?"

Cole grinned. "I get off on many things, Abigail. You'll find out very soon."

As if the moment wasn't tense enough, it was interrupted by a knock on the door. Abby pulled at the hem of her skirt, making sure it was as far down as it was supposed to be.

"Come in." Cole said, staring at Abby.

She turned to see Keith McCall smiling at her as he walked into the room.

"How are you this morning Abby?" he asked.

"I'm fine, thank you." Abby sounded falsely cheerful, but

Keith didn't seem to notice.

As Abby walked out, Cole reminded her about his meetings. "I'll be leaving in twenty minutes."

As if she could forget. She knew his schedule better than he did.

CHAPTER
Six

Cole walked out of his office at ten forty-five on the nose, and Abby was standing there, proposals in hand. She followed him out to the elevator so she could brief him on his way to his car, as usual.

"Here are the Brighton proposals," Abby said, handing Cole one stack of folders before he slid them into his briefcase. "And the Pyncorp proposals." He slid the other group into a separate pocket as they stood together waiting for the elevator.

"Liam's going to have the car waiting out front of the Brighton offices at quarter after one; make sure you're out there. You know how much that tight ass at Pyncorp hates tardiness," Abby said as the doors opened and she and Cole stepped inside. Cole pressed the button for the first floor, and Abby continued her list of commands. "I've marked your proposals with red flags, make sure you take those. I left room in the margins for you to doodle in when one of the directors gets long-winded."

"I have my best ideas when the directors get long-winded," Cole said, looking at his watch.

"I know. And I never get any bonuses for providing you with the space to come up with those best ideas. Typical stingy CEO." Just as Abby finished speaking, Cole reached over and pushed the emergency stop.

The alarm was deafening, but Abby didn't care about that once Cole dropped his briefcase and pressed his chest against hers, backing her up against the far side of the wall. Her mind couldn't process what was happening fast enough, so she gripped the railing behind her as Cole's hand slid up the side of her neck until it cupped the side of her face. Cole's eyes were the brightest blue as they searched hers.

Then Cole kissed her, completely consumed her. His fingers slid through her hair, pulling her closer to him and his other hand slid up her thigh, bringing her leg up to rest on his hip as she balanced herself against the railing. Abby couldn't get enough of his taste, the feel of his weight against her. She wanted more. More of this feeling, more of his lips. Too soon, Cole pulled away from her, resting his forehead against hers.

And then, even over the wailing elevator alarm, Abby heard Cole's words so clearly, so loudly, that she will never forget them.

"You were the best I ever had," Cole said. He was breathless, and he kissed Abby quickly before he spoke again.

"And you've ruined me for all other women."

Dumbfounded, Abby stood there. Disheveled, in complete disbelief. *Did that really just happen?*

Cole straightened his tie and combed through his hair with his fingers, then released the emergency button and the elevator continued its descent. When they reached the ground floor, he strode out in his confident manner, leaving Abby behind, completely confused and wanting him more than ever.

The following night, Cole was in his office changing into a new suit as the sun began to set. Abigail sat at her desk outside his door. Cole hadn't asked her to stay late, but there she was. He had been out of the office most of the day, stopping by for only a few minutes at lunch to pick up a few sales reports. Those few minutes had been the very best part of his day.

Now, even though she was on the other side of the door, he liked the safety of that wall. The distance from her kept his mind clear, bridled his hormones. He needed to be so careful in how he proceeded with her, but his overwhelming need to touch her was making that difficult.

Cole regarded himself in the full-length mirror behind his closet door, brushing the sleeves of his jacket. Abigail had complimented him on this suit once, and he was hoping she'd feel the same way about it this evening. As he fumbled with his tie, Cole realized that Abby probably wouldn't feel much of anything if he couldn't get the damn thing on correctly. He did this every day; he had no idea why he was having such an issue with it now.

He was interrupted by a knock on the door, followed by Abigail's sweet voice.

"Your car's downstairs. If you don't hurry, you're going to be late."

Cole turned around and looked at her, so stunning there in his doorway. He wanted to slide his hands beneath her ass and pull her close to him, to taste her sweet lips.

Control yourself, Kerrigan.

"If it doesn't affect my bottom line, then punctuality is of little concern to me," Cole replied, turning back toward the mirror and focusing on his tie. If he didn't look away from her, he was going to ravage her here, right on the spot. He had to be careful with this.

"How can you not care about punctuality when the bottle-nosed pelican fish is in desperate need of your fifteen-thousand-dollar-per-plate donation?" Abigail teased. Fuck, she was going to test his will in every way imaginable. She walked over to him and Cole watched her carefully as her delicate fingers reached out and clasped around his tie. She looped one side under the other and worked her magic until the fabric was twisted into a perfect knot. Abigail smelled of berries and vanilla, the most intoxicating scent. Cole closed his eyes briefly and breathed her in.

"Bottle-nosed pelican fish are very near and dear to my heart," he replied, gently grazing his fingers along the underside of her wrists. He saw the gooseflesh rise on her skin and smiled.

You do the same thing to me, Abigail, he wanted to tell her.

"There you go, just right." Abigail smoothed her fingers over his lapel, meeting his gaze. Her eyes were like jewels; a perfect muted green. He could get lost in them if he wasn't careful. He wanted to kiss her so badly. All he could think about was the feel of her lips on his in the elevator yesterday. He needed more, like a junkie. He didn't think he could ever get enough.

Cole kissed Abigail, fiery and fierce, and she wrapped her arms around his neck, running her fingers through the hair on his nape. He nearly moaned; that was a sweet spot for him, and of course she found it. Caution be damned, he could have a little taste of her tonight. His lips trailed down Abigail's neck and nimbly undid the first button, then the second, then the third. He gently pushed her shirt back, revealing the lacy cups of her bra. Just looking at her made him hard. He grinned, admiring the view, then kissed her again and trailed his fingers along the edges of the lace.

"Did you wear this for me?" Cole asked, his voice husky with want.

"Yes," Abigail breathed.

The tips of Cole's fingers circled Abigail's nipple and her head lolled back, offering her neck for more kisses.

God, how he wanted to lave his tongue along her neck, and take her taut nipple into his mouth. He wanted to make her moan and beg and scream his name. But he had to wait.

Just for tonight, he had to wait.

You have to be careful with her, he reminded himself.

"It's a pity I can't stay to enjoy this." Cole's arms circled Abigail's waist, pulling her against him. His erection strained against his pants, and realizing this, Abigail pressed her thigh against him. *Tease.* "I have to think of the poor pelican fish."

"Fuck the pelican fish," Abigail replied.

Cole reached down and ran his fingers along the inside of her thigh, pushing her skirt up until his hand came to rest between her legs. Abigail bucked against his hand, wanting more friction, but Cole's touch was feather-light. His fingers slipped beneath the lace on her panties, circling her clit as she moaned. He pressed one finger inside her, only for a second. Abigail's hands found purchase on Cole's back, and he laughed, taking her earlobe between his teeth before pulling away.

Then Cole ran his fingertip—still wet with Abigail's desire—along her full, pouty bottom lip. And he kissed her once more, even deeper than before, his tongue sliding against hers.

Cole had never been so turned on in his life, but he had to walk away. At least he hadn't lied when he told her he was going to make her wait. Delayed gratification, indeed. If only she could understand that it was more to help him keep a level head than it was to torture her.

Cole leaned in close to her and whispered, "Soon."

Abigail shivered in response.

Cole walked toward the door, then turned to Abigail before he left.

"Abigail?"

"Yes?"

"I want you to make some travel arrangements for me," Cole said. "I cannot stress to you how important it is that you keep this confidential."

Abigail nodded. "Okay, I'll contact your pilot. Where are you headed?"

"Chicago. I'll leave this Sunday and return Saturday morning. Call Maeve at the Peninsula. She'll know which suite to book for me."

Cole could see the apprehension in her eyes, and waited for her to speak.

Ask me, Abigail.

"Will anyone be traveling with you?"

Cole grinned as he opened the door. "You will."

CHAPTER
Seven

*F*eeling like a creep, Abby watched Becca from behind a rack of separates in the women's department of Macy's Herald Square. She dragged Becca here under the guise of needing new work clothes, but the truth was that Abby needed to talk to someone about what happened between her and Cole yesterday. The confidentiality agreement Abby had signed when she started working at Kerrigan Corp. made it impossible for her to tell Becca exactly what had happened, but she thought there had to be a way around that. Becca wouldn't know *who* Abby's boss was, only that she'd slept with him. Abby wished she had a friend who was a lawyer and could help navigate the tricky legal waters of what a girl should do when she had slept with their boss and just had to tell her best friend about it.

This was the first large chunk of time Abby had spent

with Becca since last night, and she wasn't used to having to walk on eggshells around her. Becca could usually spot a person who'd recently had great sex from miles away, and even though Becca had been asleep when she snuck in last night, she was surprised she was able to hide it from Becca this morning.

"Abby Waters, if you keep standing over there and staring at me like a stalker, I'm going to call security," Becca said, sounding highly annoyed. Abby side-eyed Becca for a few moments while she pretended to be looking at a blazer. It didn't take very long for Becca to give up the ruse of looking at clothes; she knew something was up. She walked over to the rack Abby was using for cover and began her interrogation.

"You're hiding something." Becca's eyes narrowed as she pointed at Abby. "You've been acting strange since you got home, and I know you stole my lipstick."

She is not messing around.

Still not quite sure what or how to tell Becca, Abby bit her lip and decided that the coat hangers on the rack of shirts she was looking at were entirely too fascinating.

Becca put her hand on Abby's arm and when Abby looked in Becca's eyes, she knew she was busted.

"These aren't even your size, Abby. Spill."

"I can't tell you here," Abby said, looking around as if there were cameras and/or corporate lawyers hiding out amongst the racks. Becca grabbed Abby's hand and led her to the escalator, where they headed to the cafe on the eighth floor.

Becca got a cappuccino, Abby got an herbal tea. At a

small table in the corner, Becca sat and watched Abby while Abby watched billowy clouds of cream swirling in her drink.

"You know I'm not going to judge you, right?"

Slowly, Abby dragged her gaze away from her tea to look at Becca. Abby had known her for years, and if there was anyone in this world Abby could trust, she knew it was her. Still, she was hesitant to tell Becca what she had done, even though there wasn't a single part of her that wished she hadn't done it.

Abby exhaled a calming breath before she spilled her guts to the best friend she'd ever had.

"I slept with my boss." Abby's voice was barely above a whisper, and she flinched when the words came out. She braced herself like Becca was going to throttle her. She knew she probably looked ridiculous, but it took forever for her eyes to meet Becca's after her confession.

Becca's eyes lit up as she smiled. "What do you mean, slept with him? Like, you went to a hotel room and did it, or he fucked you up against his desk?" Of course she hit the nail on the head on her first try. Becca had great intuition and she loved a good scandal, so this whole situation was right up her alley.

Abby rubbed the back of her neck, feeling a little uncomfortable talking about this in such a public place, but the cafe was nearly empty and there was no way anyone could hear them.

"Up against his desk." Abby cringed again when she said it.

Becca squealed and clapped, both embarrassing Abby

and making her laugh at the same time. Once she'd calmed down, she grabbed her chair and scooted over next to Abby.

"Holy shit, Abs. I never would've pegged you as…I'm just so proud." Abby should've known Becca would react that way, and it made her feel foolish that she ever thought twice about telling her. In that moment, Abby loved her more than ever.

"Beck, I don't know what to do now."

"What do you mean, what do you do? You do it again. And again and again until you can't do it any more. Why is this a question?"

"Well, there is the very small issue of, I don't know…my *job*."

Becca laughed, and Abby almost felt insulted.

How can she take this so lightly?

"Sweetie, guys don't fuck you and then fire you, it doesn't work that way. That would actually be the least productive thing ever. He'd either pretend it didn't happen or do his damnedest to make it happen again."

Abby took a sip of her tea. "He's doing his damnedest to make it happen again."

Becca smiled. "My kind of guy."

"Well, kind of. He's teasing me. Making me wait."

Becca's smile got impossibly bigger. "*Definitely* my kind of guy."

"It's kind of hot? I don't know. I mean, he's always been kind of an ass with me, but he's definitely got this compartmentalized. He's just completely different when we're…you know."

"If you can do it, you can say it, sweetie. Use your big girl words."

"When we're having *sex*," Abby said, feeling like an idiot.

"Have you ever considered that this isn't the first time he's done this?"

"Obviously it's not the first time he's done this," Abby replied, looking at Becca like she'd just spoken gibberish.

Becca rolled her eyes. "I mean, the first time he's done this with an assistant."

Oh god. I hadn't considered that.

"Maybe that's why your job was open."

"Shut up, Becca."

Even though Abby didn't want to hear any more, the reality had already sunk in.

What if I wasn't the first? What if this was *the reason my job was open in the first place? Cole told me my predecessor had gotten an offer from another company, but what if she'd been forced to leave?* She felt like she was going to hyperventilate.

Abby covered her face with her hands, then threaded her fingers through her hair, pushing it off of her forehead. "How could I have been so stupid, Beck?"

"Well, this thing does have an expiration date now. Start sending out your resume just in case, but have fun while you're still there."

Even though Abby allowed herself to go over the various scenarios for how this thing would ultimately play out, she chose to focus only on the good endings, because the bad ones made her sick to her stomach. She knew, deep down, that this wasn't going to be a happily ever after. But she didn't want to even begin to think about the clock ticking toward the end of it all.

Knowing Abby as well as she did, Becca knew what she was thinking.

"Lust is a powerful thing, sweetie. It makes us all jackasses. Besides, the whole power play aspect? I mean…honestly, I probably would've done it too. It's so naughty and forbidden, oh my god. I wish my own boss wasn't such a troll." Becca grinned at Abby, giving her fingers a squeeze, and in that instant Abby knew she had made the right decision in telling her. "You didn't tell me the most important thing though."

"What's that?" Abby asked.

Becca glared at her as if she was an idiot. "How was it?"

Abby couldn't help the huge grin that stretched across her lips.

"Holy shit, Abby!"

"It was…amazing. Honestly. I don't know if it was just the sex or the circumstances or both, but all together it was incredible. And-"

"And what?" Becca was getting excited, leaning forward in her chair.

"Well, last night when we were getting cleaned up, I was trying to lighten the mood."

"Oh god."

"So I teased him a little and told him that afterwards I thought he would've told me that I was the best he'd ever had and that I'd ruined him for other women. I was really lighthearted about it."

"Your lighthearted face isn't half as lighthearted as you

think it is."

"I know," Abby admitted.

"What'd he say?"

"He didn't say anything at the time. But when he leaves for meetings, I usually walk with him down to the car. Today, I handed him some proposals and told him which was which and who he should give what to-"

"I don't care about any of this, get to the good stuff."

"I'm trying! Anyway, so I was just talking to him about work stuff while we were in the elevator, and all of a sudden he reached over and pulled the emergency stop-"

"Oh my god."

"-and he kissed me. Like, really kissed me. Hand on my thigh, lifting it up to his hip kind of kissing."

Becca slapped her hand on the table and then pressed it against her chest. Abby almost laughed, but she figured she'd keep talking in case Becca blacked out from excitement.

"And when he pulled away, he rested his forehead on mine and said that I was the best he'd ever had-"

"*Stop* it!"

"-and that I ruined him for all other women."

"Holy. Shit."

Abby thought Becca was going to pass out, she was legitimately swooning.

"And then he walked out of the elevator, and I haven't seen him since."

"He's going to fall in love with you," Becca said, practically squealing.

"Don't be stupid. Just a minute ago you were telling me

that there was an expiration date on this."

"On your job, yeah. But that was before you told me that he had walked right out of a romance novel."

"He's still a jackass," Abby said, not exactly sure why she felt the need to throw that into the conversation.

"A jackass who wants to fuck your brains out and then fall in love with you," Becca said before she swallowed the last of her cappuccino.

"So what am I going to do?" Abby asked, not really sure what to take away from this conversation.

"You're going to keep doing what you're doing, look out for yourself, and let the chips fall where they may." Becca stood up and held out her hand. "C'mon, let's go."

"Where?" Abby asked.

"To lingerie."

Early Sunday afternoon, Abby stood at the foot of her bed, staring at an empty suitcase. She hadn't seen or heard from Cole since Friday evening when he told her he wanted her to travel with him to Chicago. She was nervous, to say the least.

The two of us sharing a suite?

She wasn't exactly sure how their time together was going to go, but even more importantly, she wasn't sure how she was supposed to dress for it.

Abby knew Cole expected her to work; he wasn't flying

her a thousand miles away just to be his after-hours secret hook-up. If he wanted that, he could have anyone in the entire city knocking on the door to his room with just one simple phone call. No, there would be work, but she hoped there would also be pleasure. Lots of it. Then again, Cole did seem to have a penchant for teasing Abby without offering any payoff. Well, immediate payoff, at least.

Six days alone with him in a room with no satisfaction? That would've been torture, and even Cole Kerrigan wasn't *that* heartless.

Stop second-guessing yourself, Abby.

"Whatcha doin'?" Becca asked, flinging herself across Abby's bed and making her suitcase bounce precariously close to the edge of the bed.

"Be careful," Abby said, sliding it back to safety.

Becca looked at the empty compartments, her eyebrows furrowed. "It's not like there's anything in there. Why are you even bothering with a suitcase? Just put some fresh undies in your purse and call it a day."

"This isn't Sex Fest 2013, Beck. I will actually have to work."

"Yeah you will," Becca said suggestively, laughing at her own joke.

"Stop." Abby flicked Becca with the blanket that had been spread out across the foot of her bed. "What should I take?"

"Take your normal work clothes. And your normal play clothes. And plenty of condoms. You two aren't doing something stupid like barebacking it are you?" Becca rolled over onto her stomach, gathering Abby's pillow between her arms to rest her head on.

"I'm not *that* stupid."

"Good girl," she replied, reaching for the magazine on Abby's nightstand.

"I only have, like, two sets of lingerie." Abby could not believe that this was something she was considering when packing for a work trip. The difference in her life between last Sunday and today astonished her.

"What difference does it make? Hopefully you won't be wearing it for long anyway. Men don't care about that stuff as much as they say they do. If they had to choose between seeing a woman in lingerie or seeing a woman naked, they'd choose the naked woman. Tits are magical that way, bless them."

Abby laughed as she pulled a few blouses out of her closet and hung them over the door.

"You know," Becca began in a sing-song voice, "it would be easier for me to help you figure out what to pack if I knew who it was you were trying to impress."

Becca asked Abby about the identity of her boss on several occasions since she started working at Kerrigan, but Abby had never budged. Not budging was easy considering she'd lied about the name of the company she worked for. Becca thought Abby was a junior accountant for a firm on Wall Street. That's what Abby told her, anyway. Becca was smart enough to figure out that wasn't the truth. She didn't know what the truth was, though, and Abby was going to make sure she kept it that way.

"You know I can't tell you that."

"Non-disclosure agreement be damned, Abby. Seriously, this is killing me."

Not as much as it's killing me.

In order to nip this argument in the bud, Abby asked, "Would you tell me who you worked for if doing so meant that you had a potential lawsuit on your hands?"

Becca looked up at her, forgetting the magazine for a moment. "I would, but we both know I don't usually make the best decisions."

Abby walked over to her dresser and pulled the two sets of lingerie she bought with Cole in mind out of the drawer and placed them gently in her suitcase.

"It seems like I'm not making the best decisions lately either."

And surprisingly, she didn't care.

CHAPTER
Eight

"Mom, relax," Cole said impatiently, cradling his cell phone against his ear. "We have this discussion every time I fly, and yet I'm still alive."

"I know," replied Olivia Kerrigan, Cole's opinionated, yet loving mother. "Can't I be nervous about my youngest son being propelled through the air at hundreds of miles per hour in what amounts to a tin can? The smaller planes are always the ones you hear about crashing."

Cole sighed, resting his head against the seat in the back of his limo, watching the city lights blur on his way to the airport. "It's not like I'm flying in a crop duster. I own a full-sized jet. It's very safe, I've hired a capable crew." He appreciated his mother's concern for his safety, but did not appreciate having this conversation every time he had to fly somewhere. "Besides, I'm more likely to die in this car than

I am on my plane."

Olivia was quiet for a moment, accepting the fact that she ultimately had no hand in her son's fate. "Where are you going?"

"Chicago."

"Tyler's birthday is next weekend, pick up something with the Sears Tower on it," she said. "You know how much that boy loves buildings."

Cole grinned thinking about his 4-year-old nephew. As if he could forget the boy's birthday; it was a recurring reminder programmed into his phone, not that he needed it.

"It's called the Willis Tower now," Cole gently reminded his mother, knowing how much being corrected annoyed her.

"Try to meet a nice girl while you're there. Midwestern women are very down-to-earth. That would be good for you."

Cole heard the teasing edge in his mother's voice every time she reminded him that she wanted him to settle down.

"Mother, I'm in no rush to get married."

"So the tabloids tell me."

He rubbed his eyes, trying to relieve his exasperation. "Did you send me to Yale to find a wife or to learn how to run a business? Because business is doing well right now, I need to focus on that." What he actually was focusing on was the fact that Abigail was waiting for him in his plane. He hadn't seen her in two days, which was two days too long.

"You're twenty-nine years old, Cole. It's time to start thinking about settling down."

"I can't talk about this right now, Mom. I'm running late,

and I need to board my tin can so I can be propelled through the air at hundreds of miles an hour to my certain death."

Olivia sighed. "All right. Be safe, my love. Have a nice trip."

"I will," Cole replied, grinning. "I love you."

"I love you too."

The second Cole ended the call, a message from Keith McCall popped up on his screen.

911 - Check your email

Damn it, Cole thought. He was so looking forward to spending two uninterrupted hours with Abigail, of course there would be an emergency he needed to deal with during that time. He typed a quick response.

Almost on the plane - I'll check ASAP

As if Cole needed another reminder of what this trip was all about, Keith fired off a reply that really drove the point home:

> *Have a good trip. Find out what this fucker's up to so we can nail his ass to the wall.*

Cole grinned as his car came to a stop on the tarmac. Keith was as loyal as they came, and he wanted to nab Hamilton almost as badly as Cole did.

When Cole stepped onto the plane, he saw Abigail sitting

by the window. Her hair was up in a ponytail, leaving the lovely, graceful slope of her neck exposed. He wanted to kiss every inch of that neck; he wanted to see it arched in ecstasy as he pounded into her, giving her the most pleasure she'd ever felt in her life. His cock stirred just looking at her, and Cole was sure that it was going to be a long flight.

This is business. Think about your business, he reminded himself as he climbed the steps to board the plane.

Cole spent nearly an hour and a half dealing with the issue that Keith emailed him about before takeoff. When he finally reached a stopping point, he looked over at Abigail who was dressed in a smart-looking navy blue suit. She had her laptop out, typing away.

"Do you like the jet?" he asked.

"Eh," Abigail said, shrugging. "I've been in better."

"Have you?" Cole smiled, always amused by this intriguing woman. He knew at that moment that this trip was going to be the ultimate test of his will.

"Oh, definitely. Where I'm from, they hand these out like candy. I appreciate a yacht-slash-jet combo, just to make sure that the air and sea are covered. I value different methods of transportation."

"I own a yacht." Cole said.

"Of course you do," Abigail said, laughing. "But do you own a catamaran?"

Cole laughed. "No, I do not."

"Buy one of those, and then I'll tell you how impressed I am."

Cole closed his laptop and set it aside, then rubbed his tired eyes.

"Does this thing usually impress the ladies?" She was so curious, but unable to meet his gaze.

"Which ladies?"

"The ones you get photographed with."

"Ah," Cole replied, pressing his lips together. He figured this question would come sooner or later. "Why don't you ask me what you really want to know?"

She was quiet for a long moment before answering. "Have you taken your other assistants on trips?"

"Yes." Cole was amused at her line of questioning, probably because he knew right where it was headed. "As I said before, why don't you ask me what you really want to know?"

"Have you…" Abigail stumbled on her words, uncharacteristically flustered.

"Fucked my other assistants?"

"Thank you. Yes."

Cole's plan to keep this trip mostly on the business end of things was quickly falling apart, but if anyone could multitask, it was him. Abigail was sitting on the other end of the long leather sofa that Cole occupied, which was much too far away for his liking. Unable to resist her, he turned to face her.

"This may come as a shock to you Abigail, but I do

actually have a business to run. I wouldn't be successful if I walked around screwing my employees. You might be surprised to find out that if I have a particular itch, there is no shortage of women I could find to scratch it for me."

Abigail looked as if she'd been stricken. Her eyes were wide, absolutely stunned, and Cole felt the need to clarify his statement, to ease the harshness of what he'd just said.

"However, it seems that when I find a woman appealing, I don't always follow my own rules. And," Cole continued, his gaze locked with hers, "you are the first person I've broken that rule for."

A smile broke through the tension on her face.

Christ, she is beautiful.

Abigail placed her laptop on the seat across from her and turned toward Cole. She crossed her legs, hitching her skirt up higher. He couldn't help but let his eyes travel up the length of her thigh. This woman was going to be the end of him.

"So I'm the first?"

"Yes," he replied.

"That's a momentous occasion, we should celebrate."

Cole was in trouble. *Big* trouble. But he didn't care.

"What did you have in mind?" he replied, his voice low.

Abigail grabbed his tie, pulling his mouth to hers. She kissed him—hard—her tongue brushing up against his. Cole pressed harder, needing more kisses, wanting her to remember that he'd been there long after he was gone. Abigail swung her legs over Cole's until she was straddling him, and then she hesitated a moment, looking at the cockpit door.

"No one's going to come in here," Cole whispered, attempting to reassure her as he lightly nibbled her earlobe.

Abigail pulled away to look at him. He suspected she was trying to figure out whether or not she should trust him.

"I promise."

That seemed to be enough.

Cole unbuttoned Abigail's blouse, sliding his hand down the placket, relishing in the silky softness of her skin. Then he reached up, gliding his fingers along the lacy cup of her bra and pulled it down, exposing her left breast. Their eyes met as he moved closer to her, then he licked the taut pink bud of her nipple in a lazy circle before taking it between his teeth, smiling as she stifled a moan. When he repeated the same motions on Abigail's other breast, she ran her fingers through his hair. He loved the way her fingernails gently scraped against his scalp, lighting his nerves on fire, making him want her even more.

As if she sensed Cole's need, Abigail slid one hand down his chest until it came to rest between his legs. His cock was hard, pressing against the inside of his thigh. His eyes fluttered as Abigail moved her hand in feather-light strokes over the fabric of his pants, driving him crazy.

"I want to taste you," she whispered, right against his lips.

Cole's mouth turned up in a lazy, satisfied smile. He loved it when a confident, beautiful woman took control of a situation, and he was all for Abigail having her way with him.

She kissed his neck, sucking the skin there, then slowly slinked down Cole's body, unbuttoning his shirt as she went along, kissing each spot above the button as it was exposed.

He felt as if her lips were made to kiss him; he'd never had such a reaction to another woman in his life. He wanted her mouth on every part of his body.

Abigail trailed her tongue along his abs, making his muscles tighten and his breath speed up, and blew warm puffs against the wet trail of skin. It was such a sensation, Cole couldn't help the noise that escaped his mouth. Abigail slid down over his erection until her knees touched the floor, and Cole looked at her through hooded eyes. At that moment, he was putty. Completely pliable in her hands. She could ask him for anything, and he would give it to her.

Abigail rubbed her hand across Cole's rock-hard erection and he drew in a sharp breath as he bucked his hips against her palm, wanting, no…*needing* more. The more he tried to get some much-needed friction, the lighter she would touch him. This woman knew just how to drive him crazy.

"Tease," Cole said in a low, breathy growl that spurred Abigail on.

She unbuckled his pants and slowly pulled down the zipper. He groaned when she finally pulled his boxers down far enough for his cock to spring free. She leaned back on her heels as her fingertips slid across his tender, heated skin.

"Your dick is perfect," Abigail said. Cole loved hearing dirty words come out of that luscious mouth of hers, and he longed to feel her full, warm lips around his erection.

Abigail licked her hand and gripped him, sliding her hand down his hot, silky skin. Cole sighed, long and low, and he pushed against her hand as she repeated the motion.

Too soon she let go, and just when Cole was about to

voice his protestations, Abigail pushed his legs back to give herself more room. Then, as if she was intent on driving him absolutely crazy, she kissed his abdomen, then the crease where his hip met his thigh. She kissed him everywhere but the one place he wanted her to. But, true to form, Cole didn't rush her, he just slid his fingers through her soft hair, enjoying the sensation. Then Abigail bent down and licked the stretch of skin just beneath his sack, pressing her tongue against it, nearly making Cole jump out of his skin. He drew a breath between his teeth that made a long, slow hiss.

Abigail licked him from the base to the tip of his cock with an agonizingly light stroke of her tongue. A glistening bead of precum slid down the tip, and Abigail licked it away. The texture of her tongue was exquisite.

"I want to feel your mouth," Cole said impatiently. "Now."

"Not a big fan of delayed gratification now, are you?" she teased. But Abigail was never cruel, so she took him in her mouth with voracity, her tongue swirling around him as she gently tugged his balls. The warring sensations were the best kind of agony, winding their way from his belly all the way to the hairs on his head. Just when Cole didn't think he could get any higher, Abigail took him deeper. So deep that he could feel the tip of his cock in the back of her throat. He watched her as she sucked him; her wide hazel eyes looking up at him under impossibly long eyelashes. Pink lips and a mouth that felt like heaven. She moved up and down his shaft, concentrating on all the right places before taking him deep again. Cole felt that familiar warmth creep up the base of his spine, threatening to explode.

As if on cue, Abigail slid her mouth down until she couldn't handle any more of him. And then she swallowed.

"Holy fuck!" Cole had never felt anything like the sensation of her throat squeezing the tip of his cock and his breathing quickened, his fingers wound themselves through the hair at the crown of her head. The harder he breathed, the faster she went until he couldn't hold off his orgasm any more.

Cole gently pushed her away, not wanting her to feel like she had to swallow. She refused, still sucking and swirling that relentless, perfect tongue until he exploded in her mouth, waves of pleasure rippling through his spent body.

"Christ," Cole sighed. His head lolled back against his seat as he tried to catch his breath. His post-orgasmic bliss was short lived, however, since they had to prepare for landing.

"We're approaching Chicago," the pilot's voice echoed over the loudspeaker. "Please fasten your seat belts."

Cole twined his fingers with Abigail's, then pulled her up and kissed her. His breath was still ragged as he pressed his forehead against hers.

"You don't know what you're doing to me," he whispered. Although, at this point, he had a sneaking suspicion that she did.

CHAPTER
Nine

The lobby of the hotel was unlike anything Abby had ever seen before. Being that her budget always made her a Holiday Inn kind of girl by necessity, she never dreamed she'd be staying in a place like this. She couldn't help peering out the window and watching the man in the tuxedo who was driving a horse-drawn carriage in the driveway.

Everything about the hotel was classy. High ceilings, elegant crystalline chandeliers, exotic flowers that bloomed out of vases that were almost as tall as she was. There was something in the air that made Abby want to stand up straighter, as if that would make all the rich people milling around believe that she was one of them. She wished she had a nicer pair of earrings to wear, although she knew that anyone in that lobby could spot a pair of cubic zircons from fifty paces.

"Come," Cole said, holding out his arm toward her.

Apparently when you reach the point in your life when you're able to book grand suites, you no longer have to check in like all the other plebes.

The elevator doors opened to reveal walls lined with rich mahogany. Cole swiped a card in front of a sensor before he was able to press the button for the 18th floor.

He stared at the numbers above the doors as they slowly rose. "Do you have your schedule?"

Abby nodded. "Yes."

"Be ready to leave thirty minutes before our departure time," Cole said, glancing back at Abby. "I'll knock on your bedroom door when I'm ready to go." Even though they were in an elevator a thousand miles from home, taking orders from Cole felt so incredibly familiar. "I plan to work in the suite most of the time when we're not in meetings. If you'd like to work in the common areas with me, that's fine. If not, you may work in your room. During work hours, I expect your suite door to remain open in case I need you. Outside of that, I will respect your privacy. I'll knock if I need you."

The elevator doors opened and Cole handed Abby a key card. She slid it into her pocket.

Of course he didn't address what I'm most interested in, which is what will happen outside of working hours. Then again, he seems to like keeping me guessing about that. Bastard.

Abby followed Cole out of the elevator and watched as he opened the door to their suite. She had prepared herself for luxury; plush carpets, fine furniture, antiques that were worth more than her life. But what she hadn't prepared herself for was just how huge the suite would be. Four of her apartments could fit in there easily.

The floor in the foyer was a rich, shiny marble with elegant beige striped wallpaper. The foyer opened to a living room area with twenty-foot-high ceilings. There was even a dining room with a table that could seat eight. Along the far wall were windows that stretched almost to the ceiling, each one offering a gorgeous view of Michigan Avenue. The brake lights on the cars stopped along the street reminded Abby of Manhattan.

"Do you approve?" asked Cole.

Abby was startled by his voice and surprised by how close he was standing. She shrugged, sliding her index finger along the back of one of the dining room chairs. "It'll do, I suppose."

There was the slightest hint of a smile pulling at Cole's lips. It amazed Abby how compartmentalized he could be. An hour ago he was licking her nipples, but to see him now, no one would ever know it.

"Your room is over here," Cole said, walking toward a door on the opposite side of the living room. He opened the door, revealing a plush, fluffy looking bed with an antique headboard decorated with intricate blue flowers. The room had the same view as the others, full of bright lights and city. "My room is over there." Cole pointed to a hallway on Abby's right.

"You've been here before," Abby said, noticing that he didn't need a tour and he seemed to know where everything was.

"Several times." Cole's face was impassive.

"Alone?"

Ugh, Abby. That was stupid.

Cole looked at Abby for what felt like an eternity, and Abby hung on every second of silence, hoping that he would answer her question. But the non-answer said it all. He'd been to this hotel several times, probably with several different women. Abby's heart sank, making her feel foolish. She had to keep reminding herself that this was just sex. Getting emotionally involved with this man was the absolute worst thing she could do.

"I have some work to do," Cole said, his words clipped.

Abby nodded.

"I'm just going to change."

Abby turned and went into her room, shutting the door behind her. Sighing, she flopped on the bed and buried her face in the soft, fluffy comforter. "Abby, you idiot," she said, hoping that the verbal reminder would keep her from getting too personal in the future.

After she'd had enough wallowing, she sat up and unzipped her suitcase, then picked out a pair of jeans and a form-fitting black sweater. It was cooler in Chicago than it was in New York, and since her stomach was growling from not eating since lunch, she decided she'd go out and find something to eat.

Freshly changed, Abby ran her fingers through her hair and put on a bit of gloss before she headed back out into the living room. Cole was already in work mode, sitting in front of his laptop at the desk near the dining room. He turned his head slightly when Abby walked into the room, but he didn't acknowledge her other than that. His sleeves were rolled up, and Abby could tell that his tie was beginning to come undone. She needed all the strength she could muster not to jump his bones.

"I'm starving, I'm going to go find some pizza or something. Want me to bring something back for you?"

Cole stopped typing. "If you'd like."

It was arrogant words like those that drove her crazy, made her want to scream.

"Yes," she said sarcastically. "It would be my dream to bring you dinner. Sir."

"Abigail." Cole practically growled her name as a warning.

"Mr. Kerrigan."

Cole closed his eyes and clenched his fists, then let out a long sigh. "Yes, please bring me something to eat."

Abby could tell he practically had to push the words out of his mouth and given his frustration, she felt like she won this round. She walked toward the door and just as she clasped her hand around the knob, Cole called her name.

"Yes?" she replied.

Cole turned and faced her, so Abby knew that he really meant whatever it was he was about to say.

"This trip is important, and our work here requires both of us to focus. Despite what my earlier behavior would lead you to believe, I didn't ask you here to be..." He struggled to find the right words, and Abby knew that whatever they were, they were going to sting. "Intimate. I asked you to come with me because I need your brain, not your body."

For once Abby knew that Cole didn't mean that as an insult, but she couldn't help but take it as one just the same. Of course the one man she'd like to want her for her body would want her for her brain. She nodded, unable to meet his gaze. "I understand," she mumbled, trying not to sound too disappointed.

When Abby returned with the pizza, Cole was sitting in nearly the same position he was in when she left him. He kept typing as she walked behind him, like he didn't notice her in the room. She put the hot pizza box on a marble-topped credenza next to the table, and pulled two paper plates out of the plastic bag that the cashier at the restaurant gave her.

After she served herself a slice, she put one on the other plate for Cole and brought it over to the table.

"I brought your food, are you going to tear yourself away from that screen long enough to eat it?"

Cole didn't reply, and Abby took a bite of her pizza and practically moaned. It tasted like heaven. She grabbed a plastic fork and scraped off the sauce, then the cheese, leaving her only with the buttery crust. There was a bottle of red wine on the table that she didn't recall seeing there before, with elegant glasses on either side of it.

"Do you mind?" Abby asked, holding up the bottle. Cole was finally walking over to the table, rolling his sleeves up even further. The whole rolled up sleeves and undone tie look made Abby want to jump him, and she suspected he knew that.

"It'll come out of your per diem."

Abby looked at the year on the label. "It will probably *be* my per diem. For the whole trip."

Cole laughed, and the sound of it made Abby's stomach flutter.

"Go ahead," he said.

Abby poured herself a glass as Cole sat down, and he nodded as she motioned toward the other glass. She filled it and handed it to him, then proposed a toast.

"To my brain," Abby said, trying to sound lighthearted.

Cole rubbed his lips together as his eyes met hers, and his gaze didn't waver until he clinked her glass.

"To your brain."

The look in Cole's eyes was too much for Abby, and the room was suddenly too hot and too small. His gaze was still incredibly intense, so Abby focused on her pizza, taking small bites of the crust.

"Why are you doing that?" he asked, watching her intently.

"Doing what?"

"Eating like that."

Abby couldn't tell if Cole was disgusted or intrigued, so she looked down at the pile of sauce and cheese on her plate. "I don't know, I've always eaten pizza like this."

"Is there a reason, or-"

"I eat my least favorite things first and save my favorite for last. I know it's disgusting."

"Delayed gratification," he said before taking a sip of his wine.

"In pizza, yes. I've never been very good at it in life."

When Cole finally looked away, he brought his slice up to his mouth and a huge blob of tomato sauce slid off the pizza and onto his pristine white shirt. Abby nearly laughed, because she never imagined Cole with an imperfection so common as a food stain on his shirt.

"Shit," he sighed, standing up.

Abby got up and grabbed a bottle of club soda from the bar, then a washcloth from the bathroom.

"Here," Abby said, wetting the washcloth with the soda. "This should get it out."

Abby dabbed at the stain, watching the deep red fade into a subtle, muted pink. Cole's chest rose and fell quickly beneath her hands, and Abby wanted to press her hand over his heart just to see if she could feel it beating. There was electricity between the two of them, crackling, and Abby dared to look up into Cole's eyes. As always, they were focused on her. She wanted to dive into them; they were like little portals into his soul, and she needed to know what he was thinking.

Cole reached for her hand, and his fingers trembled when they touched hers. He tossed the washcloth on the floor before wrapping his arms around her waist, bringing her closer to him, crushing her against his chest. Her arms wound around his neck and their lips crashed together in frantic, hurried kisses. His tongue brushed against hers, and she gripped him tighter as his hands slid beneath her ass.

Before she knew it, he was lifting her up. She wrapped her legs around his waist and pressed her lips against his neck.

Cole began walking, and before long he put Abby down on the soft couch. His eyes were fierce as he unbuttoned her jeans, sliding them off into a heap on the floor. Abby pulled off her sweater, too impatient to wait for him to do it. He was too busy anyway, stripping his clothes off until he was naked.

Cole spread Abby's legs and slipped between them, lifting them up until her feet rested on the coffee table behind him.

Her heart was pounding so hard she could see her pulse thumping beneath her skin, and there was a current flowing through her veins, buzzing every time Cole touched her. He reached up and pulled down her panties, tossing them on the floor, and then he slid his chin along the inside of her thigh.

"Oh," Abby whispered, loving the exquisite scratch of Cole's stubble against her skin.

She wound her fingers through his hair, desperate for whatever it was that he wanted to give her. But too soon, he pulled away.

"Show me how you want me to touch you."

Abby felt a little shy as Cole leaned back, watching her. Perhaps sensing her hesitation, he told her what to do.

"Rub your clit, Abigail," he said, his voice full of authority. "Pretend your finger is my tongue. Show me what you want me to do to you."

Abby knew from experience that he knew very well what to do to her. Maybe he got off on the voyeurism, or maybe he wanted to know things about her body that only she could tell him. Nevertheless, she couldn't resist that look in his eyes. She would do exactly as she was told.

Abby tentatively slid her hand down between her thighs and spread apart her slit, exposing her sensitive flesh. Cole licked his lips, watching as her finger circled her clit. The right side was more sensitive than the left, so she dipped her finger lower, wetting her finger with her desire, then rubbed the taut nub in a half moon motion, each stroke making her nerves sing. Lost in the building waves of ecstasy, Abby's head fell back against the pillow and she looked at Cole through hooded eyes. He gently tugged his cock as he watched her.

Seeing how turned on Cole was pushed Abby further, faster.

"Yes, that's it," Cole said, his voice gruff with desire. He brushed his lips against the inside of her thigh as her hand quickened, pushing her toward the edge. "I want to watch your face as you come, knowing that this is only the first of the many orgasms you'll be having tonight."

With that, she let go.

CHAPTER
Ten

Cole sat in front of Abigail, watching her come undone. She was so beautiful when she came; her hair a little mussed, her muscles relaxed, her body in full view as it tensed and relaxed, writhing in pleasure. Even though Cole knew every way there was to please a woman, he wanted her to show him what she liked, because he had this intense desire to be the best sex Abigail ever had. Cole wanted to be the one man that she would always remember.

When he asked her to touch herself, to show him what she liked, he noticed that she went straight for her clit. Not that he blamed her, but she completely ignored her perfect breasts and neglected those tight, pink, bud-like nipples of hers. Cole looked forward to licking her pussy; he knew that would be delectable. But he especially wanted to show her how much pleasure those forgotten, neglected areas could bring her under his expert hands and tongue.

Once Abigail had ridden through her orgasm and began to level out, Cole could sense a bit of shyness creeping up in her. She blushed under his gaze, and moved to cover herself with her hand, then draped her arm across her breast.

"No," he said, gently moving her hand, then her arm. "I want to see you."

"Why?"

The question perplexed Cole. Women that he'd fucked in the past used to ask questions like that to coax compliments out of him, but Abigail wasn't the sort. She'd never shown anything less than complete confidence around him, so this shyness seemed to come out of left field.

"Because you're fucking gorgeous, that's why," he replied matter-of-factly.

Abigail rolled her eyes. Cole grinned, because only she could be exasperated with him when the two of them were sitting there completely naked.

"Please," she said, sighing. "I have cellulite here." She pointed at her smooth thighs. "The unfortunate beginnings of love handles here," she said, grabbing her supple hips. "And stretch marks on my tits. What's there to look at?"

"Sit up, Abigail."

Reluctantly, she did as she was told. Cole leaned forward, raising himself until he was kneeling in front of her and the two of them were eye-to-eye. He would not tolerate her talking about her body that way.

"Look at my cock," he commanded. It took a few seconds for her eyes to leave his, but she did as she was told. "It's rock hard because of you, and do you know why?"

She was looking down at the floor instead of at him, so Cole gently placed his index finger under her chin and lifted her head until her gaze met his.

"Do you know why?"

Abigail blushed, and she shook her head.

Cole kissed her; long and gentle, soft and sweet, then traced the swell of Abigail's left breast with his fingertips.

"Who cares about stretch marks? Your tits are just the right size for my hands." He cupped her breast and brushed the pad of his thumb across her nipple. "See how your nipples respond to my touch?" She sighed in response, her eyelids growing heavy. Cole leaned forward and took her nipple in his mouth, laving his tongue across the puckered skin, then sucked on the nub until she moaned. "Stretch marks don't make them any less pink, any less supple, or any less sweet."

Cole splayed his hands across Abigail's sides, and slid his hands down to her waist, pulling her down so her ass was at the edge of the sofa. His hands lingered there, massaging her skin. "You think these are love handles? Fuck that."

He maneuvered her legs so that they were in the same position they were in before, her feet resting on the coffee table behind him. He skimmed the backs of his fingers along the inside of her thigh, then followed the same path with his lips, gently kissing her there. "Cellulite? No," he said, his breath against her skin. "Soft. Perfect."

"And now for the part I've been waiting for," he said, sliding the tips of his fingers along her slit. She was so wet, so warm. "You've been waiting too, haven't you?"

Abigail nodded, all her prior insecurities gone. "Yes," she sighed. "You promised me more."

"Indeed I did," Cole said, planting a soft kiss on Abigail's clit. He always kept his promises. He parted her flesh with two fingers, then traced the side of her nub, just like he'd seen her do earlier. She practically melted into him, her arms and legs turned into jelly. He knew what he had to do. He leaned forward and laved his tongue along her opening, savoring the wetness before he concentrated on her most sensitive spot. He licked her slit a few times, tongue teasing, pushing forward and making her moan. She knit her fingers into his hair, guiding his movements.

His tongue found its way to her clit and he licked her, then pressed his lips against her and sucked, flicking his tongue as she pulled him to her, wanting more. He alternated his movements: licking then sucking, sucking then licking, all the while her breath quickened as she squirmed on the sofa, desperate to find her release.

"Please," she said breathily. "More, more."

Cole gave her more. More of his mouth, more of his tongue. He couldn't get enough of her taste, of the noises she was making. It was all for him, because of him. As he worked her into a frenzy, he wrapped his free hand around his cock and stroked himself a few times, needing to relieve the ache. He would have her. Very soon.

Abigail cried out Cole's name as she came, her fingers gripping his hair. But he couldn't stop now, not if he was going to keep his promise. He continued licking, sucking, tasting her pussy, this time slipping two fingers inside of her as she moaned and quivered. Spurred on by the sound of her pleasure, he added a third finger, pressing down as he plunged inward, wanting her to feel so full.

"Faster," Abigail begged. "Please, faster." So Cole moved his hand faster, still sucking her clit. It wasn't long until she cried out in ecstasy, her muscles squeezing his fingers. Cole rubbed her legs as she came down, then kissed his way up her thigh, then her hip, then her stomach, until he reached her full, pink lips. She wrapped her arms around his neck and brought her lips to his, kissing him with more passion than she ever had before. She played with his hair, winding it between her fingers as her breathing returned to normal.

"Had enough yet?" Cole asked cockily, knowing she would say no. Selfishly, he wanted to be inside her again and he knew she wouldn't deny him.

"No. You still haven't fucked me yet."

He loved it when she told him what she wanted, and the filthy way she said it was a bonus.

Abigail stood and, confused, Cole followed her lead.

"Sit down," she said. "I want to ride you."

Fuck. He wouldn't say no to that.

Before he sat, Cole reached down into the pocket of his discarded slacks and pulled out a condom, which Abigail quickly took from him. He grinned, positive she did that so she wouldn't have to take the chance of him making her wait while he rolled it on with agonizing slowness like he had their first night together in his office.

Abigail didn't waste any time with the condom, and seconds later, she was straddling him. Cole couldn't get enough of the sight of her on top of him, so he pulled her down for a long, slow kiss. After they parted, Abigail reached down and clasped her fingers around Cole's cock, slowly sliding the tip along her hot, wet slit. It felt fucking fantastic, but he needed more.

"I want to be inside you," he growled, gripping her hips. "Now. Don't make me wait."

Cole's head rolled back as Abigail sunk down onto him, her warmth spreading all the way from his cock to the tips of his fingers. She kissed him, her hair brushing his shoulders, making every one of his nerves stand on end. Then she leaned back as she rode him, leveraging herself by gripping his knees, arching her back and offering her breasts for the taking. Cole wrapped his arm around her waist, pulling her close to him as he took one of her nipples in his mouth, then the other.

Abigail rocked back and forth and Cole loved feeling her delicious wetness on his lower belly. An unintelligible string of words fell from her lips as her internal muscles squeezed his cock, threatening to push him over the edge. Much as he wanted to help her along, he wanted to feel the glorious spasms when she came, so he kept his hands on her hips to help him concentrate.

"Rub your clit," he said, his lips pressed against the shell of her ear. "Make yourself come."

Abigail slid her hand down her belly and between her thighs, circling that tiny bud of nerves. Her hips moved faster as she worked her way closer to orgasm, and Cole pulled her down until his cock was fully sheathed in her, so he could feel every ripple of her impending explosion.

"Fuck, fuck, fuck," Abigail breathed, her muscles gripping him, milking him.

Cole pulled her down to him as he came, burying his face in her neck, peppering her skin with kisses as they both rode out their pleasure. His muscles felt like jelly and he collapsed back into the soft couch cushions. Abigail followed him, coming to rest against his chest. As the two of them sat there catching their breath, Cole traced the line of her spine with his fingertips.

He would give himself tonight. But tomorrow he had to focus on work and finding out exactly what that Hamilton asshole was trying to steal from him. Tomorrow, he promised himself, he would stay away from Abigail.

It was a promise he knew he would break.

CHAPTER
Eleven

*A*bby was wide awake before the sun came up the following morning. She was lying in bed, staring at the bright green numbers on her alarm clock, thinking about Cole. Her muscles still felt weak; no man had ever made her feel the way that he did.

Figuring she should probably just get up if she was awake anyway, Abby rolled over and looked toward the door. There was no light shining through the small sliver between the wood and the carpet; the living area was still dark. If Cole was awake, he wasn't in the common area yet. Abby sat up and dangled her legs off the end of the bed. Just as she was about to stand, she heard her phone buzzing on the nightstand.

Looking at the screen, she smiled. It was Becca.

"Do you have any idea what time it is?" Abby whispered, teasing her.

"Why are you whispering?" Becca was quiet for a moment, then she gasped. "Holy shit, are you in his room?!"

"No, I just don't want to be too loud."

"What, are you going to wake him up? How small is that room? I thought you were staying in a suite?"

"It's five in the morning, Beck. It's too early for me to be a willing participant in twenty questions."

"At least tell me about the room," she pleaded. Abby smiled at the excitement in her voice.

"You wouldn't believe it. It has a dining room and everything. Four or five of our apartments could fit in this place. It's amazing."

Becca sighed. "I really picked the wrong person to work for. So…"

Abby knew exactly what Becca was getting at. "So…"

"Did he fuck you until you lost consciousness?"

Almost.

"No." Even though she'd spilled her guts to Becca about Cole before she left, she suddenly felt protective of him. Of what they were doing. "It's been strictly business."

"You are such a liar!" Becca cried. She didn't sound too distraught over it though, both she and Abby knew that Abby would cave eventually. "If you're going to play coy, I'll hang up. But I'll get it out of you eventually."

Abby knew that she would.

"Oh, I remembered this after you left," Becca said. "Isn't the object of your long-distance flirtation there in Chicago?"

Abby gasped. *Shit. I completely forgot about Josh.*

"You forgot he even existed, didn't you," Becca said,

laughing. "That boss of yours must be giving it to you but good."

Cole didn't know about Abby and Josh's friend/flirtation thing or whatever it was. Would he even care? What she had with Josh was just flirting. What she had with Cole was just sex. Did one have anything to do with the other?

"I'm going to have to figure out what to do about that," Abby said, following her words with a sigh.

"It'll be interesting, and I'm going to nag you until you tell me all about it."

Becca was right about one thing: it would be interesting indeed.

CHAPTER
Twelve

Cole sat at the end of the rectangular conference table in the boardroom of Kerrigan Corp's downtown Chicago office. At this particular meeting, he felt like a father chastising his unruly children. It was a room full of senior vice presidents, people Cole trusted with the livelihood of his company. Even though the main point of this trip was to find out what Hamilton planned to do with the stolen data, there was some excess fat he needed to trim off of his payroll, and he was ready to do it. He hadn't announced his visit, so they all knew something was up.

Firing someone was never a pleasant experience for Cole, but he couldn't hang onto employees who didn't pull their weight, or who put his company in jeopardy. He wouldn't stand for that kind of carelessness. And perhaps it was unfair of him to do this in a room full of colleagues, but he could think of no better reminder of what would happen if one of them slacked off.

"It's true that quarterly earnings are down a bit," Jack Barton, the Senior VP of Sales said, grabbing his oversized coffee cup. "We've been looking at outsourcing some of our software production. That will lower our tax burden and shore up a more stable earnings statement by early next year."

The other men at the table seemed to relax, probably thankful that the heat wasn't on them.

Cole shook his head. "I wouldn't call twenty five million dollars 'a bit,' Jack."

Jack's face reddened. "No sir."

"You've had me out on your boat," Cole said.

Jack's eyebrows knit together in confusion. "I'm sorry?"

"You aren't able to purchase things like that by being cavalier with your money, Jack." Cole's eyes focused on his target, completely unrelenting in their stare. "I wonder then, why are you so cavalier with mine?"

"Sir, I'm not suggesting-"

"The ten other divisions of this company manage to turn a profit, yet yours is the only one that is constantly underperforming."

"Sir, the market isn't-"

Cole laughed, cutting Jack off. "Don't stand here and tell me about the market. I am the CEO of this company. Do you think you're going to tell me something that I don't already know? That you're going to come up with an excuse that I haven't heard before?"

Jack's eyes scanned the room, practically begging

someone to come to his aid. There were no takers.

"Pack your things," Cole said without a moment's hesitation. "You are dismissed."

Everyone around the table sat there, stunned. It was eerily quiet, as if all the air had been sucked out of the room.

Cole chanced a glance at Abigail, but she was looking down, engrossed in her notes. He briefly wondered what she thought of him; she'd never been present to see him fire someone.

Jack stood and left the room, closing the door behind him. Cole appointed someone to act in Jack's position until a replacement was hired, then he promptly dismissed the meeting.

Cole sat at his desk in his office on the twenty-seventh floor, in a chair that wasn't quite the right fit for him, behind a desk that he disliked. Since he wasn't in this office very often, he let the heads of the Chicago location take the plusher, more private offices. He stared out of the window that looked over a cubicle farm made of tall steel rods, wooden partitions, and sleek, frosted-glass doors. He'd always hated this office and hated the view.

Until Abigail sat at the desk on the other side of the window.

Her back was facing him, long waves falling across her shoulders. God, he wanted to bury his face in her hair.

Occasionally she'd turn to the left, so he could just see her profile, and she'd smile. He knew it was a smile for him. She'd even purposely dropped something on the floor and bent over to pick it up, flashing him her cleavage. He'd thought about marching out there and pulling her into his office, then bending her over his desk and fucking her into oblivion. But he'd never let his cock make business decisions for him before, and he wasn't about to start now.

As if she knew he was thinking about her, she stood up and knocked on his door.

"Come in," he said.

Abigail walked in, and Cole couldn't help but stare at the curves of her body, accentuated by her form-fitting sweater and pencil skirt.

"You caused quite the stir today," she told him, bending over as she sat down and giving Cole a good look at her luscious breasts. If there was any privacy in this place, he'd have her. Right here, right now.

"I don't pay attention to office gossip, Abigail. And you would do well not to pay attention to it either," Cole said, admiring the stray strand of hair that curled across her forehead.

"Do you feel bad about that? About what happened?" she asked.

"If you had to do what I just did, would you feel bad about it?"

Without hesitation, she answered. "I'd be thinking about his family. And worried about how he'd pay his mortgage."

Cole admired her compassion. But something she would

have to learn when it came to the business world was that sometimes she had to separate the person from the position. "His mortgage is not my responsibility, Abigail. I paid him—handsomely, I might add—to perform a service. He didn't deliver. It was only a matter of time before his carelessness impacted other people in this office. Other people in this company. I have a responsibility to everyone who works here, not just him."

Abigail nodded, understanding filling her eyes. "I guess that's why you're the CEO and I'm an assistant."

Cole didn't like the implication in her words, that she wasn't smart enough to be in his position. He wanted to disabuse her of that notion immediately. "Nonsense," he replied, waving his hand dismissively. "I had the benefit of a trust fund, a father with an incredible amount of business acumen and more money than he knew what to do with."

Abigail stared at him, eyes wide.

"What?"

She shook her head as a small grin curled her lips. "I'm just surprised to hear you admit it."

"Everyone knows my family history. It does me no good to pretend that it doesn't exist."

Abigail was looking at him as if she was genuinely impressed. It was a look that made Cole want to sit up straighter and stand taller. He liked what that look did to him.

"Listen," she said, staring down at her note pad. "In the meeting Jack mentioned that he was looking at outsourcing to lower the tax burden-"

"I'm not looking for a tax break, I'm looking for a profit."

Abigail bit her lip, a sure sign of frustration. Cole couldn't help but grin, even as he chastised himself for interrupting her.

"You had me take a look at our real estate portfolio a few days ago. It's true that our production is lagging in the midwest. The packaging warehouse in Kansas City is only operating at twenty-five percent of its current capacity. Couldn't we move the production center to that warehouse and combine the operations? We'd double production for only slightly more overhead, and you'd be using space you already have in an area that needs the job growth. We all know how you feel about outsourcing."

Cole loathed outsourcing; it seemed everyone understood that but Jack. He grinned at Abigail, feeling a sense of pride for her that he'd never experienced before. Every time he gave her a challenge, she shattered his expectations.

"I was wondering if you would figure that out," Cole said. It was a lie, though. He never wondered if she'd figure it out. He only wondered how long it would take her. She was a beautiful, radiant, intelligent woman. One of the best he had working for him, which is why his indiscretion with her was so utterly foolish. But what was done was done, and Cole never made a habit of dwelling on the past.

"What, it was a test?" she asked.

"Perhaps," he replied as he jotted a note to himself on his notepad.

"Did I pass?"

"Perhaps." He grinned.

Abigail was silent for a moment, and when Cole looked up he saw her wringing her hands together, twisting her fingers into white-knuckled knots. There was a nervousness about her that he didn't see very often.

"What's the matter?" he asked.

"I'm not sure how I should bring this up, because I don't want you to think that *I* think we're more than we are. But I recognize that there's…I don't know…*something* going on between you and me."

"What are you asking me?" Cole shifted in his seat, attempting to ignore the nerves in his stomach.

"I'm friendly with one of the associates here," she began, still twisting her fingers and looking at the floor. "He asked me out for drinks on Thursday. It's platonic, but I…I didn't want to ruffle your feathers, and I just thought…I don't know."

It was Hamilton, Cole knew that much. *Conniving bastard.* The thing was, Cole had come here with only a hint of a plan to somehow get the two of them together so that Josh could ask Abigail for whatever he was going to ask her for. He'd wanted to set this exact chain of events in motion, only he wasn't such a fan of the plan now that it was Josh's idea to ask her out. Cole didn't have any control over the situation, and it drove him mad. What drove him madder still, was the fact that the flirtation between Josh and Abby that Cole had only seen on paper was beginning to become real to him, and it drove him crazy.

Abigail, she was his. And he would be damned if he was going to let this thief steal her from him. But he had his company to consider…

"You're asking me for permission?" Cole said, trying to buy himself some time for an appropriate reaction.

She shook her head, grinning a little. "No. I actually don't know what I'm asking. I just wanted you to know."

"Who is this coworker?"

Abigail looked at him with that knowing smile, one that made him weak in the knees. "I'm not telling you that."

"Well, now I know," he replied. There was a bitter edge to his voice, which seemed to surprise Abigail.

"Okay then," she said, slowly standing.

She made her way out the door, all the while Cole gripped his pen, practically bending it in half as he attempted to keep the wave of possessiveness that flooded through him at bay. In that moment, Cole would've let Josh Hamilton steal everything he owned to prevent him from coming within a foot of Abigail.

That's when Cole realized that he was in way too deep.

CHAPTER
Thirteen

*C*ole left the hotel without Abby for the first time on the third day they were in Chicago. Before they had left New York, he had asked her to block off the entire afternoon on his calendar, but he didn't tell her why. Cole had a habit of being secretive, but that sort of thing became an issue when he received emergency calls from the New York office. Particularly when one of those calls was from Charles Findlay, the owner of a small software firm that Cole had been trying to buy out for the past few weeks.

What made today particularly maddening for Abby was that for whatever reason, Cole had turned off his phone.

She called Jessica, the receptionist in the Chicago office, trying not to sound frantic.

"Have you seen Mr. Kerrigan today?" Abby asked, feeling utterly ridiculous that she just called Cole by his last name.

"No," Jessica replied, sounding unimpressed. "He called a couple of times earlier this morning, but he hasn't come into the office."

"Thanks." Abby ended the call without saying goodbye.

Tapping her phone against her knee, Abby tried to figure out what to do next. If Cole was due back in the office in an hour or so, she wouldn't sweat it. But it was two-thirty, and Cole's calendar was marked off until six. She knew he didn't drive wherever it was that he went, and it wasn't like him to take a cab. That left the car service.

Abby grabbed her bag and shoved her room key inside, then ran to the elevator. In the lobby, she asked the desk clerk to call their driver, Tony. As luck would have it, he was actually at the hotel.

"Tell him I need him to take me somewhere," Abby told the clerk breathlessly. She nodded.

Abby stood out in front of the hotel, under the huge awning that covered the driveway. Since Cole was gone most of the morning, Abby was working in a loose-fitting pair of khakis and a long-sleeved cotton v-neck. She didn't even have any makeup on. Seeing how horribly underdressed she was even at the hotel, she wondered if she should go back up to the room and change. If she could convince Tony to take her wherever he'd taken Cole, who knew what kind of situation she would be walking into.

When Tony pulled around, he got out of the car and opened the back door for Abby. A hulking man, he seemed like a big teddy bear. Abby would see how big in just a second.

"Where to, Ms. Waters?" Tony asked.

"Wherever it is that you drove Mr. Kerrigan earlier," Abby told him, her voice firm. She could tell that he was reluctant to take her there.

"Mr. Kerrigan told me not to come back until six-fifteen."

Abby bit her lip, trying to figure out what to do next. Maybe the truth would work the best.

"Tony, he's turned off his cell phone, and he has an important business deal that will fall through if I don't reach him. We don't have time to wait until six-fifteen. Please," she begged. "Take me where he is and I swear you won't get in trouble." She really couldn't make that kind of promise, but he didn't need to know that.

He thought about Abby's offer for a few seconds, and then relented. "Get in."

She didn't ask him where they were going, mostly because she was afraid to find out. All she could think about were a number of different scenarios, each one worse than the one before. Would she find him in a hotel room somewhere fucking his Chicago regular? Was he out on a drug run? Could he be an addict? Maybe that's why he was so secretive all the time.

Abby, don't be a moron. No way is Cole on drugs; he's too obsessed with his body. He could be with his family for all you know. Maybe they live here in the city.

Abby's mind was spinning with one ridiculous theory after another when the car finally came to a stop. She hadn't been paying attention to her surroundings while Tony was driving. They were in a neighborhood full of apartment buildings, in front of a square brick structure that looked a lot like a school.

A school? Does he have a kid here? Abby shook that thought right out of her head. He couldn't have kept a child a secret, and even if he did have one there was no way he would've sent that kid to public school. She took a deep breath as Tony opened the car door for her, and she noticed the worried look in his eyes, still walking that fine line between wondering if he was doing something wrong by bringing her her, or if he'd be doing something wrong if he hadn't. Abby tried to reassure him.

"It's okay," she said, smiling. "I'll take the heat if he's angry." She patted his arm. "I don't know if he'll be glad I came here, but I do know that he'll be angry if this deal falls through because I didn't try to find him." Abby realized that she sounded like she was trying to reassure herself, too.

"He went in there," Tony said, pointing to a pair of red doors to their right, on the far side of the building.

Abby nodded, thanked him, and told him to come back at six-fifteen like Cole asked him to. Her heart was racing as she approached the building, pumping nervous electricity that vibrated throughout her body. She took a deep breath as she opened the door. The handle was cool against her fingers.

She crossed her arms in front of her chest as she stepped inside. It was too late to turn back now.

CHAPTER
Fourteen

*H*igh-pitched squeaks from the bottoms of tennis shoes on hardwood floors echoed throughout the gym as Cole dribbled the basketball, standing at least two feet taller than any of his opponents. He was so sweaty that his hair stuck to his forehead and his soaked t-shirt clung to his back, but he felt incredibly alive and was having the time of his life. He always had the time of his life when he was in this building with these kids.

"You're cheating!" a little boy named Ramon yelled as he laughed, his tiny, crooked teeth jutting out from his huge smile.

Cole playfully placed his palm on Ramon's forehead, preventing him from making a play for the ball.

"Here's a life lesson for you," Cole said to the kids gathered around him, hanging on his every word. "Using something to your advantage isn't cheating. I'm tall, so I have long arms. Using my height and my arm length to keep the ball away from you isn't cheating, it's strategy. Just like being short is an advantage for you."

"Not in basketball!" Ramon cried, is little arms flailing.

"Sure it is. If you stole this ball from me, it'd be easy for you to keep it away. You have a lower center of gravity than I do and can make plays closer to the floor," Cole said as he dribbled the ball.

"Show us!" a girl named Alicia yelled. Cole had only met her a couple of times, but he liked her curiosity and the fact that she wasn't afraid to take charge and ask questions.

"Okay, first-" Cole cut the sentence short when he turned and saw Abigail standing on the far side of the gym, right next to the doors. He blinked, certain she was a figment of his imagination, but she remained right where she was.

What in the hell is she doing here? Cole fought to quell the burning anger that was building inside him. He'd specifically told her to block off this time and that the appointment was private. *What on earth would possess her to come looking for me?*

Cole marched toward her with a furrowed brow, tension rolling off of him in waves. He knew he must've looked harsh when he saw the expression on Abigail's face: wide eyes and red cheeks. She looked like she wanted to run. He never wanted to see that expression aimed at him again, so he made it a point to take a few breaths to calm himself down before he spoke to her. When he finally reached her, he felt cooler, more at ease.

"What are you doing here?" he asked, his voice low so that the volunteers sitting on the bench a few feet away wouldn't hear him. "I told you to block off this time. What I do with it is none of your business." He clenched and unclenched his hands, trying to work out his annoyance. He didn't mean to sound so harsh.

"I'm not spying on you." Abigail explained, her words very soft.

"What are you doing then?"

"Charles Findlay called," she said in a rush, holding her cell phone out toward Cole. "He wants to make a deal, but he gave you a deadline. I was worried you wouldn't get back in time. I tried to call you but your phone is off."

Cole felt like an ass. Of course she would try to find him when Findlay called; that was her job. He ran his fingers through his hair and looked to his left. The volunteers quickly shifted their eyes, pretending like they weren't eavesdropping.

"It's okay," Cole replied, giving Abigail a small smile.

"I'll go, I shouldn't have come. I just thought you'd be angry if I waited."

"You're right, I would've been angry. You did the right thing." Cole pinched the collar of his shirt, lifted it up, then wiped his face with it. He motioned toward the bleachers. "Have a seat over there. By the time Tony gets you back to the hotel, he's just going to have to come back here to pick me up."

"Please don't be hard on him. I was adamant about coming here to find you. He was just doing what I told him to."

Cole laughed. "You think I don't know how you are when you're on a mission? Tony has nothing to worry about. Just have a seat."

Abigail turned and walked toward the bleachers, and Cole wondered if this wasn't an opportunity after all, a chance to show her what kind of man he really was.

CHAPTER
Fifteen

"You can sit here," a young woman said to Abby, patting the empty space on the bench beside her. Her skin was a honeyed brown, and her hair bounced in tight spirals that fell just below her shoulders. This woman was gorgeous, and if Abby had to guess, she'd say she was about twenty or so.

"I'm Michele," the young woman said, holding out her hand. Abby shook it, noting her firm grip.

"Abigail." Abby closed her eyes and smiled before correcting herself. "Abby, actually. Call me Abby." She'd become accustomed to being called by her full name for the past few days. So accustomed that it was strange to hear her preferred nickname spoken aloud.

The thumping of the basketball resumed as Cole and the kids continued their game. Abby sat in silence watching them until her curiosity got the better of her.

"So, what's going on here?" she asked Michelle.

"It's a pickup game. We have one every afternoon."

"But why is Cole playing?"

Michelle looked at Abby as if she had a third eye. "You don't know?"

Abby shook her head, completely confused. "Know what?"

Michelle scooted closer to Abby, leaning in so their conversation would be a little more private. "He funds this community center. Several of them, actually. Here in Chicago and a few other cities. He comes in every once in a while to play with the kids and check up on things."

Abby was completely shocked. It wasn't that she didn't think Cole had such kindness in him, but she just never imagined that it would manifest itself in this way. She watched him playing with the children, looking more alive than she'd ever seen him, looking more human than he ever had, and this tiny blossom of warmth began opening up inside of her. It started in her chest and traveled all the way down to her toes, making her legs feel like jelly.

"He funds this center?" Abby repeated. *I am a complete moron.*

Michelle nodded, smiling. "Yeah, you didn't know?"

"I didn't," Abby admitted. She wondered how many other things like this she didn't know about Cole, and for the first time since she started working for him, she was dying to find them all out. He was a puzzle, and now that Abby had found a few pieces, it would be little easier to put the others in place. She couldn't help the smile that spread across her lips.

Cole scored on two of the children: one boy and one girl. Then he lifted the smallest one of the bunch to the net so that he could dunk the ball. Everyone was laughing and smiling, and Abby longed to be a part of that. Cole huddled with the kids, and Abby tried not to look awkward as he kept glancing over at her. The kids looked, too. Cole said something and the children nodded vehemently.

What in the hell is going on?

"Miss Waters," Cole yelled, grinning. He held up the ball. "Can you play?"

Even though Abby was short, she actually could play. Quite well in fact, but she decided not to tell Cole that. Instead, she employed a strategy that Cole would be quite familiar with: concealing your abilities in order to take your opponent by surprise.

Abby shrugged. "I don't really know how."

Cole's eyes lit up the way they did when he had a great idea, or when he found a fledgling company that he could purchase for a bargain price.

"C'mon," he said, waving her over. "We'll go easy on you."

Abby pretended to be reluctant, slowly standing before she walked over. Cole tossed her the ball and she purposely missed the catch. She ran and picked it up, then set in motion a plan to hustle him. "So, are there teams or what?"

Cole grinned, completely unaware of what was about to happen to him and his poor little friends.

"Yes, there are teams," he replied condescendingly. "Matt,

Jorge, Kayla and Xavier, you'll be on Miss Waters' team."

Abby thought that Cole calling her by her last name was adorable. The four kids walking over to Abby's side of the court did not look at all pleased to be on her team. Their lack of enthusiasm made her smile.

"So, what are we playing to?" Abby asked.

Cole looked around at the kids, who already looked tired.

"Ten?"

"Ten!" they shouted in unison.

Abby dribbled the ball, bouncing it between her legs and catching it with her left hand. Cole's eyes widened and the faces of her little teammates lit up. "Ten it is."

And then Abby and her team proceeded to smash their opponents. Cole and his team of merry little misfits were no match for her kids. They communicated well, even though they had never played together. It was the most fun Abby had in months. And truthfully, she wasn't sure if Cole let them win or if her team just had better moves, but when the game was over they all shook hands. Cole's hand lingered in hers, and he began to walk away while they were still touching. "Good game," he said with a smile. "I'm going to take a quick shower, then we can go."

"I'll wait for you here."

Cole stopped at the bleachers a few feet away from where Abby was sitting, looking as if he had something he wanted to say to her. He stared at her for a long while. He was sweaty and beautiful. A complete mystery.

How can I get him to open up to me more? It was the first

time Abby didn't over-think the ramifications of caring for Cole. She just wanted to know more about him, everything there was to know.

"Hey Cole," Kayla said, grinning from ear to ear.

He didn't tear his eyes away from Abby. "Yeah?"

"Is Miss Waters your girlfriend?" The last word came out in a singsongy way, and Abby wanted to crawl under the bleachers and die.

Cole grinned, and Abby thought she saw a hint of redness in his cheeks. She was sure that hers were crimson. Cole picked Kayla up, spinning her around in a circle as she squealed with delight. The peals of laugher bounced off the gym walls, creating a wonderful echo.

"What would you know about girlfriends?" Cole asked as he put her down.

"Nothing," Kayla laughed.

"Miss Waters is my employee," Cole said, talking to Kayla and the group of children surrounding her. "And if you guys keep your grades up and study really hard, someday you'll have employees too."

"I hope they're all as pretty as Miss Waters," Xavier said.

Abby thought Cole might've stopped breathing. She definitely did.

"If you're lucky, Xavier." Cole mussed Xavier's hair as he walked away, glancing over at Abby once before he walked out the door. It wasn't until he was gone that Abby could finally breathe normally again.

Abby looked at the banners hanging up around the gym, each with a different inspirational saying written on it. It was such a warm, fun place and Abby was proud of Cole for making it possible. She wondered how long she would've gone thinking he was such a cold, standoffish man if she hadn't visited today. Because as she sat down on the bench, she realized that she had been so wrong about the kind of person he was. So incredibly wrong.

Tony picked Abby and Cole up promptly at six-fifteen, and even though they were quiet in the back of the limo, it wasn't an uncomfortable silence like it used to be. Cole was checking his Blackberry, catching up on emails he missed.

"Why do you keep all of this a secret?" Abby asked, unable to stay quiet anymore. She was dying to know the answer.

Cole pondered the question for a moment, the light from his phone creating shadows on his face that accentuated his perfect bone structure.

"It seems more charitable if nobody knows. Once people find out, it becomes exploitive. I would never use any of those children for positive press." He turned toward her, his expression tender.

"Why do that, though? You didn't grow up needing a community center."

He nodded. "I was lucky, but they are not."

"Yes they are," Abby replied. She longed to reach for his hand, but wasn't sure how he'd react to the gesture. "I'm sorry

114

I barged in there today. If I had known-"

"Don't apologize. You did what I would've expected anyone who was loyal to me to do. But there's no time limit with Findlay."

Abby was confused. "He explicitly said you needed to return his call right away."

"Abigail," Cole said, smiling. "When you hold all the cards, you don't have to play by anyone else's rules."

CHAPTER
Sixteen

At half-past seven, Cole was huddled over his laptop, wearing the same hoodie and jeans that he was wearing when he returned from the gym. He was behind on his emails and having difficulty concentrating. Ever since he'd fucked Abigail that night in his office, he hadn't been able to think clearly. He'd have the occasional streak of work time where he pounded through his daily routine without much interruption. Then he'd think of her or smell her perfume, and he'd get distracted by the memory of her taste, the memory of the feel of her skin.

Earlier today he'd slipped out of the hotel room, wanting to check in on the kids at his center. He didn't want Abigail to know about his charitable endeavors, preferring to keep the business and humanitarian sides of him separate. Cole had always worried that blending the two would make him look insincere, like if he went public with his charitable works the world would think less of him and the good that he did. But when Abigail walked through the gym doors today, after the initial shock he found that he wanted her there. He wanted her to see that side of him, to know that there was goodness in his heart. And when he saw her playing with the children and kicking his ass at basketball, he knew he was in deep. Too deep.

The woman was going to be the end of him—or at least the end of his business—if he didn't get his head on straight. But she was always there, on the periphery of every thought. Cole had always been more focused on work than he had been on his personal life, often preferring the company of The Wall Street Journal to the company of another human being.

He had never been the type to settle down. Being young and rich, he didn't even need to have much game with the ladies; whenever he had wanted female companionship, it always seemed to find him. His bed had always been open, and his cock was fairly easy to please. But since he'd met Abigail, he'd started longing for more. He craved her mind almost as much as he craved her body. A cutting remark from her beautiful mouth could turn him on almost as much as her perfect tits did.

With the women he'd bedded before Abigail, Cole had always been quick to love them and leave them. Once he'd gotten off, he began plotting an escape, making up excuses for why he needed to leave.

So, this was a situation he was entirely unprepared to

deal with.

Completely lost in thought, Cole looked at the time on his laptop, surprised to find that he'd been sitting there staring at the email he'd been trying to reply to for over fifteen minutes. He reached up and rubbed his eyes, then ran his fingers through his hair.

Inviting Abigail along on this trip was going to wind up being either the best or the worst decision he'd ever made. There was no in between where she was concerned.

He smelled her presence before she uttered a word; fruity shampoo and soap that made him want to close his eyes and breathe deep, made him want to nestle his head in the crook of her neck and smell that scent forever. He didn't turn around to look at her though. He wasn't sure if she intended on speaking to him or if she was just going to stand there, and he wanted to give her the chance to make up her mind.

"Hey," Abigail said after a few quiet moments. Her voice trembled on the word and Cole could tell she was nervous. Her nerves piqued his curiosity. He turned and looked at her, drawn in by her form-fitting jeans and sweater. He much preferred her like this. Even though he loved the way her work clothes hugged her figure, these clothes were more her.

"Hi," he replied, giving her a sleepy smile.

"I'm hungry, and there's a diner right down the street. Do you want to come grab a bite to eat with me?"

Cole wanted to do so much more than that, but for now he would settle for dinner.

"Absolutely." He stood and grabbed his jacket. He could practically see the relief on her face. Had she thought for one second that he would deny her? He'd have to do something about that.

The place was packed, but Cole slipped a waitress a twenty, ensuring him and Abigail a private booth in the less crowded back section of the diner. The waitress who sat them told them they were short staffed that evening, so there might be a bit of a wait, but that she would get to them as soon as she could. Normally Cole would find that kind of service unacceptable, but tonight he relished the thought of waiting, of having more time to speak to Abigail.

"May I ask you a question?" Abigail poked at the edge of a napkin with her fingernail. "There's something I've been curious about."

"Absolutely."

She didn't miss a beat. As soon as the answer left Cole's lips, she threw her question into the space between them.

"Do you ever Google yourself?"

All the things she could've taken this time to ask and she wants to know if he Googles himself? He couldn't help but laugh. "Do I ever Google myself?"

"Yeah." She nodded, blushing. Cole liked the look of bashfulness on her.

"I do," he admitted. And he didn't regret being truthful for one second; in fact, he rather enjoyed the look of surprise on her face when she heard his answer. The wideness of her eyes, how they shone under the bright diner lights.

"Wow."

"What?" Cole replied, wondering why she'd be so shocked. Obviously she suspected he did it or she wouldn't have asked.

"I'm just surprised you were so forthcoming. I thought you would've lied, maybe. To protect your vanity."

Cole laughed. "I have no reason to lie to you, Abigail."

She seemed to ponder his response for a few moments. "I've always wondered if famous people do that. Now I know, I guess."

"I'm hardly famous," Cole replied sincerely. He had name recognition, sure, and he'd been featured in a few of those eligible bachelor issues of popular magazines, but fame and notoriety were two different things. Besides, he didn't want to be known for his face or for his personal life, so popularity was of little value to him. He wanted to be known by the imprint he left on the business world and the good that he did with both his company and his fortune.

Abigail tutted at him. "You're not movie-star famous, but you're well-known. There's gossip about you. I see your picture in The City Whisper fairly often."

"You do?" Cole was genuinely surprised. "I never would've pegged you for someone who reads gossip."

She crossed her arms over her chest, and Cole got the distinct impression that she was embarrassed about what she'd just admitted to. "I don't read gossip, generally. My roommate's a fan."

"Of me or The City Whisper?" Cole smiled so she'd know

he was teasing her.

"Both."

He was amused for a moment, then his mood turned somber. "She doesn't know you work for me, does she?" Too late, it seemed, he was working out the ramifications of their behavior. Even now the course of their relationship didn't feel real to him. It wasn't like him to act on a whim, even though he'd fantasized about her for months. No, he chided himself, he couldn't consider her a whim.

"Generally when people make me sign contracts that say they'll sue my pants off if I let certain information slip, I tend not to let that information slip." Her voice was condescending, but Cole focused more on what she'd said than how she said it.

"You really think I'd sue you?" Cole had always held his employees to their non-disclosure agreements, but with Abigail... "If I wanted to get your pants off, I wouldn't have to get a lawyer involved."

Abigail rolled her eyes. "Yes I think that. Or I *thought* that, until just now."

Cole looked out the window, pondering her answer. This was yet another moment where he knew he needed to proceed with caution, but he found that he just didn't care. He should never have told her that he didn't consider the NDA to be binding when it came to her, but what was really the harm in telling her the truth? He looked at her, and he could tell that she was expecting him to say something. Anything. But he couldn't think of the right words.

"Isn't that the point of making people sign non-disclosure

agreements? What good are they if people don't believe you'd actually sue them?"

"I could never sue you, Abigail." Cole's voice was quiet, and he could tell by the look in her eyes that she knew that he meant it.

As if on cue, the waitress came to the table and handed each of them a menu.

Since they didn't have anything on tap, Cole indulged his child-like side and ordered a milkshake. Abigail asked for a cream soda, and the waitress brought their drinks almost immediately. Cole watched Abigail as she studied her menu, her eyes widening as she looked at different selections. She ran her fingertips along her bottom lip as she tried to decide what she was going to order, and Cole wanted to twine his fingers with hers and take her lip between his. He smiled as she closed her eyes when she took a sip of her drink, savoring it. She seemed so at home in a place like this.

Cole knew Abigail frequented the diner during her lunch breaks, and he figured there must be something about places like this that drew her in. He wanted to know more about it, figuring the answer would offer him a little insight into her.

"What is it with you and diners?" he asked as he drew his straw to his lips.

Abigail raised her eyebrows. "I wasn't aware diners and I had a thing."

Cole laughed, all the while dying to lean over and kiss her. Dying to grab her hand and pull her out of the seat and press his body against hers.

"You seem to eat in them frequently, and you..." Cole

looked at her body, unsure of how to phrase his comment so it wouldn't be offensive.

"I don't have the typical diner physique?"

Cole laughed, relieved that she understood what he meant. "Yes, precisely that."

"How did you know that I like diners?"

Silence. Cole had just done something he never did, at least he never did before he met Abigail. He showed his hand. He usually kept his cards close to the vest, and never in a million years would he have let anyone know how he got information about them. Knowing people's motivations was key to taking them by surprise, to finding a weakness. But with Abigail, he didn't want to surprise her, he wanted to know her. And if she had a weakness, he only wanted to do what he could to make it a strength.

"The delivery guy comes into the office often," Cole said, hoping that would be enough of an explanation.

Just then, the waitress brought out their meals, and Abigail's gaze locked with Cole's as their plates were placed in front of them. Abigail poured a dollop of ketchup on her plate, then dragged a fry through it before she spoke again.

"I like diners because my mom was a waitress. Eating in them reminds me of her." There was a sadness in her eyes that made Cole ache.

"You don't get to see her very much anymore?"

She shook her head, looking down at her plate. "I haven't seen her in eight years."

"Take some time, Abigail. Go see her," Cole said emphatically, tilting his head so she'd look at him. "If time off is an issue-"

"It's not an issue," she said quietly, and the sadness in her voice alerted Cole to the fact that this wasn't an issue that time off would be able to solve. When her eyes met his, they were shining with unshed tears.

"I'm sorry, I shouldn't have asked-"

"She had breast cancer," Abigail said. "We didn't have insurance, so by the time she even realized she was sick, it was too late."

"Jesus," Cole breathed. He knew things like this happened to people all the time, he just hated thinking of it happening to her. "How old were you?"

"Sixteen."

Cole felt a distinct wrenching in his chest. "Where did you go?"

"My best friend Becca's mother took me in. I lived with them until I graduated from high school."

"Did she...your mother, I mean..." Cole was unsure how to proceed with the question. "Did she leave you anything?"

Abigail had a sad, amused glint in her eyes.

"We lived out of our car. So, she left me that. I ended up selling it for a thousand dollars in order to pay for my college application fees and books. But I have a few little trinkets, things that remind me of her."

Of course, Cole was asking specifically about money, because in his privileged world, that was a parent's legacy: what kind of estate they left to their children. He felt like a damned fool for even having asked the question, but he wanted to know if she'd been taken care of.

"Trinkets?" he asked, anxiously waiting for any crumb of information she could give him about her earlier life.

"A pair of earrings," she said, pointing to the diamond studs she was wearing. "A few notes and things that meant something to her." Abigail looked as if she was escaping into a beautiful memory when she continued. "She always had this music box, when I was growing up. It was round and green," she said, smiling. "There was a little frog and some dragonflies painted on the top, and when you opened it, it would play 'Someone To Watch Over Me.' I used to wind it up and fall asleep to the music."

"Used to?" he asked. Realizing he hadn't touched his food, he grabbed his hamburger and took a bite, even though he was no longer very hungry.

"A few of my boxes got lost between Cleveland and New York when I was moving," she said, her voice wavering.

Christ, could anything more happen to this woman? Cole reached out and took her hand, caressing the soft skin on her palm with the pad of his thumb. When she squeezed his fingers, he made a silent promise that he was going to find that music box. How she was able to sit there and tell him this and still have the strength to stay upright, Cole didn't know. His heart broke for her, but it was far outweighed by his admiration for her strength. He'd never known anyone like her.

"Where was your father?" Cole asked, then immediately regretted it. He couldn't help his thirst for knowledge, but he was being nosy, and this was obviously a sensitive subject. But, Abigail surprised him once again.

Her smile was kind. "I wouldn't have told you any of this if I minded the questions." She pushed a fry around her plate, smearing ketchup along the edge. "I haven't ever met him."

This life of hers was so foreign to his own. He knew he was privileged, but he'd never truly felt the extent of it until he was sitting across from this amazing woman. "She would be proud of you. Your mother, I mean."

"Why do you say that?"

"Many people in your position would've felt sorry for themselves and given up. You, you finished college at the top of your class, moved to New York, and now you're following your dream."

Abigail laughed as she swirled her straw in her drink.

"What?" Cole asked.

"I'm not following my dream."

"You mean working for me isn't your life's goal?" Cole pressed his hand against his chest, pretending to be wounded.

"It's up there," she said, grinning. He was beginning to appreciate the strength behind that grin. "But not quite the pinnacle for me."

"Then what is?" he asked. He wanted this piece of information more than any of the others.

"What, so you can fire me?"

"So I can help you reach it." After being around Abigail for the past few days and learning what he'd learned about her over the past hour, those words didn't surprise him, but they certainly surprised her.

"Honestly?"

"Yeah," he replied, nodding.

"I want to own a candy store." She almost looked embarrassed when she said it.

"A candy store?" He was surprised by her answer, to say the least.

"Gourmet candy. I like to make chocolate."

"I didn't know that. Why haven't you ever brought any into the office?"

"I have," she said, giving him a chastising look.

"I've never seen it."

"I gave you a box at Christmas." Even though she had every right to be angry that he didn't remember, her good humor was evident in her smile. "You probably threw it away or gave it to someone to test for poison."

Cole attempted a laugh, but it didn't feel right. He'd been an ass to her. Occasionally it was to get under her skin, but sometimes it was because he was genuinely an ass. He was going to have to be better about that. Realizing he was still holding her hand, he gave it another squeeze.

"I apologize for that. I'd love to taste it some time."

She nodded. "Sometimes I set up a stand in the Union Square Market on Saturdays."

"So, if I want to try them, I'll have to buy them?" Cole teased, smiling at her.

"Maybe," she teased back. "Eat your burger."

Cole winked at her as he took a bite, and the two of them ate and made small talk. At the end of the meal, when Cole was paying the check, Abigail asked him a question that truly floored him.

"Do you have any community centers in New York?" She

fished in the bowl of candy by the register and picked out a swirly red peppermint.

"Yes," he replied. "In Brooklyn. Why?"

She shrugged as she popped the candy in her mouth. "I liked spending time with the kids today, and I was thinking about how nice it would've been to have a place like that to go to when I was a kid. I think it would've helped me. I'd like to volunteer."

Cole nodded slowly, taking in what she'd just said to him. "I'll talk to Antonia; she runs the center."

"Great." Abby grinned at him before she turned and headed for the door.

He was watching her walk away from him when the realization hit him.

He was falling in love with her.

CHAPTER
Seventeen

Cole and Abby stepped out into the crisp night air, both of them quiet as they walked down the sidewalk and back to their hotel. Abby, who was usually never at a loss for words, was having a difficult time coming up with light conversation after she'd just spilled her guts to Cole while they were eating. She never expected to want to tell him so much about herself. In the past, a part of her had worried that he would use that knowledge against her in some way, but that was before she paid attention to the kind of person he was.

During this trip—today especially—Abby had really begun to *see* Cole. She knew he would always have command of whatever room he walked into; that was part of who he was, what made him so successful. But now, she could see what was behind that unrelenting confidence. It wasn't ego like she initially thought, although he certainly had that in spades. It was a genuine desire to do well with what he'd been given in life. He knew how lucky he was, and he didn't want to take that for granted. But most importantly, he wanted to give the people who weren't so lucky a chance at succeeding, too. It was such an admirable trait, and one that Abby probably never would've realized if she hadn't come on this trip with him.

That desire in Cole was part of what had made Abby tell him the story of her past. The confession was even a bit easy for her, strangely enough. She wanted him to know everything that made her who she was, everything that made her tick. That was a rare thing for Abby, who was usually very reserved about her past. Because confessions like hers usually come with a price, and Abby could tell that Cole wasn't sure exactly how to react to her now. What do you say to a woman who told you she lived in a car until her mother died when she was sixteen? The answer, at least in Cole's case, was that he didn't say anything at all.

Abby crossed her arms over her chest, rubbing her upper arms with her hands to generate some extra heat. The wind whipping off the lake made Chicago colder than New York, and she hadn't thought to bring a jacket when she left the hotel earlier. It wasn't long before Cole slipped his jacket over Abby's shoulders. He pulled her closer to him, and she tucked herself under his arm, snuggling up to the warmth of his body. She turned her head and breathed in the smell of the collar of his jacket before looking up at him for the first time since they left the diner.

"Thank you," she said.

Cole smiled at her with sadness in his eyes. Sadness that made Abby's heart sink.

She hated that look. She had spent most of her life on the receiving end of it, and that was why she so seldom told anyone about her mother. When she had decided to tell Cole, she had hoped that this would open up an easy understanding between the two of them, not make him treat her like a wounded bird.

Her anger and frustration grew as she and Cole approached the hotel, coming to a head when they were in the elevator and Abby glanced over and caught him looking at her with that sadness in his eyes again. She didn't want to see that sadness ever again; all she wanted to see when he looked at her was that fire, the unbridled desire that always seemed to come out when he kissed her and couldn't keep his hands off of her.

Abby was determined to do whatever she had to in order to see that look again.

Cole slipped the key card into the lock, and held the door for her as she walked inside. The second the door closed, Abby stood on the tips of her toes and pressed her lips against his, frantically trying to make things right again, to get them back to a more physical place in their relationship. Cole seemed surprised at first, but it only took a moment for his body to respond to her. His hands were everywhere: her neck, the small of her back, her ass. When they finally broke apart, Abby rested her forehead on Cole's chest and worked at the button on his jeans.

"What are you doing?" he asked, breathless. "Not that I'm complaining, but…" He tilted her head up until their eyes met, and there was that look again, like he wanted to scoop her up in his arms and hold her.

Abby gripped Cole's hoodie, needing something to hold onto while she said what she was going to say. Those crystal-blue eyes of his were flooded with uncertainty and watching her so intently that she didn't know what to do with herself. She didn't know if she would be able to get this out the way that she wanted to.

Abby took a deep breath, focusing on the way the soft cotton of his hoodie felt beneath her hands in order to distract herself from his perfect, beautiful face. Then she looked up at him, resolute.

"Don't pity me," she said, her words hard as stone.

He furrowed his brows. "I don't pity you."

He was a liar.

"Yes you do," she insisted. "I've seen that look enough to know what it is, and I hate seeing it on anyone's face, especially yours. Nothing can change the past, Cole, so there's no reason to be sad about it. Look how far I've come." Cole's hands wrapped around hers, and the warmth of his skin made it difficult for her to concentrate. "I'm so much better off than other people who grew up like I did, you know that. I want you to look at me the way you did in your office that night; like you can't get enough of me, like nothing in the world could make you keep your hands off me. Not like this."

Cole searched Abby's eyes, taking in everything she'd just said, but it was too long for her. She reached forward and slid her hand along the crotch of his jeans, and his eyelids fluttered. He was already hard, just from one kiss. She cupped his erection and he bucked against her hand as his expression completely changed from pity to desire to absolute raging lust.

"Nothing in this world *can* make me keep my hands off of you."

And for the first time since they left the diner, Abby liked the way Cole looked at her.

CHAPTER
Eighteen

*I*f Abigail didn't want Cole to look at her with pity in his eyes, she made it incredibly easy when she touched his cock like that.

This woman does things to me that no woman has ever done before. Cole didn't mean that in the physical sense, although Abigail was exceptional in that area, but he wanted to let her get to know him, to show her parts of himself that he'd never let anyone else see. He wanted to crack himself open like a book and let Abigail read every single page of him. Everything he thought, everything he had ever done, everything he wanted to do; he wanted her to know all of it. But Cole would have to push that desire aside to make room for one of a more carnal nature, because when she put herself on offer the way she just did, he had no choice but to indulge himself.

Usually he liked to tease Abigail, make her wait until she was desperate for him, but tonight he didn't take his time with undressing her or bother with seduction. He wanted her now. *Needed* her now, right here in this foyer. As if Abigail could sense his urgency, she peeled off her clothes, tossing them into a pile on the floor. Cole did the same, needing to quench the fire that burned for her inside of him, to ease the ache he felt for her body. When they were naked, Cole kissed Abigail and picked her up, then she wrapped her legs around his waist. He could feel the wetness of her desire against his cock and he kissed her again hungrily, his lips and tongue eager for her taste.

Bed? He couldn't even wait to walk that fifty or so feet. Instead, he set her down on top of the table in the foyer, knocking over the antique vase that was there in the process.

Fuck it, he thought. *I'll pay whatever it costs.*

Abigail laughed when the vase fell and she looked down at its cracked remnants on the floor. Cole brushed his fingers beneath her chin, bringing her gaze back to his. Then they kissed, their tongues moving perfectly against each other. Cole loved the way she tasted, always so sweet, even now. Like cream soda and salt and perfection.

As Cole ran his fingertips along the swell of Abigail's breast, he felt a surge of possessiveness crash over him. Even though he'd felt something similar toward her a couple of days ago, the feeling was still foreign to him. He'd never really cared much what any of his other partners did once they were finished fucking. But with Abigail, he wanted her to keep coming back for him. He wanted to be the only one who was privileged enough to kiss her lips, lick her breasts, and be cloaked in the cape of her body. He wanted to be the only one who could make her wet, who could make her come.

"You're mine," Cole growled, pressing his lips against Abigail's ear as he slid his fingers along her wet slit.

She drew in a sharp breath through her teeth, resting her head against the wall. She lifted her legs until her feet rested against the top of the table, giving Cole full access to her.

"I'm yours," she breathed, wrapping her fingers around Cole's wrist.

He'd never wanted to hear two words as much as he wanted to hear those, and they spurred him on as he slipped two fingers inside her. "No one else can make you feel like I do."

"No one makes me feel like you do." She exhaled a long breath as he curled his fingers, finding her G-Spot. Her eyes rolled back and she wrapped her arms around him, pulling him closer for a kiss. "No one."

Abigail gently clasped her hand around Cole's cock and slid the tip back and forth along the folds of her pussy, making him groan. She felt so good that he splayed his hands out across the table on either side of her hips and leaned forward, not confident in the ability of his legs to keep him upright any longer. He wanted, more than anything, to push into her and feel her along every centimeter of his cock, skin to skin, nothing between them. Cole had promised himself when he first began things with Abigail that he wouldn't do anything to jeopardize her future, and in hindsight he supposed that he already had. He had to keep himself from thrusting, knowing it would be such a stupid thing to do. But he needed it so badly…

Abigail must've known what Cole was thinking, because she cupped his cheek with her hand as she leaned in very close and whispered, "I'm on the pill."

Cole searched her eyes, those deep, rich, hazel eyes, and he knew that she wanted to feel him as badly as he wanted to feel her. Just to give him a little extra reassurance, she pushed her hips forward until the tip of his cock was enveloped in her soft warmth. Cole groaned, then slid the rest of the way in until he filled her to the hilt.

He could've stayed right there for the rest of his life and died a happy man.

"You're heaven," Cole whispered, unable to say anything else. He kissed Abigail's neck, then slid out of her only so he could feel the exquisite pleasure of pushing back inside of her again. He thrust a few more times, relishing the velvety warmth of her, living for the sounds she made as he rubbed her clit with his thumb. Just when he was teetering on the edge of orgasm, Abigail stilled his hips.

"On the floor," she said, eyeing the marble beneath them. Cole was game for anything she desired, so he reluctantly pulled out of her and lowered himself onto the cool stone. Before he knew her intimately, he would've never guessed that she was this kind of partner. He loved the way she took control and told him what she wanted, because whatever that was, he wanted to give it to her.

"Lie back," Abigail told him, gently pushing Cole's chest

until he was prone on the floor. She straddled his hips, and not wanting to give her full control yet, he laced his fingers with hers and pulled her forward until her knees were on either side of his head. He brushed the inside of her thigh with his chin, knowing his stubble would tickle her.

Abigail squealed and wiggled her hips, taunting Cole. He parted her flesh with his fingers then laved his tongue along her clit. Abigail moaned, leaning back and resting her hands on Cole's chest. He couldn't get enough of her taste, her smell. Her hips were moving rhythmically to the tempo of his tongue, and he wrapped his arms around her hips so she couldn't escape him. He sucked and licked her until her muscles tensed and weakened and she had to lean forward and rest her palms on the floor to hold herself up.

Cole grinned, satisfied, and when Abigail went to reciprocate, sliding her body down the length of his until her mouth was level with his cock, he was surprised by his next move.

"No," he said, taking her hands and pulling her back up so that he could plant a kiss on her lips. It was a kiss that lingered, a kiss that made him want more. "I just want to be inside of you." He'd never turned down head before and couldn't make sense of it. He just knew that he needed to be as close to her as he could, and he needed it now.

Abigail slowly sank down on him, arching her back, accentuating the perfect tits and curves that Cole thought about whenever he closed his eyes. He caressed her nipples with the pads of his thumbs, then gripped her hips and helped her move as her muscles squeezed his cock. Cole couldn't take his eyes off of her body as she took him in, and he loved the way her wetness made his skin glisten. Abigail twined her fingers with his as she rode him, and Cole pressed his hips up against her, offering himself up for her pleasure. To help her along and because he loved being inside her when she came, he circled her clit with his thumb, taking her higher and higher until she collapsed on top of him and pressed her lips against his, her muscles tensing and relaxing, driving him crazy.

"Oh, fuck," she sighed, trying to catch her breath. She sat back on her heels and rocked her hips, then closed her eyes as she cupped her breasts, enjoying the fading waves of pleasure. Cole loved hearing filthy words fall from her lips, and wanted to hear them again. He pulled her down on top of him until their chests touched.

"Hook your arms under mine and hold on," he said. As always, Abigail did as she was told. She buried her face in his neck, kissing and sucking the skin there. He wrapped his arms around her waist and thrusted up, pounding into her, making their skin slap together. Abigail could barely catch her breath, each thrust drawing a short moan from her lips. She came quickly a second time, and her orgasm snuck up on Cole. He couldn't hold on any longer.

Cole withdrew quickly and stroked his cock as ropes of come decorated her belly. Abigail sat up and slid her finger into the slick seed, then licked her fingertip. He nearly came again on the spot.

This woman, she was going to be the death of him.

Cole sat up and drew Abigail into his chest, holding her

close as he kissed her. He heard his Blackberry ringing, but he couldn't bring himself to get up.

Business could wait just a while longer.

CHAPTER
Nineteen

*A*t three in the morning, Abby woke up for no apparent reason. She rubbed her eyes and rolled onto her back, then stared up at the ceiling, grinning. She had a wonderful ache between her legs; the one that came from having tons of sex. She'd had more in the past week than she had in the past year, which was a sadness she didn't really like thinking about. But Cole more than made up for her year-long drought.

Abby thought back over the time that she and Cole had spent in Chicago. She'd come here hoping for sex and lots of it, but she never would've dared to hope for the level of—dare she think it—intimacy they were slowly building. While the feelings that she had expressed regarding her hatred for Cole looking at her with pity last night were truthful, she did appreciate the fact that he even felt pity for her at all.

Not long ago, she would've thought his capability to feel true compassion for another person was completely impossible. Now, she realized, he was much, much deeper than she ever could have believed.

After finding out about Cole's community centers, she wondered what other kind of charitable endeavors he participated in but would be reluctant to admit to. There was a whole wealth of knowledge about him just waiting to be discovered, and she couldn't wait to devour every bit of it. In the hopeful hours of the early morning, Abby began to let herself dream about a future with Cole outside of the office, and didn't let her ever-present doubt creep in this time.

Abby rolled over onto her side and hugged her pillow. It was then that she saw the steady stream of flickering shadows from the television through the crack beneath her door. She grinned at the thought of Cole having fallen asleep in front of the television, and she couldn't stop herself from getting out of bed to check on him. She tried to tell herself that this was her duty, all part of being his assistant, but deep down she knew that wasn't true. Something about Cole had always drawn her to him. She used to think that it was his confidence and business acumen, but now she knew that it was something more.

She felt as if she was attached to a string, and whenever Cole pulled it, she moved. And she *wanted* to.

Abby slowly opened her door, then peered outside. She could see Cole's arm dangling off the sofa, and even though she couldn't see his face, she knew he was sleeping. She smiled as she grabbed a folded blanket from the foot of her bed, then walked out into the living room.

Cole's face was smushed against the sofa pillow, his body contorted in an odd way, twisted at the waist. She carefully moved his legs, bringing them to rest in line with the rest of his body. He burrowed into the cushions, then gripped a pillow, hugging it to his chest. Abby unfolded the blanket and spread it over him, tucking in the edges so it wouldn't fall off of him during the few hours they had left before daylight.

Cole looked so peaceful like this, such a stark contrast to the way he was when he was awake, all businesslike. Abby sat on the edge of the sofa and took a minute to appreciate the tranquility of his expression. She gently slid her fingertips through his hair and felt that familiar warmth creep up inside of her again, only this time its presence didn't confuse her. She knew exactly what it was, what it meant, and how much trouble it would cause her.

She didn't want to fall in love with him. She didn't want it at all, but her heart had other plans.

Then, Cole did something that shocked her senseless.

"Abby," he sighed. His eyes were closed and Abby was certain he was still sleeping. His voice sounded like a dream. "I love you."

CHAPTER
Twenty

*T*hursday evening, Cole was sitting at the desk in the living room of the hotel suite, reading through a never-ending stream of emails. His eyes felt sandy and tired from constantly staring at a computer screen. He missed his office in New York and the familiarity of his routine, preferring to work at his own desk instead of in a hotel room. But the discomfort was worth spending time with Abigail.

Cole rubbed his eyes with the heels of his hands, then sat back and rolled his neck, trying to work out the kinks. He'd fallen asleep on the couch last night, which was completely unlike him. He woke up in the early morning light, warmed by a blanket that Abigail had covered him with at some point during the night. He grinned at the thought of her getting up in the middle of the night and looking for him, then caring enough to make sure he was warm. She'd always taken care of him at work, which was part of her job. That she was taking her own time to do it outside of working hours opened up a floodgate of emotions inside of him that he wasn't quite sure how to name. Was it fondness? No, that wasn't strong enough. Love? Perhaps.

Cole could hear the shower running in Abigail's room. Tonight was the night she was going out with that asshole Josh Hamilton. Even though it was something that Cole both wanted and needed her to do, a surge of jealousy coursed through his veins and he realized that his hands were balled into fists. What was he doing letting her go out with Hamilton? Only a week ago, when he first came up with the idea to bring her here, Cole still thought of Abigail as an employee, as a means to an end. Now, he thought of her as so much more.

Cole sat there, clenching and unclenching his fists. If he was smart, he would tell Abigail what Josh was up to. But she was such an intelligent woman, she'd put the pieces together immediately. Cole would have to admit that he spied on her and that he asked her here hoping she would find out what Josh was up to. It would unravel the carefully knit cloth of trust and intimacy they'd gained over the past few days, and he didn't want to risk that.

If Cole were able to be honest with himself, he'd realize that gaining that intimacy was the precise reason he'd invited Abigail on this trip in the first place. His 'plan' to corner Hamilton was flimsy at best, not at all up to Cole's usually high standards. He'd found out about Abigail's limited involvement with Josh and used that as an excuse to bring her here, to spend time with her outside of the office. There were other, more fool-proof ways of finding him out. But Cole was already knee-deep in this mess and he had to see it through to the end.

Conveniently, he decided not to think about what would happen if Abigail didn't get any information out of Josh, if she did get the information and decided not to tell him, or worse—if Josh and Abigail's outing this evening really was a date.

Cole wanted to crawl out of his skin thinking of Abigail going out with that slime. His two biggest instincts were at war: the instinct to protect his business, and the instinct to protect the woman he was...falling in love with? Was that really what it was? Cole wasn't familiar with love, only lust. Love had no place in Cole's life because he hadn't been willing to make time for it. Before Abigail, that is. He wanted to make time for it with her. But she was his employee, how would he handle that? As exciting as it was, he couldn't keep carrying on a secret relationship with her at the office. Having her around was distracting enough now, surely he'd wind up losing his handle on his company if he tried to deal with a girlfriend at work. No, he couldn't keep her, he'd have to help her find employment elsewhere. And then he would lose the best assistant he'd ever had.

Love really has a way of fucking everything up, Cole thought. Love. He smiled just thinking of that word when he assigned it to Abigail. If he didn't love her already, he was well on his way, but he was going to have to be sure of it before he told her. He'd rather lose KC-23 to another company than hurt her.

Again, if Cole was honest with himself, he would've known at that moment to tell Abigail the truth.

But he didn't.

Just then a message popped up on his computer screen, pulling him out of his thoughts.

Did you find out what that dick head is up to yet?

It was Keith, who Cole imagined was probably sitting at his computer, gnawing on his fingernails and waiting for an answer.

Not yet, but probably tonight.

Cole wasn't going to tell Keith how he planned to get that information.

I hope you have something good up your sleeve.

Cole grinned as he typed back:

Don't I always?

But he didn't, not this time. All he had on his side was hope, dumb luck, and a woman who changed the orbit of his universe.

"Hi," Abigail said, standing in the doorway to her room. She was dressed as she would've been for work, in long black slacks, a pink blouse and a black blazer. She looked so lovely, but not at all like she was meeting someone she was remotely interested in. This realization made Cole relax somewhat. Her hair framed her face in subtle waves, and those beautiful eyes of hers sparkled when she looked at him. He could see the slightest bit of apprehension in them, and he thought about what a bastard he was for not telling her to ditch Hamilton and stay here with him instead. That's what he should have told her.

Soon, that's what he'll wish he had told her.

But tonight, Cole was going to let her go through with it and hope things turned out in his favor.

"Is everything okay?" Abigail asked.

Cole nodded, trying to muster a smile. He managed one, but he was sure that it was weak. "Everything's fine. Keith was just checking up on things, wanted to know how the trip is going."

"How *is* the trip going?"

Cole stood and walked over to her, then placed his hand on her hip. He wanted her to stay here in this room with him tonight. He wanted to kiss the curve of her neck and the tender skin between her breasts where he could feel her heart pounding beneath his lips. He wanted to make her his.

"It's going better than I could've possibly expected," he

said, pushing a stray curl behind her ear. Her eyes fluttered shut as he caressed her cheek.

"I should probably go," she whispered, not sounding like she wanted to go at all.

It gave Cole some satisfaction that she seemed reluctant to leave him. He was reluctant to let her go.

He should have told her to stay, but he didn't.

"Enjoy yourself," he said, but the sentiment was empty. He was a bastard, letting her go and hoping she had a miserable time.

Abigail gave Cole a half-hearted smile as she turned to go and meet another man.

Cole felt the burning hot rip of possessiveness cut through his skin and he grabbed her wrist and pulled her to him. He wanted her to remember his lips, his kiss, his taste. He wanted her to see his face when she looked at Hamilton. He wanted her to know that she belonged to him, even though he couldn't claim her. He wanted her to return to him. Soon. He pressed his lips against hers and she knit her fingers through his hair as their mouths collided. Cole memorized the soft noises Abigail made as she kissed him. He wrapped his arms around her waist and pulled her close, his hand finding purchase on her lower back. He wanted every part of her against his body, wanted the smell of her to remain on his clothes for the rest of the night.

When they finally parted, Cole touched Abigail's forehead with his own, searching her eyes as he caught his breath.

Then, too soon, Abigail sighed, tenderly running her

fingers along the slope of Cole's jaw before she turned and walked out.

Cole missed her the moment she was gone. He stood there, looking at the door, waiting for her to come back and hating himself for being selfish enough to let her leave in the first place. He fought the urge to follow her so he could make sure Hamilton didn't lay a finger on her. No, he couldn't do that; it was the first step down a very slippery slope. Instead of doing one more thing that could push Abigail away from him, he decided to do something that would bring her closer.

He went back to the desk and picked up his Blackberry, pulling up Keith's secretary's number on the screen.

It rang only once before she picked up.

"Hello, Mr. Kerrigan," she said cheerily. "How may I help you?"

"Listen…Abigail is out for the evening, and I need your help."

CHAPTER
Twenty-One

*A*bby cradled her cell phone as she walked down the street to the bar where she was meeting Josh Hamilton. She hated herself for leaving Cole, but she wanted to do this. She had hoped that Cole would stop her, but he hadn't. That hurt, but she didn't want to let on. There was a small part of her that wanted him to be jealous knowing that she was having drinks with another man. It was immature, sure, but she couldn't seem to help herself from wanting it anyway.

"So, how hot is this guy?" Becca asked. She sounded excited as always, living vicariously through her friend.

"I don't know, maybe a eight? I've only seen him in company pictures."

"Christ, Abby. What is it with you? Do you have magical pheromones or something? First your boss and now this dude?"

"I don't even know for sure that this guy is even interested in me like that. This seems like it's going to be work related," Abby said as she waited at a crosswalk.

"Oh my god, corporate espionage!" Becca sounded like a kid on Christmas.

"Don't be crazy," Abby replied, laughing. "I would never spy on my boss." She'd nearly said Cole's name and was relieved she caught herself.

"I was just teasing you. So…what if he makes a move?"

I'd turn him down, Abby thought, but she wanted to spare herself a lecture so she didn't say that to Becca. "I don't know," she replied instead. She'd been thinking about the possibility that Josh was after more than work-related conversation. She didn't think it was likely, but she wanted to be prepared.

"Why don't you know? What's a little innocent flirting-slash-sex between coworkers?"

Abby was silent. What was a little innocent flirting-slash-sex between coworkers? Her heart was telling her that it was a pretty big fucking deal, but only when that coworker was Cole. She had absolutely no interest in Josh, but she didn't want to hurt his feelings.

"Holy shit, you're in love with him." Becca's word had an undercurrent of pity, the very thing they shouldn't have when she was talking about something as glorious as love.

Abby wanted to tell her that he'd said he'd loved her. But he'd said it when he was sleeping and even though Abby desperately wanted it to be true, she couldn't hold him to words he'd spoken when he wasn't even conscious.

"No," Abby replied, taking a beat too long to deny it.

Becca sighed. "Yes you are." Abby hated the tentative lilt in Becca's voice. "Oh, Abby. Sweetie, you're going to get hurt."

"No I'm not," Abby replied, trying to sound light. "I'm not in love with him, Beck." She didn't want to have this conversation in the middle of the street while Becca was a thousand miles away. It would have to wait, especially because Abby was at her destination. "Look, I've got to go. I'm right outside the bar."

"I'm sorry I teased you. I just love you and I don't want…" she paused, probably realizing that this wasn't the time to say what she wanted to say. "Eh, I hope you have a good time tonight. I can't wait for you to come home. I miss you more every time I look in my makeup drawer and realize that it's all still there."

Abby laughed, thinking it was pretty rich of Becca to accuse *her* of being a makeup thief. "I miss you too. I'll see you day after tomorrow."

"'Kay. Have fun."

"Bye." Abby grinned as she turned off the phone and slid it into her purse.

Josh was already at the bar waiting for Abby when she walked through the door, and he called her over to him with a friendly wave and a smile. Abby waved back, forgetting how charming he could be. She was surprised that he hadn't spoken to her more often during the time she'd spent working in the Chicago office, but he seemed to want to keep his distance. At the time she had wondered if that had something to do with Cole or something to do with whatever it was he had wanted to talk about on the phone. She was beginning to think that the two things may be related.

Josh stood and pulled out Abby's chair, hugging her quickly before she took a seat. She ordered an Amaretto sour from the bartender as Josh took a pull from his beer.

"How are you enjoying the city so far?" he asked, tattering the edges of a napkin with his fingers.

Abby shrugged. "What little bit I've seen of it is very nice. Apart from going to the office though, I haven't really ventured out of the two-block radius around the hotel."

"Cole's working you pretty hard, huh?" Josh gazed at Abby for a moment before turning his attention back to his drink.

Abby felt foolish for even thinking that this meeting might have something to do with anything other than business. It relieved her in a way, knowing she was off the hook for having to let Josh down easily. But the fact that Cole was the topic of conversation put a knot in Abby's stomach. She didn't want to talk about him with Josh, it felt disloyal and wrong. But the side of her that always looked out for Cole and made sure that he was taken care of stood at attention. She was going to have to be very careful with how she played this, whatever it was.

"Yeah, he keeps me pretty busy." Abby took a sip of her drink, hoping the alcohol would calm the nerves in her stomach.

"Can you believe he fired Jack the other day?"

Abby nodded. "It was a performance issue."

Josh rolled his eyes. "That guy did more for Kerrigan than he'll ever realize."

Having seen the sales reports and having been in the room when Cole ran down the reasons why he was firing Jack, Abby seriously doubted that.

"Cole had his reasons. He didn't become a billionaire by being reckless." Abby swirled her drink with the straw and watched the ice cubes circulate and bump up against the glass. She wanted to leave. Immediately.

"He became a billionaire by being a prick," Josh replied, laughing. And it broke Abby's heart that the reason Josh was talking about him like this in her company was because not too long ago she would've been saying nasty things about him too.

Abby attempted a giggle, but it fell flat. It didn't seem like Josh noticed.

"Do you ever think of leaving?" he asked.

"The company?" Abby replied dumbly.

"Yeah." Josh looked halfway between nervous and anxious.

Dumbfounded, Abby searched for an answer. "I don't know, I haven't ever given it much thought."

"Would you consider leaving?"

Abby paused. "Are you offering me something?"

"It depends."

"On what?"

"I need something from you."

Abby was both intrigued and sickened.

"You have access to Cole's emails, right?"

Oh, no. No. No. No.

"What does that-"

"I need the spec sheet for KC-23."

Abby balked. "I can't get that." She *could* get that for him, she just wouldn't.

"Can't or won't?"

"Won't. Do you know how much trouble that could get me into? He could sue me for everything I've ever had, and everything I ever will have." Cole might not have sued her over a non-disclosure agreement, but he would surely sue her over his company's most important project.

"What if I could offer you protection?"

"Protection from what?"

"Legal protection. Monetary protection."

"You can't do that."

"I can." He shifted in his seat, looking around as if he thought someone might be eavesdropping on the two of them.

"How?"

"I've put my heart and soul into that project and I'm barely making enough to pay for my mortgage. I can improve the design; Cole's plans for it aren't big enough. He lacks the ability to see the big picture and realize everything it can do."

It could guarantee hack-proof protection of worldwide banking systems. Was there a bigger picture than that? Panicked, Abby knew that in order to get all of the information she could out of Josh, she was going to have to go along with this at least for tonight, in order to give Cole the tools he'd need in order to safeguard his work.

"What, are you going to sell it to someone?"

"I have several interested buyers, Abby. I can offer you a position in research with me. Double, even triple your salary. We both know you're too damned smart to be an assistant."

"Who are you going to sell this to?" He'd have to be a moron to tell her this, but maybe since she held the key to getting him the information he needed, he'd be a little lax with the details. Besides, Abby knew better than to underestimate the hubris of a man who thought he was pulling something over on someone.

"Yamamoto or Minghella. I haven't decided which yet. Actually, they haven't fully committed to bid until I can get them the final spec sheets."

Yamamoto or Minghella. Abby repeated in her head. She couldn't forget those names. Swallowing down the bile that rose in her throat, she asked Josh when he needed the information.

"As soon as you can get it to me."

"It won't be until I get back to New York."

"Monday," Josh said.

Abby was tempted to ask Josh why he was doing this, but that was probably a question that was better left unasked if she wanted him to believe she was going along with him. He had an ego, he thought he was smarter than the guy who hired him, and he didn't think he was being paid what he was worth. Knowing that, she didn't really need to ask him for his motivation.

"Obviously I don't need to tell you to keep this between us?"

The nervousness was rolling off of him. Abby could tell he'd rather do anything than ask her for what he was asking her for.

"I won't say anything at all."

She swallowed the rest of her drink and Josh stood, putting a twenty down on the bar.

"I've gotta go," he said. He handed her a card with a hand-written number on it. "When you get the specs, give me a call on this number, okay?"

Abby took the card, tucking it safely in her purse. "I will."

Josh reached out and clasped her hand in his. "I'll see you later, Abby."

"See you later."

Abby watched him as he walked out. Even though she was desperate to run to Cole or to call him, she stayed put and kept her phone in her bag just in case Josh was watching her. She decided to wait it out at least a few more minutes and ordered another drink from the bartender. She couldn't drink it, though. She had to get back to the hotel. She had to tell Cole.

CHAPTER
Twenty-Two

Cole stood at the window in the suite's dining room, staring out at the traffic below as he sipped a glass of red wine. The suite was too quiet, almost eerily so. Even though he was used to being alone at home in the city, he'd grown accustomed to having Abigail around. He *missed* her. So much that he gave more than a passing thought to calling her and making up some kind of work emergency just to get her to come back. Even though his phone was in the palm of his hand, he resisted pulling up her number. He wasn't quite ready to venture into obsessive boyfriend territory.

The task he'd sent Abigail on wasn't dangerous, and it required no risk on her part. It did, however, come with great risk to Cole. If she found out that he'd used her this way, he might lose her twice. Once as his assistant, and once as a… lover? A girlfriend? Cole wasn't even sure what to call her.

If she found out what he'd done, he might not be calling her anything anymore.

Cole usually wasn't one to get too stressed out about anything, but the tension in his body was making his muscles ache. He set his glass on the table and loosened his tie, then rolled his neck to relieve some of the tightness that was building there.

Everything will be better when I get back to New York. When he got back to New York, he'd figure out what was going on with Abigail and focus on that.

Just when Cole was reaching for his phone again, he heard Abigail's key card click the lock, then the door swung open. She stood there with a stricken look on her face and concern welled up through his veins. *What did he do to her?*

"What's the matter?" Cole asked, rushing toward her. *If that prick hurt her, so help me I will make him pay.*

Stunned, she looked up at him, worry deep in her beautiful eyes. Cole put his hands on her shoulders, caressing the sides of her neck with his thumbs, hoping to calm her down.

"Josh wants to steal KC-23," she finally said, her eyes wide.

That much Cole had known, but he found that he didn't really care about the project at this point; he only cared about her.

"He asked me to get the final spec sheet for him," she said, her voice wavering.

Cole took a deep breath, looking up at the ceiling. He was an idiot for not seeing it, he should've known. This was the very reason why he had different departments work on different phases of the project, so that if anyone tried to sell information it would be incomplete. It didn't matter now, Cole would put a stop to it.

Still, Hamilton had asked Abigail to steal from him, but she'd raced here right away. Cole felt a surge of affection for Abigail in that moment, completely separate from his romantic feelings for her. He was…proud? Relieved? He couldn't place it.

"What did you tell him?" Cole asked.

Abigail looked up at him with a twinge of fear in her eyes. "I didn't want to say no, because I was worried about what he'd do if I didn't go along with his plan. I said I would get the plans for him, but not until we got back to New York. I would never steal from you, Cole."

Unshed tears threatened to fall, and Cole caressed Abigail's cheek. "I know you wouldn't," he said. *Beautiful, smart, fierce woman.* Abigail leaned into his touch, allowing him to cradle her face in his palm.

"He's going to sell it to either Yamamoto or Minghella." Her voice was very quiet.

Cole surprised himself by not really caring about who had the potential to get the info. This trip had stopped being about the project a long time ago.

"Did he make you any promises in exchange for this information?"

Abigail took a few moments to respond to him, although Cole couldn't quite make out why she would be nervous about telling him.

"He said he would give me a job at a higher salary and that he would protect me if you filed a lawsuit."

Cole felt a rage boiling inside of him the likes of which he'd never experienced before. He turned away from her, not wanting her to see the anger in his eyes, and he clenched his fists as he walked to the window, needing to look elsewhere as he worked himself through the urge to walk out of this room and kick Josh Hamilton's ass. Not for the stealing, but for what he'd done to Abigail. He had lied to her; he could offer her no such protection, and he was counting on her being ignorant enough to not know that. He was counting on her being greedy and disloyal enough to betray him.

Josh Hamilton didn't know her at all.

"He can't do that, can he?" she asked. "Protect me from a lawsuit?"

Cole shook his head as he looked out the window. "No."

"Asshole," Abigail said under her breath.

Cole grinned.

"Couldn't you sue him, too? What could he possibly have to gain?"

"People with large egos often think they're above the law," Cole said, shrugging. "Who knows what kind of deal they offered him for the plans. That software has incredible potential, he may have believed the risk would have ultimately been worth it."

"I guess it doesn't matter now."

Cole turned to face her. "No, it doesn't." *But I will make him pay for using you.*

"What are you going to do?"

He took a deep breath before he answered. "First I'm going to fire him, then I'm going to make sure he never works for another reputable company again."

Worry flashed across Abigail's face, and Cole walked toward her, wanting to comfort her. "He'll know I told. What if he tries to-"

Cole brought his finger to her lips, stopping that thought from even being spoken aloud. "I will *never* allow anything to happen to you," he told her. It wasn't just a promise about retribution from Josh Hamilton. He wouldn't allow anyone to touch her, to harm her, to put this worry in her eyes ever again. He wrapped his arms around her until she was pressed against his chest, her head tucked under his chin. He'd never felt so protective of anyone in his entire life.

"Is there anything I can do to help?" Abigail asked.

Cole kissed the top of her head. "You already have."

CHAPTER
Twenty-Three

*A*bby didn't sleep well at all that evening, tossing and turning as she thought about her meeting with Josh and the look on Cole's face when he told her that he would never let anything happen to her. She knew he meant what he said, but she wanted to believe that he was speaking of more than business when he offered her such promises. Abby felt safe with Cole, safer than she'd ever felt with another human being. And it was funny to her that she could feel so secure around a man who offered such a great possibility of a broken heart.

It was only six-thirty in the morning, and the dim morning light was creeping through the curtains in Abby's room. She slipped on her robe and climbed out of bed, then shuffled to the bathroom to brush her teeth. She stared at herself in the mirror when she was finished, piling up her hair on the top of her head and examining her profile in the mirror. She was still too short, too plain. She thought back to the model whose name she couldn't remember in the gossip mag Becca had shown her last week. Abby knew she couldn't compare to the women Cole could attract, so there was a niggling voice inside of her that warned her that this would all be fleeting. It was fun here in Chicago, but things would go back to normal once they were back in New York. No way would Cole be interested in her long enough for this fling to amount to anything.

Abby yawned as she made her way towards her door, looking forward to a little caffeine. She noticed, however, that the smell of freshly brewed coffee was already in the air. When she opened the door, she saw Cole standing beside the dining room table, the morning paper in one hand and a cup in the other.

"Did I wake up too late?" she asked, panic in her voice.

Cole wore a soft, happy grin when he looked at her. "No, I'm going to head into the office in a few minutes. I'd like you to work from the suite today."

Abby could tell from the look in Cole's eyes that he didn't want her in the office when he fired Josh. She was a little relieved; she didn't want to be there either. Not to mention the fact that part of her was still worried that he was going to take this out on her. Still, Cole would protect her. She had to believe that.

"Okay, I will," she replied.

Cole set down his cup on top of the paper and walked toward Abby, coming to rest a few inches from her. He smelled so clean, and Abby found herself wanting to wrap her body around his, to imprint his smell on her body.

"Listen," Cole said, trailing his fingers along the edge of the collar of her robe. He cleared his throat before he spoke. "I've been invited to a dinner this evening, and I'd like you to come with me."

"Okay."

"Would you like to come?" He sounded nervous, the thought of which made Abby smile.

"I wasn't aware I had a choice," she replied playfully. He was paying her after all, she would do whatever he wanted her to.

"This is a request, not a requirement," he said, looking in her eyes. "I'd like for you to be my date."

Abby's stomach fluttered, and warmth spread throughout her body. He wanted *her* to be his date. He wanted her to be his *date*.

"I didn't bring anything to wear." She could've smacked herself for that reply, what a stupid thing to say to a man who looked like that, made her feel like he made her feel. She should've said yes immediately. Shouted it from the rooftops.

Cole seemed amused by her answer, thankfully. "I didn't ask if you brought anything to wear," he replied with a laugh. "I asked if you would like to be my date."

"Yes," Abby said, blushing. "I would like to be your date very much."

"Good." Cole sounded genuinely pleased. "I've asked someone to come over later to help you pick out a dress."

"Pretty sure of yourself, aren't you?" Abby was teasing

him, but there was an edge of truth to it, one that Cole heard loud and clear.

"I hoped," he said, wrapping his arm around her waist. "I always hope when it comes to you."

Cole drew Abby in for a kiss, long and slow, and she wanted a hundred more. It had been too long since she'd tasted his lips. Unfortunately, the car was downstairs and the business Cole had to attend to today couldn't wait for matters of the heart.

"I'll meet you at seven," Cole said, running his fingers through her hair as he brushed his lips across her cheek. "Right here." He lingered for a few more moments, then grabbed his briefcase and walked out the door.

CHAPTER
Twenty-Four

Cole sat quietly in his Chicago office, directly across from Josh Hamilton, who was flanked by two of Kerrigan Corp's finest lawyers. The HR director was standing by the door, her head down, marking off some exit interview checklist. Josh's eyes were wide, like a scared deer staring into a pair of oncoming headlights. It was one of Cole's favorite looks to see on an opponent, especially one like Josh.

"Do you know why you're here today, Josh?" Cole asked, tapping his fingers along the surface of his desk.

Josh shook his head slowly, looking at the lawyer on his left first, then the one on his right.

"No, sir. I'm honestly clueless."

Cole let out a short laugh. He was clueless all right.

"Last week, I was on a conference call with my Tokyo office, and the VP of marketing in Japan, Keiko Tanaka, told me that she had received an interesting letter from an anonymous source that Kerrigan had a top-secret software project it was shopping around Japan," Cole said, watching Josh as he shifted uncomfortably in his seat. "Included in the envelope was a jump drive that had the specs for the part of the project your group was responsible for on it."

"Cole, I-"

With one cold, steely look, Cole silenced him.

"I suspect that this news doesn't surprise you. But what will surprise you is that each copy of the specs was embedded with a serial number that is specific to the person it was sent to. So, I knew immediately that this one was yours. What I didn't know was exactly what you were planning on doing with it. I had IT search your computer for anything they could find, but you were at least smart enough to cover your tracks in the office. It might've taken me a while to figure out what you were up to, but luckily for me, you played right into the only hand I had available."

"Which hand was that?" Josh asked cockily.

Cole had to give the guy credit; even though he knew exactly where he'd misstepped, he was going to play dumb until the end.

"Abigail."

"You have no idea how much she despises you," Josh said. His angry eyes formed narrow slits.

Those words wounded Cole, even when he took into account who they were coming from and why they were being said. He had to pretend, both for his sake and for Abigail's, that they didn't bother him at all.

"Apparently she doesn't despise me enough."

"That bitch." The words came softly from Josh's mouth, whispered under his breath. But they reignited the rage Cole felt yesterday, and this time he didn't have to hide it. Cole banged his fist on the desk and then stood, towering over Josh. His lawyers gave him warning looks, and Cole took a deep breath before he spoke again. He was not going to give this little prick the satisfaction of suing him for anything.

"Security is standing right outside of this door. They'll escort you out."

"What about my stuff?"

Cole let out a bitter, cold laugh. "Nothing in this office belongs to you, no matter how much you wish it were so."

Josh was indignant. "So, you fire me and then I walk out of this door and find another job in seconds. With my education and credentials, anyone would fall over themselves to have me."

"See, that's where you're wrong," Cole replied, smiling.

"What do you mean?"

"Employers generally don't like to take chances on people who steal their work. In order to be employable, you have to be trustworthy." Cole could see that the reality of what Josh had done was just starting to sink in. "I am a very well-known and well-respected businessman, Joshua. You will soon find out that I have a very long reach."

Josh stood, but he was no match for Cole. "Wait until my father hears about this!" he yelled.

Coming from the background Cole came from, he wasn't surprised by Josh's threats to contact his father. In fact, he'd anticipated them. Rich, influential parents were usually the safety net of spoiled, entitled brats like Josh.

"Your father and I both serve on the Yale Alumni Board of Governors. He's already aware of what you've done. I don't think he'll be rushing to help you anytime soon."

Cole walked over to Josh, looking him straight in the eye. "Abigail told me that you offered her a job as well as legal protection from my team." Cole eyed him with the iciest glare he'd ever used. "We both know that you could offer her no such protection."

"Cole-" a lawyer warned. Fuck the law, he was going to say what needed to be said.

"You've shown yourself to be lacking in every single mark of a man, Josh. And conning someone into doing your dirty work for you is the lowest of the low. Since you seem to be incapable of taking responsibility for your actions, I would feel remiss if I didn't tell you that Abigail is off-limits to you now. You will not call her, you will not email her. You will not see her, you will not threaten her. The walls have eyes now as far as you are concerned, and if I find out that you so much as breathe the air within a two-mile radius of her, I will end you. And that, Mr. Hamilton, is a promise."

Cole motioned for the security guards standing outside of the door. "Get him out of here."

CHAPTER
Twenty-Five

"What color is the dress?" Becca asked, sounding like she was ready to jump out of her skin. She was the best kind of friend to have; sometimes Abby thought Becca was happier for her than she was for herself. Tonight seemed to be one of those occasions.

"It's red. Boatneck collar, cowled back."

"Make sure you wear your hair up." Becca sounded like a kid on Christmas.

"I am. I'm almost finished with it," Abby told her as she curled a strand of hair around her finger and pinned it to her head. She probably should've paid to have someone do her hair for her, but a messy up do always seemed to work for her and tonight was no exception.

"Have you been doing your hair all this time?"

"Yes, thanks to the technological wonder that is speaker

phone."

"Take a selfie and send it to me."

"Okay," Abby replied as she brushed back a few stray hairs. She misted a little hairspray on top of her chignon, just to make sure it stayed in place. "Hold on a sec."

Abby pulled up the camera app on her phone and snapped one picture of herself from the front and one from the back in the reflection of the full-length mirror on the back of the bathroom door, then texted them to Becca.

"I sent a couple," Abby said, placing the phone on the bathroom counter so she could give herself a once-over in the mirror. Her makeup was perfect, her hair was flattering. There was nothing else to be done but meet Cole. She wondered if she should walk out into the living room or wait for him to knock on her door. It was close to seven already.

"Holy shit!" Becca yelled. "Oh my god, Abby. You look… you just look amazing. Do you get to keep that dress?"

"I don't know, someone came over with a rack full of dresses and I picked this one out. She left me shoes and jewelry too. She told me it had already been taken care of."

Becca sighed. "I want to be rich. Seriously, rich people don't know how good they have it."

"Hey, do you think I should walk out to meet him or wait until he knocks on my door to see if I'm ready?"

"I'd probably wait until he knocked on my door, so you should do the opposite. Go out there and let him know you're ready to go."

Abby took a deep breath an exhaled. "Okay, wish me luck."

"Call me tomorrow and tell me all about it. First thing."

"You're picking me up from the airport tomorrow evening, Beck."

"Like I said, call me first thing in the morning and tell me all about it."

Abby laughed. "Okay, I will."

"Have fun tonight, Abs. You look beautiful."

After Abby ended the call, she gave herself a once-over before she grabbed her tiny evening bag and gripped the doorknob. She took a deep breath, then pulled open the door.

Cole was sitting at his computer, unable to let go of work even for the few minutes before a night out on the town. His head turned the second Abby's door opened, and he stood when he saw her, wearing a dopey, love-struck look on his face that made Abby smile.

"Hi," she said, feeling slightly unnerved because he was just standing there staring at her.

It only took a moment for Cole to remember himself; he shook his head and then gazed at Abby warmly while he walked toward her.

"Abigail, wow," he replied. Abby didn't cringe at his use of her full name. She thought it felt fitting this evening, while they were both dressed to the nines. She expected him to say something else, but he was frozen there, staring at her. She took that as a compliment.

"You look handsome." Abby admired Cole's broad chest under the clean lines of the tux. He always had a way of turning a simple garment into something spectacular, something you couldn't take your eyes off of.

"Thank you. You look so…" He paused, seemingly unable to find the right words. "Beautiful. Gorgeous. Perfect."

"Thank you." Abby grinned, feeling a blush rise to her cheeks.

Cole stood there looking at her for a beat longer before he held out his arm. "Shall we?"

Abby hooked her arm around his, and they made their way to the elevator.

The curious stares of fellow hotel patrons followed them as they walked through the lobby. Even though Abby usually did what she could to avoid being the center of attention, she thought it was nice for once. Especially since most of the people in the hotel were probably stinking rich, and they'd most likely seen plenty of couples on their way to elegant dinner parties before. Abby was turning heads tonight, an experience that was completely new to her, but it made her confident that she'd chosen the right dress, the right hairdo and the right makeup. She hoped Cole thought so, too. A week ago Abby never would've guessed that she would so desire his good opinion, but tonight she was desperate for it.

Abby and Cole were mostly quiet in the car, exchanging pleasantries that quickly died out. Cole wasn't his usual unshakable self; he almost seemed…nervous? The two of them were sitting close together. So close, in fact, that Abby could feel the heat from Cole's thigh against hers. Her hands were folded in her lap, and his rested on his knees. Never before had Abby been so desperate to reach over and twine her fingers with Cole's. She wanted to be connected to him in any way that she could, and this was the first time she'd felt that way towards him that wasn't related to sex. For now, it was enough for her just to be close to him, to have him near.

It wasn't long before the car pulled into the small driveway of another hotel. When they came to a stop, Cole let himself out, and Abby heard him tell the driver that he would be opening her door. She quickly skimmed her fingertips across her hair to smooth it down, wanting to look perfect. The car door opened, and Cole held his hand out for Abby to take. She held onto him for support as she stood.

Once the door was closed, Abby and Cole stood face-to-face next to the car. She reached up and straightened his tie, which had become ever so slightly crooked. He looked into her eyes, smiling softly, and his fingertips skimmed the back of her hand for a fleeting moment before his cool confidence returned. Cole held out his arm, and Abby linked hers with his as they walked into the hotel.

Inside, Cole introduced Abby to several people whose names and faces she recognized from newspapers and magazines. She was feeling very frazzled and out of place, even though every time she shook another hand her nerves abated, she was never truly at ease. Not until she and Cole were finally seated at a table, sitting side-by-side. They exchanged small talk with other couples nearby, and Cole schmoozed some investor and his wife who were sitting across from them. Abby frequently chatted with a woman sitting next to her who, for some reason, spoke about ten decibels higher than everyone else in the room. Every once in a while Abby glanced over at Cole, who was listening intently to whomever was talking to him as he ate. Just as often, Abby would catch Cole looking at her, and he'd smile at her warmly before engaging someone else in conversation.

Abby wasn't sure what exactly was going on between them, but it was obvious to her from the very start of the evening that something had changed between them in a very real, tangible way.

After dinner was over and the dessert dishes were cleared, a small band began to play on the stage near the edge of the ballroom. Abby already knew that Cole didn't much care for dancing, although she couldn't help but hope for a change of heart. He had been speaking to a gentleman named Robert throughout the dessert course.

After the first few bars of music had been played, Robert looked at Abby. "My wife can't dance like she used to, and I know Cole here doesn't like to do anything remotely fun. Care to join me for a spin around the floor?"

Abby looked to Cole, who grinned and nodded his approval.

Itching for a chance to dance in such a fancy place, Abby nodded. "I'd love to."

Robert stood and helped Abby up out of her chair, then led her out onto the dance floor.

CHAPTER
Twenty-Six

"She's lovely," said Robert's wife, Victoria, as she and Cole watched Abigail and Robert dance.

"Indeed she is," Cole agreed, admiring Abigail as she moved. She and Robert were engaged in a lively conversation, and Cole felt something inside of him stir when she laughed, tossing her head back in that carefree manner she had about her. He wanted her badly, in a way he'd never wanted another woman before.

"I hope you can help me Cole, I'm a bit perplexed," Victoria said, leaning closer to Cole.

"About what?"

"I've known you since you were a boy. I'm not sure who this woman is, but I do know that she is completely unlike any other woman you've brought to one of these functions. And, truth be told, I've never seen you look at anyone the way you look at her."

Cole grinned, remembering why Victoria and his mother were the very best of friends. The two of them had a way of nagging him like no other women could. He found it difficult to be too annoyed, however. Because she was completely right.

"Your point is," Cole asked dryly.

"My point, young man," she said, picking up her wine glass, "is that you're a fool if you let this one slip away. And sending her out there to dance with my husband isn't doing you any favors."

Nodding playfully, Cole leaned in closer, engaging her in her reprimand. "What do you suggest I do then?"

Victoria took a sip of her wine and rolled her eyes. "I suggest you go out there and get her, you adorable imbecile."

Cole threw his head back and laughed, then took her hand and kissed it before he headed out to the dance floor to reclaim Abigail.

"May I cut in?" Cole asked.

Robert looked surprised, but he nodded and stepped aside. "I was wondering how long it would take you to get your ass over here," he said quietly, so only Cole could hear him. Robert patted Cole's arm before he walked away.

Cole placed his arm on the small of Abigail's back, and laced his right hand with her left as they began to move to the music.

"Are you enjoying yourself?" he asked, his eyes meeting hers.

"Very much. I've never been to anything like this."

"The novelty wears off, I'm afraid."

Abigail laughed, sounding nervous. "I don't know that getting all dressed up and wearing pretty clothes would ever get old to me."

"I don't think pretty is the right word to describe it," Cole said.

"What is the right word?"

"Stunning," Cole replied, gazing at her. Abigail looked down, unable to hold his eyes. But she was smiling; he could see it. He didn't like her hiding her smile, so he crooked his finger beneath her chin and tilted her head up. "Do you want to get out of here?" Cole wanted to take her to the hotel room, take her anywhere the two of them could be alone. Just him and her and that smile.

"What about the rest of the benefit?"

"I made a sizable donation to the foundation already. They have my money, they don't care if they have me anymore." He took her hand and brought it to his lips, pressing a kiss against her knuckles. "Please tell me you want to leave with me." He so desperately wanted her to himself.

Abigail's beautiful smile lit up her eyes. "I want to leave with you."

In the car, Cole sat close to Abigail, staring at her hands, debating whether he should reach over and twine his fingers with hers.

Christ, she's making me nervous. He wanted to laugh; he couldn't remember the last time a woman had made his stomach flip the way Abigail did. He felt like he was back in high school. Just as he was about to reach over to take her hand, he heard her stomach growl over the low hum of the engine. Cole felt Abigail stiffen from embarrassment, and he grinned.

"Next time I'll have to take you to a seven-course dinner, since it seems the five courses weren't enough."

Abigail laughed, clutching her stomach. "I didn't want to say anything."

Cole was confused. "Say anything about what?"

Looking contrite, Abigail made her admission. "I'm allergic to shellfish."

Cole recalled the shrimp, lobster and scallops they'd been served for dinner. "We should get you something to eat. What do you want?"

"Honestly, I could really go for a hot dog."

Cole rolled down the window separating the back of the car from the front. "Tony," he said, smiling.

"Yes sir."

"We need hot dogs. Take us to the best place around."

Twenty minutes later, Abigail was sitting on the back of the town car, hot food in hand, while Tony leaned against the hood devouring his food. Cole stood behind the car, watching Abigail open the bag. He'd slipped a waiter a hundred-dollar bill in order to avoid the long line, and the look of appreciation on Abigail's face made that little gesture completely worth it.

"Oh god," she said after she took a bite. "This is the best thing I've ever eaten."

Cole watched Abigail as she enjoyed her food. "Did you have fun this evening?"

"Any night I avoid dying from anaphylaxis is counted as a win in my book."

Cole laughed, loving the way she always lightened him up, made him forget about all the things in his life that ultimately didn't matter. "Do you have any other allergies I should know about?

"No, just shellfish. And vacuuming, I guess. You?"

"Nope, nothing."

"I should've known," Abigail said before taking another bite.

"What does that mean?"

She shrugged. "You're Cole Kerrigan. Of course you have no weaknesses."

"Allergies and weaknesses are two different things. I don't have allergies, but I do have weaknesses."

Cole caught Abigail's eye and held her gaze for a moment.

"If you say that your weakness is beautiful women or something cheesy like that, I'll kick you in the shins."

God, he wanted to kiss her. He'd never let himself just feel the anticipation of a moment before he met her; he'd always given in to temptation at the first chance. There was a crackling in the air between them, an electric charge. He wanted to keep it going.

"Beautiful women are every man's weakness, Abigail. It would hardly be worth mentioning."

"What's your weakness then?"

"Honestly?"

Abigail nodded as she chewed.

"Dogs. Puppies, I guess. Golden retrievers, specifically."

Abigail laughed. "Seriously?"

"Yes, seriously. Is that so difficult to believe?"

"Why don't you have one?"

"With the hours I work, it would hardly be fair to an animal. My parents own several; I see them when I can. They have a large yard, too. Better than living in an apartment."

"Where do your parents live?"

"Upstate New York."

"In an estate, am I right?"

"I guess you could call it that."

Abigail nodded, but didn't say anything. For a split second, Cole seemed wounded.

"I'm not embarrassed of my money, Abigail. Nor am I embarrassed of my parents' fortune."

"I never suggested that you should be," she explained,

wiping her fingers on a napkin. "I apologize for being petty. Taking little digs at your wealth is my way of feeling…I don't know, like I'm on the same level as you are."

For someone who always seemed so self-assured, Cole was surprised at her admission. "You're on the same level as me always, Abigail. Money has nothing to do with it."

"If I'm on the same level as you are, then maybe you should stop calling me by my full name. And stop paying fifteen thousand dollars for a plate for me at benefit dinners."

Despite his earlier declaration, he did seem embarrassed at that. "I didn't pay for that plate for you, I did it for me."

Abigail looked shocked, her beautiful eyes narrowed. "Why?"

"I spend a lot of time at stuffy dinner parties and benefits, and for once I wanted to know what it would be like to have fun at one of them."

"I made tonight fun?"

He nearly laughed at her self-doubt. Surely she knew how much better she made his life. Just in case she wasn't being coy, he made sure to tell her. "You make everything fun."

She grinned, her shyness making her look down.

"C'mon," Cole said, taking her hand and helping her off of the trunk. Inside the car, he followed the instincts he'd been having all night and laced his fingers with hers. He didn't let go until he slipped his key card into their suite door's lock.

Abigail placed her purse on the table in the foyer, pressing her palms against its marble top. Only last night he'd fucked her in this very spot. And it was at that moment that Cole felt shame for the fact that he'd never taken her to his bed. His desire for her had always been so frenzied, so immediate, that he'd fucked her against his desk, on the sofa, in the foyer. He'd never taken the time to savor her, to worship her the way she deserved. He'd never made love to her on a bed. Cole wanted to show her how he felt about her, and it all started with him breaking down the last barrier between them.

Cole walked up behind Abigail and slid his fingers down the sides of her arms. She melted into him, her back against his chest. He brushed his lips against the slope of her neck, then wrapped his arms around her waist and she placed her hands atop his.

He leaned in and whispered, "Abby."

CHAPTER
Twenty-Seven

*H*e called her by her nickname.

Abby's heart skipped a beat. Cole finally, *finally* called her by her nickname. He whispered it, like a prayer.

Abby turned around and faced Cole. He looked unsure, something she was entirely unaccustomed to with him. His eyes were wide and earnest, waiting for some kind of reaction from her. The sound of her name was still echoing in her ears, and she needed to hear again the way his voice sounded when he said it. She looked up and ghosted her fingertips along the ridges of his brows. His eyelids fluttered shut.

"Say it again," she whispered.

"Abby," Cole breathed. A slow grin spread across his lips before he turned his head and kissed her palm.

Abby gently slid her hands down the sides of Cole's face, then they twined together behind his neck. She used him as leverage to pull herself up and plant a kiss on his lips. It was long and slow, and when they finally broke apart, Cole picked her up.

Abby squealed, and then Cole carried her into her bedroom since it was the closest.

Cole was taking his time with her tonight, savoring every touch, every kiss. He had removed her dress slowly, gently sliding it off her shoulders and into a pool on the floor. He took care in removing her bra, then caressing and kissing her breasts. She had thrown his jacket across the room and kissed his chest as she unbuttoned his shirt, had slid her fingertips along his hot skin as she'd pushed his pants, then his boxers down to the floor. Until it was just the two of them together, naked.

Cole's hands rested on Abby's hips, his erection pressing against her belly as his tongue brushed against hers during a long, heated embrace. Abby wanted to memorize the planes of his skin, learn every curve of his body by heart.

It wasn't long before the kissing was no longer enough, and Abby climbed onto the bed with Cole following close behind her. He wrapped his arms around her shoulders while she was still on her knees, bringing his legs to rest on either side of hers, pulling her back into his chest. His hard cock rested against the small of her back as he lowered his hand to cup her breast and wrapped the other arm around her waist, sliding his hand down between her thighs. Abby gasped as Cole's fingers found her clit, building immeasurable pleasure in her belly as he peppered her neck with kisses. She rested her arms and hands over his, not wanting him to stop what he was doing to her.

"No one makes me feel like you do," Cole said, pressing his lips against the shell of her ear. "Only you, only you."

Just as Abby was about to come, Cole slid inside her, stretching her in the most wonderful way. The heel of his hand pressed against her belly as he thrust, each move of his hips hitting that perfect place inside of her, his fingers working in concert with the rest of him to completely push her over the edge. Abby turned her head and kissed Cole, wrapping her arm around his neck as she reveled in every lick of pleasure he pushed through her body.

Too soon, Abby's knees felt weak, and she pressed her palms into the bed, bent over, desperately trying to hold herself up.

"Let go," Cole whispered, his chest against her back. "I've got you."

Abby did as she was told. She lay down on the bed, and the duvet felt soft against her breasts. Cole settled himself over her, slipping one hand around her hip to tend to her clit. He rested most of his weight on his elbow, twining his free hand with hers as she rolled her hips against him. She was so close that within a minute or two of switching positions she was able to find her release. Cole kissed Abby's neck, across her shoulder blades, and then the small of her back before he gripped her waist and turned her over onto her back.

Cole's mouth found hers again, the wet sounds of their kisses filling the air between them. As if he sensed what Abby needed, where she wanted him the most, he laved his tongue along her sensitive nipples, then her ribs, her belly button. Then he pressed his cheek against the inside of her thigh and parted her flesh with one long, sure lick.

Abby's clit was still thrumming, her delicate skin still buzzing from her orgasm. She knit her fingers through Cole's hair as his tongue rocked against her, building pressure, pushing her towards yet another climax. And she wanted it, she really did. But tonight, she just needed him close to her, wanted to be able to look in his crystal clear eyes as he moved inside her. She touched his arm, diverting his attention, then she took his hands and pulled him up until they were kissing.

And then, suddenly, there was too much air between them, too much distance even though they were so close together. Abby pulled him to her, until she was comforted by the weight of his body on hers. They didn't need words, just kisses, just touches, just each other. Cole slid Abby's arms up over her head, twining her fingers with his as he pushed into her with a long, satisfied sigh. Abby thought Cole's eyes were so beautiful when they looked into hers, and there were so many things that she wanted to tell him, but words didn't feel like they'd be enough. So she showed him with her body, with each buck of her hips that made his eyes flutter, with each kiss that made him come back for another. She wanted everything about him to be imprinted on her, so she could carry a piece of him around with her forever. Nothing mattered anymore but the two of them together, lost in pleasure. Tonight, she wasn't his assistant or his employee. She was just his.

It was a slow, perfect rush when they came, their lips pressed together, breathing each other's air. Cole didn't move right away, instead spending the moments as they came down from their high kissing Abby, caressing her hair. Whispering sweet words in her ear that made her drift off into some warm, soft place with a smile on her lips as she fell asleep in his arms at last.

The next morning, Abby woke up wrapped firmly in Cole's embrace. He was already awake when she opened her eyes, looking gorgeous as ever with his happy smile and his hair all unruly from sleep. Abby found herself wanting to wake up like this every morning.

"Hi," he said.

"Hi." Abby curled against his side, relishing in his warmth.

"I've been waiting for you to wake up." Cole pressed a kiss against the top of her head. That wasn't enough for Abby; after last night, she wanted every little bit of him she could have, and since they were leaving in a few hours, she was going to have to take what she could get while she could get it. She tilted her head up, intending to kiss him, then at the last minute she remembered that she probably had morning breath and she ducked her head, covering her mouth.

"What is it?" Cole asked, laughing.

Abby spoke under the cover of her hand. "I wanted to kiss you, but I was worried about my breath."

"I'm not worried about your breath." Cole playfully rolled her over until she was resting on his stomach, and he gave her a long-awaited kiss. It deepened quickly, and Abby was alerted to another need Cole had so early in the morning. His erection rested against the inside of her thigh, and he drew a hiss through clenched teeth when she moved her leg to tease him. Wanting to relive the endless pleasure she felt last night, Abby reached down and slid her fingers along his length.

Cole thrust against her with that needy look in his eyes, urging her on. She continued touching him, rubbing him, stoking his desire until he rolled her onto her side. He lifted up her left leg and brought it to rest over his, pulling her against his chest as he entered her from behind. Cole wrapped his arms around Abby, holding her close and kissing her as his fingers circled her clit. He moved leisurely, unhurried, seemingly content just to be inside of her. It was a slow build for the two of them, the kind of pleasure that came in steady, small waves.

After, the two of them drifted in and out of sleep, finally waking when the sun was shining through the curtains.

"What are we going to do today?" Abby asked. Their flight left at six, but there were so many hours to kill before then, so many things they could do to each other in that span of time. Abby's toes curled just thinking about it.

Cole glanced at the clock on the beside table. "I'm due at

a meeting in an hour, but after that I'm yours."

"All mine?" Abby asked, kissing a trail up his neck to his lips.

"All yours." Cole sighed happily when Abby's lips were on him.

"I guess you should shower then."

"Probably," he replied.

He rolled out of bed, and Abby admired the muscular planes of his body as he stood, throwing off the sheets. He didn't even bother to cover himself.

"You?" he asked.

"I'm going to make some coffee."

"Save some for me," Cole said, winking at her as he stood in the doorway.

Abby followed Cole out into the living room, playfully swatting at his ass with the belt of her robe. He turned for retaliation, wrapping her in his arms and assaulting her with kisses. They got caught up in one another for a while before Cole finally broke away to continue his day. Abby walked over to the kitchenette and poured some water into the coffee pot, then waited impatiently for her caffeine fix.

It was then that she noticed the flashing chat notifications on Cole's laptop.

"It looks like you're pretty popular," Abby shouted, hoping Cole would hear her.

"Yeah?"

"You've got about ten chat windows up."

"Will you check them for me, please? And my emails, too. Make sure nothing is urgent."

It felt strange, the transition between being Cole's lover and being his employee. Abby did her best to shake off the discomfort.

Abby walked over and sat down in Cole's chair, then clicked on each of the windows. All of them were from Keith; short messages asking Cole to call him back, telling him that Keith had received his email. There were notes of congratulations. She'd seen Josh's name several times.

Her stomach sank as the realization hit her, and she pulled up Cole's sent messages, knowing exactly which one she was looking for. It was the last email he'd sent, last night before they left to go to dinner. The subject was *Josh Hamilton*.

She paused for a moment before she opened the email because she knew, whatever was in there, that it was going to change things between her and Cole. She knew it in her gut, with every fiber of her being. She figured she should do this quickly, like ripping off a bandage. So, she clicked the mouse and the email popped up.

Keith,

> *I got him, he was just as stupid as we thought. He took Abigail out for drinks last night and offered her a job in exchange for the plans for KC-23. She*

came back to the hotel and told me right away. I
should give her a bonus.
Fired him this morning.
More later.

-CK

Abby felt like she was going to vomit. Everything was starting to make sense to her. Why Cole brought her here, why he was even interested in her in the first place. She thought back to the night she left to get drinks with Josh, how she was desperate for Cole to tell her not to go. Now she knew why he wouldn't, why he *couldn't*. That evening was the whole point of their trip.

What would Cole have done if Abby hadn't told him about Josh asking her out? She'd wanted him to show a bit of jealousy when she mentioned the invitation, but he didn't, and this was why. He knew what Josh was up to and was just waiting for him to slip up and hoped he'd be stupid enough to do it with Abby. He was.

And Abby was stupid enough to believe that he actually saw something in her, but…everything was a lie. Every smile, every touch, every kiss. And last night was…what? A reward? Abby's hands shook as her breathing quickened. She was such a fool.

"Anything important?" Cole called out from his room.

Everything important, Abby thought. She swallowed against the growing lump in her throat. "Nothing at all." Her voice was steady, she almost believed herself.

Abby heard the water turn on and she stood, trying to figure out what she was going to do. There was only one thing she *could* do, and it was what she knew would happen eventually ever since the night her and Cole first kissed in his office. She couldn't cry, not yet. She had to take care of business.

She reached over a stack of Cole's files and grabbed a sticky note and a pen.

Then, she began to write.

CHAPTER
Twenty-Eight

"That coffee smells good," Cole said, stepping out into the suite's living room. It was eerily quiet, and instantly he knew that something was off.

"Abby?" She wasn't sitting in his chair; she hadn't even poured herself a cup of coffee. She wasn't in the foyer or the sitting room. Cole quickly walked to her room. He didn't see any of her things; not the underthings he'd thrown on the floor last night that he'd had to step over this morning. Her bathroom was empty, no clothes were in her dresser drawers. The dress she wore last night was hanging neatly on a rack in the corner.

A rising tide of panic crashed against his chest. He walked back into the living room, where he noticed her laptop sitting on the chair, the cord neatly wrapped around it. When he looked at his computer screen, his heart sank.

"Fuck. Fuck!" He wrapped his fingers into a fist and slammed it against the desk. The email he'd sent to Keith last night was pulled up on the screen, obscured by a small square piece of paper with two simple words written in Abby's impeccable handwriting.

I QUIT

Cole grabbed his wallet off the desk and shoved it in his pocket as he ran for the door.

CHAPTER
Twenty-Nine

*S*afely back home in the comfort of her shoebox-sized apartment, Abby watched as Becca paced across the kitchen.

"I don't know who he is, but I'm going to fucking *kill* him," Becca said, scooping a giant heap of chocolate ice cream into a bowl. Becca walked over to where Abby was sitting on the couch and handed the bowl to her, but she politely declined. She didn't think she could stomach anything at this point, not even her all-time favorite comfort food. "What did he say when you told him you read the email?"

"He didn't say anything, because I didn't tell him I read it. I wrote that I quit on a sticky note and took off before he got out of the shower."

Becca stood there, the handle of the spoon she was scooping the ice cream with hanging out of her mouth. "You did what?" she asked, her words slurred by the silverware pressing against her tongue.

"I wrote 'I quit' on a sticky note and stuck it to his laptop screen. Then I left my work phone and computer there and left. I headed to Midway since I figured he'd look for me at O'Hare and I got out on the first flight available. You have to jump through some hoops to change flight plans on private aircraft, so since his jet wasn't scheduled to leave until six, I figured I was safe."

"Yeah," Becca said sarcastically. "No way could that gazillionaire just hop on a commercial flight to find you."

Honestly, Abby hadn't thought of that. "My heart was broken, Beck. I wasn't exactly thinking through all my options."

Becca's eyes softened, and she came over and sat beside Abby on the sofa, then gave her a hug. "Did he even try to call you?"

Abby pulled her personal cell phone out of her pocket and showed Becca the missed calls.

"*Two-hundred and seventeen*? My god, Abby. Are you going to call him back?"

Am I? Abby wasn't so sure. She shrugged and looked at her watch.

"It's four now. What I'm going to do is head down to the office and pick up my stuff before he gets back."

"Do you want me to come with you?"

Abby smiled and sadly shook her head. She knew this was one time Becca was asking just to be her friend, not because she wanted to know who Abby's mysterious boss was.

"No, it's alright. I can go alone." When she stood, Becca grabbed her hand.

"You should let him explain," she said. "Maybe it's not what it looks like."

Abby felt the sting of welling tears behind her eyes. "What happened to the theory that this had an expiration date? You're on his side now."

"No, I'm on your side," Becca said, attempting a sad smile. "But I've never seen you look like this over an expiration date."

The office was quiet when Abby walked in, completely abandoned for the weekend. She walked with careful steps toward her desk, anxiety and anticipation building, wondering who or what she would find when she finally got there. As it turned out, she needn't have worried. Everything was in the same place it was when she'd left last Friday evening, and Cole was nowhere in sight. She went to the storage room and picked out a file box, then brought it back to her desk and began packing all of her personal belongings. Only once did she look at Cole's door, but the longing and pain in her heart was ever-present.

Abby was putting the last framed photo in her box when she heard the front door open, and she knew it was him. Even though he'd broken her heart, the rest of her body was so hyper-aware of his presence that she didn't even need to see his face to know that he was near. Her heart picked up speed, thrumming against her chest, and she quickly put the photo in the box, not wanting Cole to see her hands shaking.

He stopped a few feet away from her, just outside of the shadows of the unlit office.

"Abby," he said quietly, his voice so full of remorse that it made the one piece of her heart that was still intact shatter into a hundred pieces. "I was on my way to your apartment and I saw you walking toward the subway. I figured you were coming here and I…I wanted to see you. To talk to you."

Abby swallowed against the painful lump in her throat and swiped at her eyes. *Damn it*, she didn't want him to see her cry.

"I'm just collecting my things," she said, her voice wavering. "I'll be out in a minute."

He stepped forward into the light, breathtakingly handsome as always. "Please don't go." The words were raw emotion, reflected in his eyes.

All of this was just too much for Abby to bear. Why couldn't he have just wanted her? Why did there have to be strings attached? She was so angry at him for ruining this that she could scream. She'd wanted to get out before she felt this way. She'd wanted to end it before she was forced to.

Nothing, it seemed, was ever going to go according to plan. And she was so angry with him that she wanted to scream.

"Please don't go?" She sarcastically repeated his question. He'd done everything possible to make sure that's all she wanted to do. "You got what you wanted, why do you want me to stay?"

He took another step closer. "I didn't get what I wanted," he said, and foolishly, Abby looked into his eyes.

"What was the point of all this?" Abby asked angrily. "No, no," she said, shaking her head as she reached for the lid to the box she'd packed her things in. "I know what the point of it was. I just wish you hadn't felt the need to make a fool out of me in the process."

Cole's eyebrows knit together, his eyes dark. "I didn't make a fool out of you."

Abby laughed bitterly. "Do you have any idea how your own company works, Cole? You didn't encrypt the message you sent to Keith. All the assistants in this office have access to their boss's email. His assistant is the biggest gossip in the place," she said angrily. "Do you know how that makes me look? Like I'm just some…some whore."

Cole took two steps forward. Abby could tell he was angry, and she steeled herself against what he was getting ready to say.

"Don't say that. Don't you dare talk about yourself that way."

"That's the way you treated me," Abby said, matching his anger.

"No, it's-"

"Either I wanted you too badly or I was too stupid to realize what was going on. And now not only do I get to feel like a complete fool, but soon the whole company will know. Even if there was nothing going on between us, I wouldn't be able to stay after something like that."

"I'll fire her if she dares say anything about you."

Abby sighed, shaking her head. "For what? She didn't do anything wrong, I did. And I knew better. But I wanted you so badly that I just didn't care. The great Cole Kerrigan showing someone like me attention…I just didn't know what to do with myself. Besides, you fire her for something like that, then the rumor mill will be twice as bad, and then people really will think I'm trash."

He actually looked pained to hear the words aloud. "Please," he begged. "Stop talking about yourself like that."

"You used me, and it hurts to hear that out loud, doesn't it?"

"I didn't use you," he said adamantly. "Abby, I didn't even think of doing it until-" he stopped himself, knowing he'd gone too far.

The words hit Abby like a punch to the gut anyway. What more could hearing the rest of it hurt? She was numb at this point.

"Until what?"

He stared at her a long while, as if he were memorizing her. As if he needed to remember what she looked like because he knew that after he said what he was getting ready to say that he'd never see her again. Finally, the words came. "Until later that night."

Abby had lied to herself; she wasn't numb. She wasn't anywhere in the vicinity of numb, because the admission hit her like an arrow to the chest, pain splintering out and breaking her into tiny pieces. More tears fell, only this time she didn't bother wiping them away. She wanted him to see what he had done to her. But she had to know one thing.

"Why didn't you just ask me to talk to him? I would've done it." *I would've done anything for you*, she wanted to tell him. But she didn't.

"I was worried that you'd tip him off to the fact that I had some idea of what he was up to."

So now I'm untrustworthy too.

"So, you just took me up to Chicago hoping he'd ask me out and tell me his grand plan? That sounds like a huge stroke of luck, even for you."

"No," Cole replied, at least having the decency to look embarrassed. "I knew he had been calling you, and I figured he was using you to get to something."

Abby felt a fresh wave of tears falling. "Yeah, I guess it would make sense for him to be interested in me only to get to you. Apparently that's my main appeal, getting people what they want."

Cole stepped forward and reached for Abby's cheek, but she flinched away from him. "That's not what I meant," he said, sounding very sad and resigned.

"Will you please just let me box up my things in peace?"

Cole stood next to Abby, lingering as if he was waiting for her to change her mind, for everything to go back to the way it was just hours before. "I want you to understand, that I ultimately went about this the way that I did because I didn't want you to feel like this."

"What a consolation that is." Abby threw the top on the box, just wanting to get out of the office and out of his presence as soon as possible.

"Abby," Cole said, and there was a tenderness in his voice that made Abby look up at him. "I don't know how to be in a relationship. I never have."

"Clearly."

"The truth is that I've never wanted to try it as much as I want to try it with you."

Abby felt an ache somewhere inside of her, one that took the place of the thrill she should've felt from hearing those words. She would've felt it just this morning, before one email changed everything.

"And I've never wanted to get out of here as much as I want to get out of here right now." She grabbed the box and shoved past him, walking as fast as she could to the elevator bank. She was no match for his long stride though, she knew he was following her.

"Wait," he said in a rush. "Please, wait."

Abby had waited for him for months. She couldn't wait any longer. She couldn't hurt any more. The elevator doors opened seconds after she pressed the button. She stepped inside and Cole pressed his hand against the door to prevent it from closing.

His eyes mirrored her own sadness. So much so that she almost believed that he was hurting as much as she was. That he was truly sorry for what he'd done. But Abby knew, deep down inside of her, that was only her desire for things to be back the way they were. He gazed at her sadly.

"The truth is that I don't know what to do without you."

"You'll find another assistant," Abby said, pressing the

button for the bottom floor.

"But I won't find another *you*."

She wished she could just be angry at him, that every single word didn't rip her insides to shreds. She wished she could just walk away from him and stop caring. It would've been easy if she didn't love him so much.

"Please let me go," she begged.

Cole tapped his fingers against the door and Abby could tell he was just waiting, hoping that something would change. That she would give in.

He was used to that.

Finally, he pulled his hand away. Abby looked down at the floor, unable to look into his eyes one last time.

CHAPTER
Thirty

Cole settled into a luxuriously soft chair in his brother's den, cradling his month-old niece Alexandra in his arms. She grabbed his index finger with her curiously strong newborn fist, and despite all the inner turmoil he felt, he couldn't help but smile at her.

"I haven't seen you in a while," Scott Kerrigan said as he set down a bottle of water on the table next to his brother. "Nice of you to finally stop by."

"It's funny how you look like my brother but sound like my mom," Cole said, gazing lovingly at his niece. He wasn't going to let his only brother irritate him, not today. Not when he needed his advice more than ever.

"Okay, okay," Scott said, holding his hands up as he laughed. "We'd like to see you more is all. Tyler was asking about you the other day."

"I'll stay until he wakes up from his nap." Cole looked at his brother and smiled, letting him know that he was making an effort.

"He'd like that."

"I picked up a model of the Sears Tower for him while I was in Chicago. I thought he'd like that for his birthday."

"The Willis Tower," Scott corrected.

"Whatever."

"Tyler idolizes you, you know." Scott leaned back in his chair and crossed his legs.

"Well, he shouldn't."

Scott gave him that brotherly look; the one that told Cole that Scott knew that something was going on. "Usually holding the baby soothes the self-loathing."

Cole's heart warmed as his niece gripped his finger tighter and let out a wide, toothless yawn. Then, he looked at his brother with anguish in his eyes. "I messed up, Scott."

"Want to tell me about it?"

"No, I just stopped by to mooch off your Evian supply."

Scott rolled his eyes, but didn't offer a reply like he usually would have.

"Yes, I want to tell you about it," Cole said, resigned. He smoothed Alexandra's whisper-fine hair with the backs of his fingers and had a fleeting thought of what it would be like to look down into the face of his own sleeping infant. It was a warm feeling. "I can't do it while I'm holding her though."

"Jesus, what did you do?" Scott stood and gently lifted his sleeping daughter, then carried her over to the bassinet in the corner of the room.

Cole waited until his brother returned to his seat to start talking.

"My assistant…"

"Annabel?"

"Abigail," Cole said before he caught himself. "Abby."

"What happened?" Scott eyed Cole suspiciously, and rightfully so.

Cole paused for a moment, dreading the look of judgment in Scott's eyes once Cole told him what he'd done.

"I slept with her." That wasn't enough of an explanation and didn't nearly do their relationship justice, but it would have to do for now.

Scott sighed, tilting his head back. "Christ, Cole. I thought you knew better than to shit where you eat?"

"I do, I just…" *Couldn't resist her. Fell in love with her.*

"Do you have any idea how big of a liability this is? You've just left yourself wide open for a lawsuit."

Cole loved Scott dearly, but he was always an attorney, even when Cole just needed a brother. "I know that."

"She can't even really give consent, Cole. With you as her superior, she could make a case for harassment and coercion."

"I know, Scott. I didn't come here for legal counsel, I have a team of lawyers for that."

"Do they know about this?" Scott asked.

Cole looked down and shook his head. "No."

"If you were smart you would tell them."

"I'm not worried about her filing a suit." Abby should do that, but she wouldn't. She cared for Cole, she had told him as much. She wanted him to erase what he'd done, and no lawsuit was able to do that.

"You should be."

"I need advice," Cole said, sounding exasperated. He was tired of the third degree; it was making him feel shittier than he did already. "I don't know how to make it right."

"Make what right?"

"I got word last week that one of my employees was shopping top secret project specs to potential buyers in Japan. I knew what he was trying to sell, I just didn't know if someone else was in on it and I wasn't sure exactly who he was selling to. I wanted that information before I fired him so I could make sure that we didn't leave ourselves open to theft or corporate espionage."

Scott shook his head. "It amazes me that you thought that through so carefully, but not your sexual relationship with your assistant."

Cole glared at his brother, but it only took a few seconds for his gaze to soften. Scott was right to reprimand him; what he'd done was incredibly stupid. "Well, as it turns out, I didn't think that through so carefully, either."

"What do you mean?"

"I had IT pull everything from his computer. Every outgoing communication. Nothing. His phone records turned up several calls to one person in particular."

Scott sighed. "Abby."

Cole nodded.

"Was she in on it?"

"No. I was hoping that if I somehow got the two of them

together that he would be dumb enough to spill. Turns out that he wanted to use her to get to me."

"So…"

"I took her with me on a trip to Chicago, which is where the office this man works out of is located."

"And then you slept with her to get what you wanted."

Cole could hear the disappointment in Scott's voice. "No," Cole said quietly. "That happened before I knew about the thief. But only by half a day."

"Christ, Cole. Why didn't you just tell her what you were up to?"

"That would've been the easy and smart thing to do. Strangely enough, I didn't want her to feel like I was using her."

"But you were, just not in the way you thought you would be."

"I know that now," Cole replied, his eyes downcast. "Being the amateur I suspected he was, this guy made contact with her quickly, then offered her a job in exchange for her stealing some information from me."

"She didn't take him up on this offer."

"No, she came to me immediately. But Keith left for Tokyo on Tuesday and we're on opposite schedules, so I sent him an email letting him know what happened, including the fact that this man had asked Abby out and that she'd come to me with the information, and-"

"She saw the email," Scott said, intuitive as always.

"And assumed the worst."

"It sounds like even the best is a little sketchy."

Cole had to admit that Scott was right. "She quit."

"That's probably for the best."

Cole nodded. "It is for the best," he said, looking down at his hands before his eyes met his brother's. "Because I'm in love with her."

Scott shook his head, smiling despite the heaviness of their conversation. Cole was certain that was because Scott had never heard him utter those words before.

"I never thought I'd hear you say," Scott said.

"I'm doing a lot of things lately that I never thought I'd do."

Scott took a sip of water. "Then you're in bigger trouble than I thought you were."

"I am. She won't take my calls anymore." Cole was relieved at the shift in the mood, glad that things were finally lighter.

"Since when has that stopped you?"

"This is true, I just…she asked me to let her go, and I don't want to make her angrier with me than she already is."

"You've got to lay it all out on the line, Cole. Put yourself out there and let her know how you feel in a way that lets her know that you're not trying to manipulate her into keeping her job. It has to be honest."

"What, like a grand gesture?"

"A *sincere* grand gesture, yeah. What does she like to do?"

Cole thought back to the discussion that he and Abby had at the diner, when she'd told him her dream of owning a candy store. She mentioned that she sold her candies on Saturday at the Union Market on the weekends. *There,* he thought. *I'll do it there. She had just quit her job, so surely she'd set up a stand this weekend to earn some extra money.*

Scott must have recognized the spark of an idea in Cole's eyes, because he leaned forward, resting his head in his hands. "I think we have the beginnings of a plan."

Later that afternoon as Cole walked through the office, he stopped briefly at the empty desk outside of his door. He felt an ache every time he saw Abby's empty chair, even though it had been four days since she quit. Four days since he'd seen her. Every once in a while he'd close his eyes and imagine her smile. It was then that he wished he had told her how beautiful she was more often.

He entered his office and closed the door behind him. On his desk was a small box, wrapped in plain brown paper. Puzzled, he unwrapped it, impatiently pulling at the paper. When he pulled back the flaps on the top of the box, he thought back to when he'd called Marley and asked her to help him find this.

And here it was, with no recipient.

In two days, Cole was going to change that.

CHAPTER
Thirty-One

$\mathcal{B}$usiness was slow at Abby's stand that Saturday, despite the fact that she and Becca spent most of the morning handing out samples. It was like this sometimes, so of course Abby expected it, but there could not have been a worse time for low crowds at the market. She'd been second-guessing herself all week; even though she needed to get away from Cole, it had been so foolish of her to quit her job before she had another one lined up. Luckily for her, Becca had pulled a few strings at her office and got Abby an interview with a director in another section of her company, but she was going to have to start at the bottom again.

She didn't even want to think about the job that one of Cole's colleagues called to offer her a few days ago, but it seemed that was all Becca could talk about. Abby willed some customers to walk over to offer her a distraction.

"You should've taken that job," Becca said, popping one of the samples in her mouth. "Not that I don't want you working with me, I mean. I'd love that, but this guy would've given you way more money and a much better position."

"And then I'd be beholden to C-" Abby caught herself before she said Cole's name, pretty sure that Becca didn't notice her slip. She was too busy eating the chocolate. "I'd be beholden to my boss. I need to cut all those ties."

"Who was the guy?"

"Someone he went to business school with. I Googled his name when I got off the phone, and I know that I've seen his picture in my boss's office before. They're golf buddies or something."

"He still cares about you," Becca said.

Deep inside of Abby, a small flicker of hope made itself felt.

Two hours later, Abby and Becca were still at the market, refusing to give up. Business had picked up a little, but Abby's had better Saturdays.

"I can't believe how many people are here," Becca said, peering out from under their booth's canopy.

"If only all these people would buy my chocolate," Abby lamented, looking at all the unsold goodies on the table in front of her. Quite a few people were still tasting samples, but few had actually purchased a piece for themselves. "Go out there and flash them or something, Beck. We need something interesting to drum up some attention."

Becca swatted Abby with one of her flyers. "I never thought I'd say this, but I liked you more when you were depressed."

"I wasn't depressed," Abby said, attempting to sound lighthearted. Sad, yes. Heartbroken, yes. But depressed? No. And as much as it hurt her to admit it, Abby missed Cole. Not just the sex, even though that was obviously great, but she missed *him*. The person she'd come to know during their trip together. Cole was in nearly every thought Abby had. But she knew she'd move on in time. She just wanted that time to pass as quickly as possible.

"You were borderline depressed, Abs."

Becca was right. "But I'm better now."

Becca twirled a strand of Abby's hair around her finger, then smiled the smile of a friend who had been in a similar place one too many times before. "Yeah, you're getting there."

Abby allowed herself a moment to lean against Becca, taking comfort in the hug of a long-time friend. But she didn't want Becca to feel like she had to walk on eggshells around her forever. "Let's cut this emotional crap and sell some chocolate before I wind up having to give this stuff away for free."

Then, Abby heard a voice that was so familiar it made her heart ache.

"Never give your product away for free, that's not the way to run a business."

Shocked, Abby looked up at Cole. Her heart wanted to

explode. She wanted to kiss him and run away at the same time. He looked really bad. Good, as always, but bad. Like he hadn't been sleeping, like he'd been just as messed up over what had happened between them as Abby had.

"What are you doing here?" Abby asked, sounding more defensive than she meant to.

Seemingly unfazed, Cole looked at Abby and simply said, "My favorite chocolate maker once told me that she liked to come here on Saturdays."

Nerves made Abby's heart sink into her stomach, and she wasn't sure if she was ready or able to believe that Cole's intentions were honorable, were real.

"Don't do this, Cole." Abby looked down at the table, afraid to meet his gaze, knowing that she was helpless when he was around.

He touched her hand, just a fleeting graze of his fingertips across her skin, and her heart beat double time.

"Just listen to me, Abby. Please, just hear me out."

Chancing a look over at Becca, Abby found she was still standing right beside her, staring at Cole, her mouth agape in shock. Surely she recognized Cole. Abby nearly laughed. Seeing Becca's face reminded Abby of Cole's precious confidentiality agreement.

"There are people here," she said, looking around at the crowd. "They might see us talking and get the wrong idea."

Cole reached over and lifted Abby's chin until she looked at him. "Or they might get the right idea. I don't care, let them hear."

"Then say what you need to say."

He caressed Abby's cheek, and the memory of his touch flooded Abby with warmth. "I'm sorry I hurt you. It's no excuse, but you have to know that wasn't my intent. I'm a businessman, Abby. I've spent my whole life caring about the bottom line, and I've never had any qualms about using someone for my own benefit-"

Abby looked at him sharply. "Is that supposed to make me feel better?"

"Let me finish," he said, smiling nervously. "I never had any qualms about using someone for my own benefit until I met you. Because I care about you more than I've ever cared about any other woman in my life."

"Stop," Abby said, feeling foolish. "Just stop with this, okay? You apologized, I accept. You can leave here with a clear conscience."

Cole's eyes softened. "I *can't* leave here with a clear conscience."

"Why can't you?"

"Because I've fallen in love with you."

Those were the words Abby most wanted to hear, but never thought she would. Not from Cole. She wasn't sure whether she could trust them. But oh, how she wanted to.

Cole cupped her cheek, swiping away a tear that had fallen.

"I need you, Abby. I need you to give me another chance. Please," Cole pleaded. His eyes never left Abby's.

There was a small crowd beginning to gather. Either they finally were ready to purchase her candy or they recognized Cole and wanted to eavesdrop on whatever he was doing.

Either way, they had the worst timing.

"When you've upset the woman you love, you bring her chocolate, am I right?" Cole stared at Abby a moment longer, then turned to the small group of onlookers who had gathered around them, There was a smattering of approval from the crowd. "Am I right?" Cole repeated, raising his voice. The men laughed, the women cheered, laughing.

Turning to them, Cole said, "There's no better chocolate in the city." He reached out and took the sample tray from Becca, who was still standing there wide-eyed like she'd been smacked in the face. He grabbed the stack of Abby's business cards and schmoozed the crowd, handing out samples and cards. Most of the people who took a sample from him bought a piece of chocolate. Abby and Becca couldn't keep up with the demand. It seemed as if everyone wanted one. Cole really turned on the charm.

It didn't take long for Abby to sell out. Abby had been longing for a steady flow of business, but she never anticipated such a rush. When they had sold the final piece, Cole set the tray down on the table and offered his hand to Becca.

"Hi, I'm Cole," he said, flashing a winning smile.

"Kerrigan," Becca said before she could catch herself. She shook her head, embarrassed, and Abby just had to smile. "I'm sorry, I'm Becca."

Cole grinned. "You must be Abby's roommate," he said, laughing. Abby had spent so much time fretting about that damned non-disclosure agreement that she never took the time to wonder about what Cole would be like around her friends. "It's nice to finally meet you."

"Likewise," Becca said, blushing. She glared at Abby in an excited way, like she couldn't believe what just happened.

Cole gently grasped Abby's upper arm and walked to the edge of the tent where they had a bit more privacy.

"I meant what I said about wanting a second chance."

Cole's eyes were so intense that Abby could barely look at them.

"I'm considering it," she said, although her words were soft. There was no consideration to be made; if he wanted a second chance, she would give it to him.

Cole crooked his fingers beneath Abby's chin. "Let me see you tonight."

Abby knew it was more than a request. She thought about spending the night with him, going to a fancy restaurant like she was sure he'd want to do. A place where she would feel out of her element. It was then that she began to think about what he had just told her. He had fallen in love with her. In love. With *her*. Their week together in Chicago had been a fantasy, but this…this love, this relationship, *this*…whatever it was, needed to be based in reality. And the reality of their situation was that he was a billionaire. She was not.

"Okay," she said, feeling giddy at the sight of the relief in his eyes. "But I have one condition."

"Anything."

"I want you to come over to my apartment."

Cole looked a little shocked. No doubt he had something more elaborate planned, but if he was reluctant to agree to her plan he didn't show it. "What time should I be there?"

"Seven," Abby replied.

"Okay. Should I bring anything?"

"No. I'm making dinner." From the look on Cole's face, Abby could tell that few women had ever made Cole dinner. "And dinner is all that we'll be having."

Cole smiled.

Abby knew they could not have sex tonight. Because if they did, she'd lose all her resolve, and resolve was the one thing she needed right now.

"I'll see you at seven," Cole said, leaning in toward her. Abby could tell that he wanted to kiss her, but he stopped himself. Part of her ached for the feeling of his lips on hers, but she wasn't quite ready for that yet. The sting of his betrayal was still too fresh despite today's events.

Not five seconds after Cole walked away, Becca was by Abby's side.

"I just cannot fucking believe that you…you…you know, you did whatever with Cole Kerrigan. Christ Abby, it's like I don't even know you!"

Abby grinned. "I told you, I signed a-"

"I know, I know. You signed a non-disclosure agreement. Ugh, you lucky bitch!"

Becca flipped her hair over her shoulder in faux outrage. "I *am* pissed! So pissed, in fact, that I probably won't make it home tonight." She winked at Abby then leaned in to give her a hug.

Becca really was the best friend she'd ever had.

CHAPTER
Thirty-Two

Cole wanted to take Abby to his favorite restaurant and order her the most divine prime rib she would ever taste, then take her back to his place. He wanted to make love to her, of course, but he found that tonight he craved her company. He craved the knowledge that she was near him; that he could see her, touch her, talk to her whenever he wanted. Instead, she'd invited him to her tiny walkup in Brooklyn. Even though his plans were dashed, he couldn't have been more pleased. He'd get to see her in her element. He couldn't have asked for more than that.

Cole had been to her apartment building before, although Abby didn't know that. He found himself standing on her front steps on the evening that she quit, right after she left his office. He had planned on going up to her door, falling on his hands and knees and begging her for forgiveness, for just a moment of her time so that he could explain. But he knew, deep down inside of him, that for once he had to give up his selfish desire to have what he wanted when he wanted it. Part of loving her was giving her space when she asked for it, so that was exactly what he did. He gave her time.

And time was what brought him to her this evening.

He thought about bringing the gift he bought her along with him, but it was too meaningful and would've seemed trite on an evening like this. It would've seemed like a bribe, like he'd only given it to her to get back in her good graces. He wanted to wait before he gave her this gift. So the brightly wrapped package waited in his apartment, ready for another night that Cole was sure to come.

Cole wore a steel grey button-down shirt with black slacks, and his heart pounded against his ribcage as he knocked on Abby's front door. He could smell the delicious dinner she was cooking even here in the hallway, and his stomach growled at the thought of a home-cooked meal. It would taste even better because Abby was the one who made it.

Abby opened the door and gave him a shy smile, her cheeks a perfect blush. She was so fucking beautiful it made him ache for her. Just to stand next to her, to smell her, to be near her.

"Hi," Abby said, standing aside so that Cole could walk in.

"Hi." Cole held out the bouquet of roses he brought for her and she smiled as she thanked him. He followed her into her apartment and stood in the small living room as Abby pulled out a vase from below the sink.

"I'm making Coq Au Vin," she said as she filled the vase with water. "I hope you like it."

"I like it very much." He would like whatever she made him.

After Abby placed the vase on the small table just outside her kitchen, she placed her hands on her hips as she smiled at Cole.

"This is the place," she said, outstretching her arms. "I'd show you around, but this is pretty much it."

"It's very you," Cole said, taking in the colorful fabric of the curtains and pillows, and the numerous photos on the mantle and the wall.

"What, small?"

"No, welcoming. Warm."

The corner of Abby's mouth curved up into a smile as she turned and walked back into the kitchen. "Dinner will be ready in about five minutes. Would you like a glass of wine?"

"I'd love one."

As Abby popped open the bottle, Cole motioned toward the photographs on the wall. "Do you mind if I look?"

"No," she replied, smiling.

Cole's eyes were immediately drawn to a small, somewhat blurry photo in a bright blue frame, of a woman who had Abby's eyes holding a toddler who was most definitely Abby. "Is this your mother?" he asked.

Abby nodded. "And me. It's one of the very few photos I have of her."

"She was beautiful," he said, sliding his finger along the

edge of the frame.

"She was," Abby replied sadly.

Cole looked around at the pictures of Abby and Becca, and pictures of other friends whose names Cole didn't know but hoped to learn.

"So, can I ask the obvious?" Abby said as she pulled two plates out of a cupboard. "How are things in the office?"

Cole had anticipated this question. "It's awful without you. And I mean that in every sense of the word." He hated going into work and not seeing her face. He hated not talking to her whenever he wanted, not seeing her at her desk when he walked out of his office.

"I'm sorry I quit the way that I did. Regardless of the situation, I should've been more professional."

"I deserved it."

"Maybe, but that doesn't make it okay. It's probably for the best."

If this night and the ones that followed it went the way Cole hoped they would, Abby was right. "Probably."

The dinner spread was perhaps the most delicious thing Cole had ever smelled, and after he tasted a piece of of the tender chicken, he decided it was perhaps the most delicious thing he had ever tasted.

"This is phenomenal," he told Abby as he cut himself another piece.

"I'm glad you like it."

"Like isn't a strong enough word," he said before taking a bite.

"If you're nice to me, I might cook for you more often."

Cole put down his knife and fork and leaned in close to her, a fierce look in his eyes. "I plan on being more than nice to you, Abby."

"I like that," she said, smiling.

"Like what?" Whatever she liked, Cole planned on doing as often as possible.

"The way you say my name. You spent so long calling me Abigail that hearing my nickname is…nice."

"I've been an ass to you," he said, self-loathing flooding over him. "I don't know how I can ever make it up to you."

She grinned, placing her hand on top of his, and he didn't realize just how much he'd missed the feel of her skin until she touched him again.

"You'll think of something. But for now, you can start by enjoying your dinner."

Cole and Abby finished their dinner while making polite conversation. It wasn't until after they were finished, when they were both nursing glasses of wine, that the heavier subjects made appearances.

"So," Abby said, swirling what was left of her glass of red. "That thing you said to me earlier." She looked at Cole with those gorgeous eyes, and it took every ounce of willpower in him not to slide all the dirty dishes onto the floor and take her there, right on that small table in the middle of her apartment.

Instead, Cole searched his memory, trying to figure out which 'thing' she was talking about. "That I said I had fallen in love with you?"

She inhaled a sharp breath at the words, and instantly Cole knew he had found the right ones.

"Yes, that was the thing."

"What about it?" he asked nervously.

She looked down, as if she was measuring her next words very carefully. Cole found that he was nervous, wondering if she was going to let him down easy. He wasn't sure how he would deal with that, despite the fact that he would've rightfully deserved it.

"I can't say it back. Not yet."

Even though Cole's heart sank, he couldn't say he hadn't expected this reaction. Still, it wasn't easy to hear. The corner of his mouth turned up into a sad smile. "That's understandable. After everything I put you through, I figured I owed it to you to put my heart out on the line first."

"You said that you don't do relationships." She was playing with the corner of her napkin and was clearly very nervous.

"No," Cole said, reaching out and touching her hand. He took it as a small victory that she didn't shy away. "I said that I didn't *know how* to be in a relationship. But I want one with you."

"That's still the truth?"

He squeezed her fingers. "Very much so."

"You think the two of us will work as a couple?"

Cole's eyebrows knit together. He was confused. "I don't understand what you're getting at."

Abby rolled her eyes as if her issue was obvious. "You're a billionaire. I'm a...I'm an assistant. People will talk, won't that bother you?"

"I don't give a fuck what people think or say about me, Abby. If I did, I wouldn't be where I am today."

"But you're a-"

"A billionaire," Cole said with a light sigh. "I know. It's just money."

"Spoken like someone who actually has it," Abby teased.

Cole smiled and was tempted to bite his tongue, but he figured they better put all their cards out on the table if they were going to really try to make things work out between them. "You ask me if it bothers me, but it sounds like it bothers you."

"It does," she admitted. "Not in the way you probably think, but we can't—at least, I can't—pretend like there isn't an income difference between the two of us. Our lifestyles, I mean...there are a lot of things you'll want to do that I won't be able to."

"Don't allow my money to define me, and don't allow our income discrepancy to define us. I'm a man who wants you, Abby. Desperately. And I'll want to buy you nice things and take you out to dinner. Take you on trips. I understand your issue," he said, squeezing her hand again. "Honestly, I do. But I need you to accept that about me and allow me to do it."

Abby nodded, although Cole could tell she wasn't quite sold on the idea. Yet.

"You once told me that part of the thrill of business for you is winning the unwinnable. Attaining the unattainable. The thrill of the chase. What happens when you finally have me?"

And there it was. She was worried that she wasn't interesting enough, smart enough, intriguing enough, sexy enough to keep him interested. He was going to have to disabuse her of that notion immediately.

"Then," he said, "I will be a very happy man."

"Won't you-"

"You're asking me for guarantees, and I can't give them to you. Even if I did, you know better than to believe them, Abby. You're too smart for that. But I will love you with all of my heart, I promise you that."

A smile spread across her lips, but she didn't say anything.

"Since we're talking about promises," Cole said, standing as he gathered their dirty plates. "I need you to make a couple. First, that you'll let me do the dishes. Second, that you'll allow me to see you again. Tomorrow night."

Abby made quite the show of considering Cole's request. "Okay," she finally replied.

Cole washed the dishes, Abby dried. They chatted about things people typically chat about on first dates. Cole couldn't get enough of her smell, her clear eyes, her radiant smile. He practically had to tear himself away from her at the end of the night.

Standing in Abby's doorway, Cole gazed down at her, longing to press his lips against hers. The electricity between them was palpable. Regardless of what happened between them in other areas of their relationship, their sexual chemistry was ever-present. Cole leaned against the doorway and Abby stood in front of him, fiddling with a button on her shirt. She licked her lips as she looked up at him to say goodnight. Cole grew hard just looking at her mouth, and he longed to taste, to feel her lips.

But tonight, Abby wanted to tease him.

And he was going to let her.

CHAPTER
Thirty-Three

Ten dates.

Abby told Cole that sex was completely out of the question for ten dates. It seemed like a good idea at the time, considering they were two people whose hormones went wild when they were around each other. Abby wanted to take the time to make sure this was real, that their hearts were in it just as much as their bodies were. That their attraction was just as much mental as it was physical.

Ten dates, no sex. After that, well…Abby had plans and she was sure that Cole did too.

Tonight, they were on their second date. Abby agreed to let their dinner the night before count as the first. Tonight, probably to show her that he didn't always live a high-end lifestyle, Cole was treating Abby to dinner at her favorite diner, two blocks away from his office.

"I miss this place," Abby said, swirling a fry in a small dollop of ketchup.

"It's not like you can't come here. You quit the job, not the city."

"I know," Abby replied quietly. Even though she'd agreed to give Cole another chance, talking about her quitting her job and the events that led up to that was still a sore subject for Abby.

Perhaps sensing her unease, Cole tried to lighten the subject. "You should come here and meet me for lunch one day."

Abby narrowed her eyes. "You don't take lunches."

Cole lifted a fry off of Abby's plate and popped it into his mouth. He wore a sly grin that made Abby want to kiss him, want to forget about her stupid ten-date rule. Why had she made that again?

"I've been thinking that I should probably start taking them." The fleeting humor of the previous moment was gone, and Abby met Cole's gaze, which was suddenly serious.

"What made you think that?"

He smiled. "You did."

"Really?"

Cole reached across the table and gently pushed his hand against hers until their palms were touching, then laced their fingers together. It was a simple gesture, but it stirred a few butterflies in the pit of Abby's stomach.

"Really. When I nearly lost the woman I love because I put my work ahead of her feelings, I decided I needed to examine my priorities."

The woman he loved. Abby didn't think she'd ever get used to hearing those words fall from his perfect lips.

Abby laced the fingers on her free hand with the fingers on his. "And what are those priorities?"

"You," he replied, squeezing her hand. "My family. I don't see them as often as I should. I've spent all my life living up to my last name, doing what I thought was expected of me. The business side of my life was always fulfilling, but my personal life was severely lacking. But now..." Cole drifted off, gazing into Abby's eyes.

"Now?"

"Now I want more."

Abby closed her eyes, taking in the conversation. Tonight's Cole was such a drastic change from the way he normally was. Of course, Abby realized she usually saw him in work mode, with only glimpses of this one, especially when they were in Chicago. She liked work Cole, but she had fallen in love with this Cole. Maybe almost losing her really had rattled him. A calming warmth spread throughout her body as she thought about what that would mean for her. For them.

"So, what. You're going to retire?" she teased.

"No," Cole replied, laughing. "I'm just going to make sure I take the time I need to in order to enjoy my life."

He reached into his back pocket for his wallet, and as he pulled out a credit card to pay for dinner, Abby caught a glimpse of a photo of him holding a baby.

"May I see?" she asked, motioning toward his wallet.

Cole grinned and handed it to Abby. She looked down

at the picture, sliding her finger along the edge of the plastic that held it. She knew he had a nephew who was about five years old and that his niece was born about a month ago, but she'd never seen pictures of either one of them. Cole was notoriously private about his family, and while Abby respected that, she was sad she'd never seen this picture before tonight. Cole was gorgeous holding his niece. He wasn't even looking at the camera, just staring down at her, absolutely smitten. A thought entered Abby's mind of a time far into the future, when he might look at their child that way. Admittedly, she'd had these thoughts before, but she always pushed them away, believing them to be out of the question.

Abby held tight to this thought. It felt right.

"Her name is Alexandra?"

He nodded, smiling.

"She's beautiful."

"Tell me about it."

Abby made a gesture with her little finger, indicating that the baby already had Cole wrapped around hers.

He laughed. "That's definitely true."

Abby flipped to the next picture, which featured Cole and his nephew playing with toy dinosaurs. The next was of the two of them in a swimming pool. Cole was holding his nephew over his head and the two of them were dripping wet and laughing hysterically. Abby couldn't help but grin. She'd never known what a family man he was. She assumed he was all work and no play, but was happy to be proven wrong.

"What's that smile for?" Cole asked, looking at Abby as if

he was longing for her approval.

"This," Abby replied, holding up Cole's wallet and pointing at the picture of him and his nephew playing. "I never knew this about you."

Cole's expression grew tender. "There are a lot of things you don't know about me."

Abby couldn't wait to find out every single one of his secrets.

Later that evening, Cole's driver pulled to a stop in front of Abby's apartment building and Cole walked her up to her door. He stood incredibly close to her as she fished through her purse for her keys; so close that she could feel his breath on the back of her neck. She wanted to fall back against him, to feel the security of being in his arms. Her hand shook as she tried to insert the key into the lock, and Cole laughed. He ran his fingertips down the backs of her arms intending to calm her, and even though it set every nerve in her body on edge, her skin immediately warmed from his touch.

Abby finally managed to get the door unlocked, and then she pushed it open to reveal an empty living room. Becca was out for the evening.

"Would you like to come in?" Abby asked, turning and facing Cole.

He smiled wistfully, looking over her shoulder for a moment before his gaze returned to hers.

"I want to more than anything, but I don't think that's a good idea," he said. He dropped his hands to his sides and Abby missed the feel of him immediately. "I wouldn't be able to leave, and I promised you I would respect your wishes."

Eight more dates.

Her hormones were in overdrive, and she knew she was doing the right thing. "Okay," she replied, trying to mask the disappointment in her voice. It was her fault it was there in the first place.

"I want to see you tomorrow."

Abby nodded. She had a fleeting thought of playing hard to get, but Cole was going to get her. Even he knew that. The rest of this was just an exercise in restraint and letting their hearts catch up to their hormones. "Tomorrow."

"I'll pick you up at seven-thirty."

Abby licked her lips.

Cole watched.

Then, he knit his fingers through her hair and she pushed herself up on the tips of her toes, closing her eyes as his lips brushed hers. The kiss was tender and full of longing, but too quickly he pulled away, breathless.

"I have to go before I-"

"Yeah," she said, before running her tongue along her upper lip.

Abby backed in the doorway and held his eyes as she closed the door. Once it was closed, she leaned against it, needing something sturdy to hold her up.

Seconds later, there was a knock. Abby flung open the door and was immediately wrapped in Cole's arms, kissing her deeply this time. His lips pressed against hers like he never wanted to be parted from her, and their tongues brushed together like they'd been kissing their whole lives. They clung to each other like their lives depended on it. When the kiss ended, Cole held her close, his forehead touching hers. Then they slowly, reluctantly untangled their limbs and grinned at each other like a couple of love-struck teenagers.

"I'll see you tomorrow," he said, rubbing his bottom lip with his fingertips, as if he wanted to ingrain the feel of her in his memory. She watched him walk down the hall until he disappeared into the stairwell, then retreated into her apartment, floating on air.

On their third date, Cole took Abby dancing.

For the fifth, they went horseback riding through Central Park.

The seventh was a romantic, candlelit dinner for two.

It took them nearly two weeks to get to their tenth date, which was a surprise that Cole wasn't going to spoil no matter how much Abby begged him to. It was such a surprise that Cole wouldn't even allow his driver to take them to wherever it was they were going. They walked hand-in-hand down a street near his office; one that was bustling during the day but a little less busy at night. Even though there were other people walking nearby, Abby felt like she and Cole had the entire block to themselves.

Cole couldn't wipe the smile from his face, and Abby loved the fact that Cole having her on his arm made him look like that. She loved the way that look made her feel, just knowing that he was happy. And it was then that she said the words she'd been dying to say for the past month, without even a thought before they left her mouth.

"I love you," she said. She felt it so much in that particular moment that she just wanted to tell him. She *had* to tell him. It wasn't a grand, sweeping declaration, but it was the truest thing she'd ever said.

Cole stopped dead in his tracks, the already present grin on his lips spreading wider.

"I'm sorry I just said it on the street like that," Abby rambled, realizing that maybe she should've waited for a more intimate moment to share her feelings. "I just felt it so much that I wanted you to know."

Cole cupped her cheek, then kissed her, long and lingering.

"I love you too," he whispered against her lips, and she'd never felt so bright inside. "C'mon," he said, clasping her hand as he led her further down the street, seemingly energized by the sentiments they'd just shared.

"Will you just tell me where we're going?"

"No!" he laughed.

"Damn it, Cole. You're driving me crazy. Don't make me take back the thing I just told you!" she teased.

Cole looked over at Abby, grinning. "You couldn't take that back even if you wanted to."

Damn him, he was right. She could never, *would* never

take that back.

"Just give me a hint."

Cole stopped right in front of an empty storefront, it's darkened windows standing out along the line of lit up shops.

"We're here."

Abby looked around, wondering exactly where "here" was, and Cole pulled a key ring out of his pocket. Confusion clouded Abby's brain. Cole held the door open for her, and she tentatively stepped inside. The store was immaculately clean, but empty.

"What is this place?" she asked, running her fingertips along the bright white shelving that lined the wall.

"It's the site of my next business venture."

Abby turned to him, her eyebrows knit together. "You own this place?"

Cole smiled tenderly at her as he pulled a piece of paper from his pocket.

"No, you do."

CHAPTER
Thirty-Four

Cole held his breath as Abby processed what he had just told her. He had to admit that he was concerned about her reaction; he just hoped she would hear him out when he explained why he decided to give her this gift. And hope that she would accept it.

Abby took a measured breath before she said anything, and when she spoke her words were very slow.

"You...you bought a building for me?" Her eyebrows were scrunched together in an adorable way, and Cole wanted to kiss the confusion from her face.

"Well, a retail space, yes," Cole replied, smiling.

"A store," Abby said dumbly, her eyes wide.

"A store."

There was a fleeting moment of silence when Cole thought Abby was going to accept the gift without any protestations. It was a lovely moment.

"Cole, what were you thinking? This is just..." Abby looked around at her surroundings, still unable to believe this belonged to her. As if she needed a reminder, she looked down at the deed Cole had handed to her. "I can't accept this. I mean, it's a lovely gesture, but-"

"Will you allow me to explain myself?" he asked, taking her hand in his.

She opened her mouth to object, but then thought better of it. "Okay."

"Abby," Cole said, touching her cheek. He loved the surprise in her eyes, the awe. The disbelief that this actually belonged to her. He hated to admit this to himself, but a small part of what drove him to do nice things for other people was exactly this reaction, of knowing he could help them in ways they could never help themselves. With Abby, the satisfaction was ten-fold. Because he loved her, he worshiped her, and he wanted her to succeed at everything life had to offer. "I had more money the moment I was born than most people will ever see in a lifetime. I inherited a substantial fortune when I turned twenty-one, and I invested it in my company. I work very hard, but I started out on the ladder two rungs from the top. Few people are as lucky as I am, I know that. What good does all this money do me if I don't share it? If I don't make life better for the people I love?"

She considered what he told her, although doubt still clouded her perfect eyes. "Then give me business advice," she said, her eyes pleading. "Not a building."

"A retail space," he said, hoping to lighten the mood.

"Stop correcting me, damn it," she replied, laughing.

Cole smiled. "It's my fault that you're no longer working for me. I can't say that at this point I'm sorry about that." Cole looked deep into Abby's eyes, and she blushed at the meaning behind his words. He hoped she wasn't sorry, either. Still, he wronged her, and he needed to make it right. "You have so much potential, and selfishly, I put myself above that. You would've gone far at my company."

"Would you rather I come back and work for you?"

Cole pulled Abby close, then planted a kiss on the top of her head before letting her go. "No, I'd rather have you just like this. But I do bear some responsibility in knocking your career off course and I didn't do right by you. I want to do that now."

Abby looked around, and Cole could tell that she was beginning to imagine what she could do to this store to make it her own.

"So, say I accept this gift of yours," Abby began as she walked along the far side of the wall. Cole wanted to tell her she didn't have a choice in the matter, but this didn't seem like the right time to bring that up. "There's one important thing you're forgetting."

Cole was certain she was wrong, but he humored her. "What's that?"

"I have no idea how to run a business."

"The important thing that *you're* forgetting is that I do. I know a lot about it, actually."

"And you're going to help me?"

"Absolutely." What, did she think he was just going to

throw her into the water without teaching her how to swim?

"May I ask the question that I probably shouldn't ask?"

Even though Cole knew this was coming, his stomach dropped to his knees. He nodded.

"What happens if things don't work out between us?"

"That's something I'd rather not think about," he said. "But in any event, as I said before, this belongs to you. It's yours to do with as you wish. If we break up, and that's a very big *if*, this space will remain yours. Continue to run your business from it. Sell it, rent it out. Whatever pleases you."

Abby looked at him for a long while after he said those words, searching his eyes. She must have liked what she saw there, because she continued walking around, looking at the counters, the cabinets, the floors. She seemed to still be in a state of shock, so Cole continued speaking.

"It needs a little bit of work done cosmetically, but I can hire a designer to come in here and give you some options. I've gotten a few names already. And I'll have a consultant come in here to help you figure out what kind of machinery you'll need."

Abby made her way back over to where Cole was standing and looked up at him with watery eyes. "Why are you doing this?"

"Because I love you," Cole said, brushing her hair behind her ear. She closed her eyes, resting her cheek against the palm of his hand. "And I want your dreams to come true."

Abby took Cole's hand in hers and looked down at their fingers as they laced together.

Worried, Cole wondered if perhaps the events of the

evening had been too much for her.

"Do you want me to take you back to your place?" he asked.

"No," she replied, looking up at him and smiling through her tears. "I want you to take me to yours."

CHAPTER
Thirty-Five

Cole's apartment didn't look at all the way Abby expected it to. She was anticipating hard lines and black leather, more modern-styled furniture. She was anticipating abstract sculptures and strangely simplistic art. But Cole's home was much like its owner: unexpectedly charming. While it was undoubtedly masculine, full of soft, worn leather and impeccable wood, there was a feminine touch to it. Abby was certain that a woman had a hand in decorating this space, because the rich browns contrasted with creamy whites, deep reds, and a few blink-and-you'll-miss-them florals. There were personal touches, too. Family photographs and keepsakes peppered the shelves that lined the walls.

"Do you like it?" Cole asked, the heels of his shoes clicking on the hardwood floors as he walked closer to Abby.

"Very much."

Cole grinned, and Abby liked the way her approval looked on him. "Is this what you thought it would look like?"

"Honestly, no. But I mean that in a good way."

"I'll take your word for it," he said lightheartedly.

"I was just thinking that everything in here would be…" Abby paused, having difficulty articulating her thoughts. "I thought you would have, like, one of those uncomfortable Swedish sofas that looks like installation art or something." She ran her fingers through her hair, feeling foolish.

"I can't watch football on installation art," Cole replied, laughing. He walked up behind Abby, pulling her to him. He slid her hair to the right side of her shoulder, exposing her neck, and her body was electric. His fingers fluttered across her shoulders and down her arms, leaving tiny goosebumps in their wake. Then he took her hand, grinning, and led her into the next room.

"C'mon," he said. "Let me give you a tour."

Cole walked Abby through the apartment, pointing out his favorite features in each room. He had a flawless kitchen, with counter space Abby would've killed for. *Such a shame*, she thought. *So much space wasted on a man who has never cooked a day in his life.* His den was filled with beautiful leather-bound books and limited editions. His guest room had a fluffy king-sized bed that Abby wanted to dive into. She could've done laps in his bathtub.

Cole saved his bedroom for last.

They walked inside and Abby was completely taken by the view: floor-to-ceiling windows with the bright lights of Manhattan twinkling beyond the glass. Even though the decoration was somewhat sparse, the room still felt comfortable and lush. Abby's eyes were drawn to the bed, which looked down and soft with simple white linens. It was perfectly made.

"I have a maid," Cole said, as if he knew what Abby was thinking. "If it were up to me, I'd never make that bed. She comes three times a week, and you should see how awful it looks on Sundays."

Abby enjoyed Cole admitting his flaws. Sure, it was just his habit of not making his bed, but it was a little piece of him that no one else knew about. Abby would've bet that he made his bed meticulously each morning, every fold and tuck of the sheets creased and exact. She loved finding out that she was wrong about him. She loved the thought of his messy bed and the fact that he admitted he had a cleaning lady. She loved that his high school football jersey was hanging up over his desk in his den.

But most of all, she loved him.

Abby's eyes scanned the room and came to rest on a relatively small box that was on top of his dresser, wrapped in lavender paper with a vibrant purple bow. It was presumptuous of Abby to assume that it was for her, but somehow she knew that it was.

He has to know that I see it.

"Just so you know, I don't keep a gift in my bedroom at all times, just waiting for a beautiful woman to come over and open it," Cole said as he took Abby's hand and walked her over to the dresser.

"Is this bribery?" she teased.

Cole shook his head. "Do I need to bribe you to make you want me?"

"No," Abby whispered, meeting his gaze. There was a flurry of desire behind his clear eyes which made Abby's skin buzz with anticipation.

"Open it."

Abby picked up the package, but she looked at Cole tentatively. "You can't keep giving me things," she replied, even though she was desperate to find out what was inside.

"I can and I will. I want to give you everything."

"What if what I want isn't material?" she asked.

"What do you want?"

She was amazed that she felt confident enough to tell him what she not only wanted, but what she needed.

"Your love, your heart." *Your body.*

Cole smiled softly. "They're already yours." He gently pushed the box toward her. "Open it, please."

Abby's hands trembled as she reached out, but Cole steadied them with his own. She knew that whatever was in the box was significant; Cole wasn't the type to give away meaningless trinkets. Abby took hold of both ends of the ribbon, slowly pulling until the knot gave way. She handled the paper like precious silk, gently pulling the tape from the seams to keep the paper in one piece. The box was plain white, with absolutely no writing on the outside to indicate what kind of treasure she would find inside.

"I hope you like it," Cole whispered, watching Abby intently as she pulled open the top.

Abby gasped; she recognized the contents immediately.

Inside was a little round box with green lacquered wood, a hand-painted frog and dragonflies decorating the top. It was an exact replica of the one Abby's mother had given her when she was younger; the one she had told Cole about that night in the diner in Chicago. Abby took a deep breath as she wound the key on the bottom, and she couldn't help the tears that fell when she opened the top and heard the familiar tinkling song.

She felt closer to her mother than she had in years.

Abby looked at Cole, her eyes blurry with tears. "You remembered."

"I remember everything you tell me." His expression was so soft, so earnest. Abby was overwhelmed by the moment.

"Everything?"

Cole nodded. "Even from before you knew I was listening."

Abby set the box down on the dresser, then cupped Cole's cheek with one hand and ran her fingers through his hair with the other. She kissed him. It was soft and long and sweet, a promise of what was to come later that evening.

"How did you even find this?" she asked. She had searched eBay for years and was unable to find it.

"I have my ways," Cole replied slyly. "It arrived the day after we…well, I came home from Chicago." He placed a kiss on her forehead, his lips lingering there. "I'm so sorry that I hurt you."

She nodded, pulling him closer. She couldn't say she was sorry he'd done it. His mistake had moved their relationship further along than it ever would've moved if they'd returned home and continued seeing each other in secret. That pain was worth this feeling.

"Just don't do it again," she said, teasing him.

Cole didn't seem to be in the mood to take anything lightly, not tonight. "I promise." He kissed her again, and she wrapped her arms around his neck. "You're the first woman I've had in this room," he told Abby, slowly sliding his hands up and down her sides. "And I want you to be the last."

Abby wanted the rest of her firsts —whatever they were—to be with Cole.

"I love you," Abby said, those three little words drawing a smile from Cole's perfect lips.

"I love you too. And I'm tired of talking."

Abby grinned as Cole pressed his lips against hers, more urgent this time than they were before. He gripped the hem of her shirt and pulled it up over her head, then unfastened her bra and dropped it on the floor. Cole kissed a trail down Abby's neck and across her collarbone. He cupped her breasts in his hands before taking her left nipple in his mouth, circling the puckered skin with his tongue. Her head dipped back as she moaned, and she ran her fingers through his hair, gripping the nape, wanting him closer to her.

Cole's hands drifted down to Abby's hips, then he cupped her ass and picked her up. She wrapped her legs around his waist as they kissed, and Cole walked them over to the bed, gently lowering Abby onto her back. Reluctantly they parted, and Cole gave Abby a sexy smile as he unbuttoned his shirt and tossed it aside.

Abby admired the smooth planes of his chest and the

sturdy build of his body as she undid her pants, and Cole watched her as he undid his. Once he was completely undressed, Cole reached over and grabbed the cuffs of Abby's khakis, pulling them off as she giggled. He kneeled on the bed, hovering over her, kissing her as his fingertips outlined the waistband of her panties.

Abby wanted to call him a tease, to tell him she was desperate for him, but she let him have his fun. Trying to get him to hurry up would only make him go slower. Luckily for her, Cole wasn't much into waiting tonight. He pulled the lace from her waist and slid them down her legs until it was just the two of them, skin against skin. Cole grinned a wicked grin as he kissed her ankle, then her calf, then her upper thigh, until he licked the spot that made her gasp and grip the sheets. His tongue swirled around her clit, pushing her higher and higher until she thought she was going to explode.

Of course, Cole would never make it that easy for her.

He kissed and licked his way up her body until they were face to face, and he kissed her long and slow and deep. Abby bucked her hips, trying to find some relief, and Cole moaned as his erection grazed her thigh. She reached down and slid her hand along his length, but Cole only allowed her a few passes before he brought her arms up above her head and laced his fingers with hers.

And then their eyes met. Abby couldn't look away.

The only time she broke his gaze was when he pushed inside her, when she drew a quick breath and closed her eyes to savor the feeling.

"I've missed you so much," he whispered, before brushing his lips against hers.

And then all was quiet and they were the only two people left in the world.

Cole released her hands as he moved inside of her, reaching down between them to find her clit. Abby gasped and lolled her head back, offering her neck for kisses. The feeling of Cole's lips on her skin as he moved inside her was heaven; she wanted to remember every touch of his mouth on her body. It wasn't long before she felt a glorious wave of pleasure rise up from her belly, urged on by Cole's masterful fingers. Abby's breathing quickened as she desperately sought release, grinding her hips up against Cole until she came, glorious ripples of satisfaction pushing out to her fingertips. Cole squeezed his eyes shut as Abby rode out her orgasm, and knowing how good it must feel for him too, she pushed him over onto his back, straddling him as she rode him, rotating her hips as his muscles strained, trying to prolong the building pleasure.

"Let go," she whispered, and she pressed her forehead to his as he came, gripping her back, bringing her as close to him as he could. She loved the look on his face, his complete surrender to her. She loved that she could make this rich and powerful man so weak, that she could make his limbs like jelly.

As the two of them came down, Abby lay on his chest, their legs tangled together. Cole's fingers twisted through her hair, and they shared soft kisses and soft words.

"I'm the first," Abby breathed as her lips peppered Cole's

jawline with tiny kisses.

Cole tilted her head up until she looked into his beautifully clear blue eyes. "You're the only."

Their lips met again, and then Abby rolled off of Cole and onto the bed. Cole gripped her wrist and playfully pulled her back to him as she squealed.

Cole slid his hand up the inside of her thigh, then nuzzled her ear. "I'm not finished with you."

In her heart, Abby knew he never would be.

Epilogue

Cole pulled his Blackberry out of his pocket and pressed the number 1, which was pre-programmed with Abby's number. He smiled when she picked up the phone, sounding breathless. She was so busy these days, and there were other, easier ways for her to get to her meeting with her store's designer uptown, but Cole needed to spend some time with her this afternoon.

"I just got in the car and I'm leaving my office now. I'll be there in about ten minutes."

"I can take the train, you know," Abby said, with a hint of humor in her voice. His overprotectiveness with regards to her safety in the city did border on ridiculous sometimes, but today he was being selfish.

"I know that," Cole replied gently. "I just need you."

Understanding what he meant, Abby relented. "Okay."

If he didn't know better, he'd swear she sounded excited. "I'll see you in a few."

Cole hatched this plan this morning when they left their apartment. He so loved the way her legs looked in the skirt she wore, and he had been thinking about them all day, the ache in his cock growing by the hour.

It had been six months since Cole had taken Abby to Chicago. They'd seen more of the world together since then: London, Paris, Tokyo. Abby moved out of her apartment and into Cole's nearly four months ago. Waking up next to Abby every morning made Cole the happiest he'd ever been in his life.

Abby's store would be opening in a little over three weeks, and she was busy putting the finishing touches on the design and training her new employees. Cole was going to take her to his parents' house upstate this weekend for a short trip to de-stress. Cole's mother had been nagging him to bring Abby for another visit. While Olivia Kerrigan adored Abby, Cole suspected her urgency had something to do with her wanting some of Abby's candy, which was quickly becoming a favorite in the Kerrigan family, much to Cole's delight.

Abby had fit into his family (and his life) seamlessly; it was almost as if she was meant to be there all along. She also dealt with the stresses of being his girlfriend like the beautiful, patient woman that she was. Luckily for both Abby and Cole, the press attention that Cole garnered when he was one of the city's most eligible bachelors had died out. Turns out monogamy had made him less interesting to the New York gossip rags. He wouldn't have had it any other way.

But the thoughts of paparazzi faded away when Cole's car pulled up in front of Abby's shop and he saw her standing on the curb, the early autumn wind blowing her hair around her gorgeous face. The first thing Cole saw when she stepped into the car were her long, luscious legs. He reached out to take her hand and help her inside, and when she sat down, he pulled her to him, taking her face in his hands and pressing his lips against hers.

Abby seemed surprised at first, but the kiss deepened quickly. Needing more contact with her body, wanting to feel her weight on him, Cole wrapped his hands around her waist and pulled her on top of him. Abby broke the kiss quickly, checking to make sure the partition behind the driver was closed.

Cole laughed. This was not the first time they'd done this and it certainly wouldn't be the last, but she always had to check that damned window.

"I missed you," he said, running his fingers through Abby's hair.

She grinned at the sentiment, then her eyelids fluttered shut as Cole slid his hands up her thighs and around to the swell of her ass.

She's wearing a thong. Perfect.

"It's only been a few hours," Abby replied, peppering kisses down the side of Cole's neck. He loved days like this, the ones where they just couldn't get enough of each other.

"A few hours too long," he replied, as he pulled yesterday's tie out of the interior breast pocket of his coat.

Abby's eyes grew wide with excitement when she saw the

silk garment, and offered her wrists to Cole immediately. His practiced hand had her bound in seconds, and she lifted her arms up and over his head, hooking them around the back of his neck. They kissed again, and Cole slid his fingers between Abby's thighs, along her slick flesh.

"Wet already?" he asked, taking her earlobe between his teeth.

"From the moment you called me."

Shortly after they first started dating, Abby told Cole that she missed their trysts; the kind of sex they used to have when Cole was still her boss, when there was a naughty, off-limits quality to their encounters. While Cole enjoyed having Abby in his bed (and other places around the house), he had to admit that he missed their trysts too, and did what he could to keep the spice level high in their relationship. Abby could usually tell from Cole's voice when he was up to something, and today was no different.

Knowing time was not on his side, Cole circled Abby's clit, and she sucked in a breath through clenched teeth, leaning her head back as Cole kissed his way along her collarbone. She shifted her weight, brushing her thigh against his erection, and he had to have her. Now.

Cole grabbed her waist and turned her body until her knees came to rest in the middle of the limo's footwell. He kneeled down behind her and wrapped his arms around her, pulling her to him until he could feel every inch of her. Vixen that she was, she pressed against his cock with her ass, knowing that would spur him on. Cole unzipped his pants quickly, then lifted Abby's skirt, gently smacking her ass before he slid inside her, overcome by her tight warmth.

"Fuck," he breathed in Abby's ear. "You feel so good like this." In and out of her he thrust, completely lost in ecstasy with every move of his hips.

"Oh, right there." Already, Abby's body was completely relaxed, willing him to give her pleasure. And giving her pleasure was what he intended to do.

Cole unbuttoned the top few buttons of Abby's blouse with one hand, cupping her breasts with his palm, gently pinching her nipples with his fingertips. She writhed against him, desperate for more as the rumble of the car heightened every sensation.

"More, please," Abby begged, moving quicker as she chased her orgasm until she was teetering on the edge of it, so obviously wanting to fall over but relishing in the anticipation.

Slowly Cole rubbed Abby's tender flesh, timing the strokes of his fingers with the strokes of his hips until her quickened breaths were all he could hear. Abby turned her head and kissed Cole as he relished in the velvet brush of her tongue.

"You're perfect, you're so fucking perfect," Cole chanted, willing himself to hang on long enough for her to come. She made it so damned difficult when she squeezed his cock like that. "I can't…I have to…" He pressed against Abby's clit, and she leaned against the seat in front of them, unable to hold herself up any longer. Cole bent over her, sliding his fingers across her clit and kissing her to muffle her cries of pleasure as she came.

Abby's breathing was still uneven when she straightened up, the movement of her body threatening Cole's tenuous grasp on keeping his orgasm at bay. She moved forward and Cole slid out of her, missing the feel of her immediately.

Cole looked at Abby, confused, but she had that wicked gleam in her eye that let him know she was up to something.

"Sit down," she said, her hair a little wild, the corners of her mouth tilted up in satisfaction.

Cole did as he was told, knowing that soon he would feel the exquisite perfection of Abby's mouth. He unbound her hands, tossing the tie onto the seat across from him. Abby pulled her hair back as she took Cole's aching cock into her mouth. She swirled her tongue around the head, then took him deep until he hit the back of her throat and swallowed, making Cole's head loll back against the seat. She repeated the circuit once, twice, and on the third time he couldn't take it anymore, knitting his fingers through her hair as he exploded in her mouth, reveling in the pleasure of it all. Abby swallowed every last drop of him, then raised up on her knees to tenderly kiss his lips.

Abby and Cole had come down by the time the car pulled up in front of Abby's designer's studio. Cole got out to open the door for her and after she stepped out she gave Cole a long, lingering kiss goodbye.

"We're having dinner tonight?" she asked as she smoothed her hair with her fingertips.

"Yes, I'll pick you up at our apartment at seven." *Our apartment.* He still loved the sound of that. "Wear that red dress I like."

Abby grinned. "Do you have another surprise for me later?"

He did, but not the kind that she was expecting. He answered her with a sly smile. "I love you," he said.

"I love you too," she said before she stood on the tips of her toes and kissed him goodbye. "I'll see you tonight."

He nodded as she walked away.

He would see her tonight.

Tonight, when he was going to ask her to be his wife.

Tonight, when he knew she was going to say yes.

Bonus Book:

The
BILLIONAIRE'S
Wedding

CHAPTER
One

*A*bby Waters stood in the back room of her store, *Sweet Talk*, with her cell phone pressed against her ear and her hand pressed against her hip. She was surrounded by stacks of hundreds of shiny, hot pink boxes, each of which had *Sweat Talk* written across the lid in silver embossing.

"Craig, listen," she said, her voice a little louder than usual, but still surprisingly calm given the circumstances. "This is a gourmet chocolate shop, not a gym. I can't sell people candy in boxes that have the word 'sweat' on them, do you understand? Sweet talk is the name. Two e's. *Sweet*, as in what I'm not going to be to you if you don't pick up these boxes and deliver new, correctly spelled ones in the morning."

Craig was usually very thorough and was currently falling all over himself to please the fiancée of one of the most powerful men in the city. Not that Abby would ever hold Cole's status over someone's head; she liked to use his power for good instead of evil.

"Yes Ms. Waters, I completely understand. We'll get a new batch printed up and sent over first thing."

"You'll double-check them before you deliver them?"

"Absolutely. And we'll recycle the incorrect tops," he replied, anticipating Abby's next question.

Abby sighed, her insides finally loosening from the knot they'd been tied into for the past week and a half. Well, if she was honest with herself, that knot first got tied the night Cole slipped the engagement ring on her finger, and it'd only gotten tighter in the months since. Soon though, she'd tie a different knot.

"Thank you, Craig," Abby said after Craig wished her a good night. Once Abby ended the call and slipped the phone back into her pocket, she leaned over her desk, her hands splaying out over the smooth, cool wood.

Jayne, *Sweet Talk*'s manager and Abby's right-hand woman, stood next to Abby, clutching a clipboard. Jayne was tall and lanky, her bleached-blonde hair pulled back into a severe ponytail that sharpened her otherwise soft features. She was quiet and kind, the type of person you'd go to if you had a bad day, someone who would have a plate of warm cookies ready for you to eat while you spilled your secrets. Abby wished she had a plate of cookies in front of her right now.

Jayne tapped on her clipboard with the end of her pen. "I'll go over there in the morning before I come in and I'll make sure they have the name spelled right before they go to printing, okay? Relax," she said, reaching over and placing her hand on Abby's shoulder, giving it a gentle squeeze. "You can cut the cord, Abby. We'll be okay here without you for a couple of weeks."

"I know," Abby sighed, and she really did mean that. But Jayne was misreading Abby's tension. Abby wasn't so much worried about leaving the store in someone else's care during her vacation, so much as she was worried about getting everything done on her 'to do' list before she left for that vacation, which wasn't really a vacation at all.

It was going to be a honeymoon. A honeymoon that she and Cole were going to go on after they got married. After they got married in a super-secret (his words, not hers) ceremony that was going to take place on Saturday. The day after tomorrow.

In forty-eight hours, she'd be married. She'd be Mrs. Cole Kerrigan.

An excited, nervous wave passed through her at the thought of it, making goosebumps pepper her skin.

She and Cole were going to the Kerrigan family's summer home in Connecticut first thing in the morning. Abby's mind raced when she thought of all the things she still had to do. It was quarter to nine, and she still had to go home, pack everything she needed for the wedding, and pack everything she needed for their honeymoon. She still didn't know where they were going for that; Cole had maddeningly insisted on keeping their destination a secret.

She had to get everything situated at the store, too…and

did she mention she was getting married in less than two days? It was enough to make a girl go insane.

Abby wanted to tell Jayne about the wedding. Actually, she found that the closer the day came, the more she wanted to tell any and everyone. She wanted to shout it from the rooftops, but that would defeat the purpose of keeping it a secret in the first place. And she was the one who had pushed for the small ceremony, just wanting to be able to spend the day with Cole and the people they loved most in this world, not worrying about photographers or tabloids or upper-class society's judgment.

No, Abby couldn't pull back the curtain on the whole operation when she had been the one who insisted that it stay hidden in the first place. So, she took a deep breath and closed her eyes, letting the deep, chocolatey aroma that had settled into every single part of her store calm her nerves.

"I know you'll be okay," she told Jayne with a smile. "I trust you." Truthfully, Jayne could run the store better than Abby could. She had years of experience, and even though the store had been open for a little over seven months, Abby still had a lot to learn.

Abby glanced at her watch, then looked up at Jayne, smiling. "It's almost nine, you better get out of here."

Jayne nodded gently, offering Abby a tired grin as she put down her clipboard and untied her apron. "We'll take care of everything," she said, pulling Abby into a hug. "Have fun, and I don't want to see or hear from you until you get back."

Abby nodded, thinking about the next time she'd step

foot in this store; she'd have another ring on her finger and a different last name. The thought of it made her smile, a gesture that Jayne took to mean something different than it did.

"There we go, that's more like it." Jayne flipped her hand in a short wave before she opened the door that led into the small alley behind the shop. "Have fun."

"See ya," Abby said as she watched Jayne slip out the back door.

Abby had just picked up her phone to text Cole when she heard someone talking in the front of the store, followed by a laugh that she'd know anywhere. She walked toward the noise, feeling a warm rush and a stomach full of butterflies. She came to a stop in the doorway that opened behind the counter and crossed her arms over her chest, unable to stop the smile that pulled at her lips at the sight in front of her.

One of her employees, Tommy, a junior in high school, was hunched over a book that was open on the counter. Cole looked breathtakingly handsome in an Italian suit that Abby had picked out for him during a trip they took to Milan just before Christmas last year. He was leaning over the counter, holding a pencil as he tried to explain a calculous theorem to Tommy. He might as well have been speaking a foreign language for all Abby understood it, but that didn't stop her from grinning and picturing him doing something similar many years from now, helping one of their children with their homework.

"I'm probably breaking about ten child labor laws right now," Abby said, her heels clicking on the black and white tiled floor as she walked towards them.

"I'm off the clock, so Cole says we're good," Tommy said, looking at her with his dark, inquisitive eyes.

"Well, as long as Cole says so," Abby teased, sliding the tips of her fingers along the back of Cole's tie before she gently wrapped her hand around it and pulled him in for a soft kiss.

"Hi," Abby whispered. She hadn't seen him since this morning when his car dropped her off in front of the store. It had only been thirteen hours, but it seemed like an eternity.

"Hi," Cole replied, grinning. He looked a little lovesick and a lot gorgeous.

Abby heard Tommy let out a loud, long-suffering sigh. "That's my cue." He snapped his book shut and walked over to where his backpack was slouched against the wall, then shoved the book inside.

"Text me and let me know how you do on your test," Cole said, holding up his phone. "Get an A, and then we're going to start talking about a scholarship."

Tommy grinned. "Thanks, Mr. Kerrigan."

"We'll take you home," Abby said as Tommy ducked under the counter, stretching a bit as he came out on the other side.

"My mom's right outside, but thank you."

Tommy slung his backpack over his shoulder and gently pushed past the bodyguard that was constantly hovering in the corner of whatever room Abby happened to be in. The bell rang as Tommy opened the door, and just as he stepped outside, he popped his head in. "I forgot to say - have a nice vacation."

Cole looked at Abby with a soft gleam in his eyes. "Thanks, Tommy," he replied, then watched Tommy as he ran across the sidewalk and into his mother's car.

"Are you going to send the muscle home? For good?" Abby asked, giving Cole a look that she hoped looked a little teasing, an effort on her part to hide her annoyance with him for insisting the bodyguard be there in the first place. "No offense, Pete."

Pete's gargantuan chest rumbled with laughter. "None taken."

"Nope," Cole replied, completely unamused. There was a hard look in his sea-green eyes, one that had been there ever since last spring, when Josh Hamilton had begun showing up at the store whenever Abby was there alone, offering to buy a candy or two and leaving her with simple, vague threats. "He's staying." Cole's voice was firm, unwavering. Abby knew there wasn't much of a point in arguing with him, but she was going to do it anyway. Later.

"We're going to talk about that," she said quietly, so that only Cole could hear her.

A flash of challenge sparked across Cole's face before his eyes softened and he offered Abby something that was as close to a smile as he could manage when they were talking about her safety and security. "I look forward to it."

"Famous last words." Abby sighed as she gave the store one last once-over. She grinned as her eyes skipped over the pristine white walls and counters, brightened up by hot pink accents nestled everywhere they could fit. Sometimes she still had difficulty believing that this store was *hers,* and that it was Cole who had given her the freedom and the opportunity to be able to spend her time doing something she loved. She didn't know what she could do to even come close to repaying him for that, but she figured that promising herself that she'd do whatever she could to make him happy for the rest of his life was a start.

"You can cut out, Pete," Cole said as he shook the man's hand.

Pete grinned, something Abby would never get used to. He was always all business and completely stone-faced when he was around her. She supposed that should make her happy, that Cole entrusted her life to someone who took the task of protecting it so seriously. "We'll see you in the morning; we're leaving right at seven."

Pete nodded and turned toward the door.

"We'll see you in two weeks, Pete." Abby's voice was firm as she met Cole's stare. He'd promised her a security free wedding and a bodyguard-free honeymoon. She'd be damned if he was going to back out of that promise now. "Enjoy your vacation."

She could see Cole swallow his argument, his Adam's apple bobbing against his crisp, white collar. They'd had this argument before, and Abby wasn't going to concede to Cole's overly developed case of paranoia.

Cole turned his head and nodded at Pete, admitting defeat.

She sighed happily as she turned off the lights and then walked to the door, where Cole waited for her, his hand outstretched. She slid her fingers between his, relishing in the warmth of his touch and the way his palm fit against hers. She pushed herself up on her tiptoes, pressing her mouth softly against his.

"Thank you," she whispered, before fishing her keys out of her purse. "C'mon. We've got a wedding to get ready for."

CHAPTER
Two

Cole relaxed into the fluffy, overstuffed cushions of the chair that took up most of the corner of their living room. A piece of furniture like this never would've fit into his old apartment, but he'd given Abby carte blanche to decorate this new penthouse to her liking. He'd bought the place shortly after he decided to propose to her, wanting to start their life together with a place of their own, untainted by his bachelor past.

He surprised her with it the night he proposed. He proposed to her here, actually, just outside on the huge balcony that spanned the length of the apartment and wrapped around the eastern side. That night Cole told Abby he was taking her out to dinner, but when he picked her up, he brought her here under the guise that this was an investment property he was thinking about purchasing.

Cole had given a lot of thought to how he'd propose to her. Abby was a woman who appreciated simplicity, someone who was wholly unimpressed by his wealth. He knew that she would be far more touched by something he spent a lot of time and effort on, rather than spent a lot of money on. So, he went to that diner down the street from his office that she liked so much, and he asked the chef to show him how to make her favorite burger and fries. Cole wasn't much of a cook, and it took him ten visits to finally get it right.

That night they ate her favorite burgers and fries out on the patio under the stars. Throughout the night, Cole told Abby all the things he loved about her, without repeating a single one. *The way you laugh,* he said, before popping a fry into his mouth. *The way the bathroom smells after you shower*, he whispered as he took her hand and pulled her into his arms. He walked her to the far side of the patio, which was bathed in candlelight and covered in pink and purple tulips—her favorite. As he slid his arm across the small of her back, he held her close and told her how much he loved her, how much she changed his life. How she made him a better man. He told her he wanted to give her everything she ever needed, everything she ever wanted. He told her he wanted to give her the world, but he wanted to start by giving her his last name. He got down on one knee with tears shining in his eyes as he slipped an antique diamond ring onto her finger. "Marry me," he said, not really a question, more like a plea. Like he wouldn't be able to breathe until she said yes (he didn't, and she did).

It didn't even take Abby a second to cup Cole's face in her

hands and answer him with a soft, tender kiss. Afterwards, they christened their new home, beginning with a rousing session of the hottest sex they'd ever had, right here in this very spot. Cole would never tell Abby that was why he liked sitting in this chair so much, but he suspected she knew. She always seemed to know pretty much everything about him. And the day after tomorrow, he would finally, *finally* make her his wife. He looked down at the empty ring finger on his left hand, anxious to feel the weight of the platinum ring he'd be wearing around it.

Cole was drawn out of his reverie by an incredibly loud, angry swear, let loose by his bride in their bedroom.

"Are you sure you don't need any help in there?" he asked. He'd been banished out into the living room about an hour ago, after Abby swatted his greedy hands away from her waist, admonishing him for distracting her while she was preparing for their big day.

"No," she shouted. "I mean yes, I'm sure. No help!"

He couldn't help but smile.

Abby walked out into the living room and through to the foyer, opening the door to the coat closet and staring inside, all the while tapping her foot on the floor. Apparently she hadn't found what she was looking for, because she shut the door a little too forcefully, her tiny feet padding along the hardwood floor as she passed by Cole. He could hear her muttering to herself back in their bedroom, could hear the shuffling of fabric and the zipping of bags. Then there was a long stretch of quiet before she made another appearance in the living room, walking the same path to the coat closet.

When Abby walked past Cole yet again, hands still empty, he gently caught her wrist. "Hey," he said quietly. "What's the matter?"

Abby took a deep breath and sighed before her eyes finally met his. "We're getting married in two days," she replied, like that explained everything.

"I know." The hint of a smile teased the corner of his mouth, but he didn't dare laugh, not until he knew she was okay.

"And you're just sitting here."

He really couldn't help the full-on smile this time. "I asked if you needed help, and you said no."

"Don't you have things to do?"

He let his fingertips slide across the length of her wrist, skimming across the bone. He enjoyed watching the way the goosebumps bloomed over her skin from his touch. He didn't think he'd ever tire of that reaction.

"I packed yesterday," he told her. Of course he was already packed; he'd been ready for this. Been ready for it ever since he first slipped that diamond ring on her finger, probably even before that.

"I hate you," Abby huffed, letting out a puff of air that made her side-swept bangs fly away from her face. Cole carefully tugged her towards him, wrapping his hands around her waist and pulling her onto the chair until she was straddling him, knees planted on either side of his thighs. His hands slid across the delicate skin of her arms, until he cradled her head in his hands, the pads of his thumbs lightly brushing her pink-tinged cheeks.

"I thought you wanted to have a small wedding specifically to avoid this stress," he reminded her, his voice soothing.

Abby shrugged, looking down at him. "It's still a wedding. It's the only one I'm ever going to have. There's bound to be some stress involved, regardless."

There was something about the way she said 'the only one' that reverberated through him, made his whole body taut with anticipation. Then he noticed how every muscle in Abby's body was tense to the point of snapping, and he thought that he should do what he could to help her unwind. It would be his pleasure, after all.

Cole gently brought his lips to Abby's and kissed her. She melted into him almost immediately, and the knowledge that he had such an instant effect on her made him smile as his tongue traced her bottom lip and he licked into her mouth, drawing a soft moan from her. His hands slid down to the heels of her feet, and he kneaded his fingertips into her skin, loosening the tension. He moved up her calves to her thighs, taking his time, enjoying the friction as Abby ground her hips against him, making him hard.

"Relax," he whispered, his lips brushing the soft shell of her ear.

Abby lifted her skirt, then fumbled with Cole's belt, clumsily undoing it as the brass buckle clanged against itself and echoed through the room. She pulled down his zipper and pulled his cock out through his boxers, running the palm of her hand along the rigid length of him, drawing a hiss from his lips.

Normally he would tease her, slide her underwear to the side and thumb her clit, make her ache and beg for him before he finally slid home. Tonight, he just wanted to be inside her, to feel the soft slide of her skin on his as she rocked back and forth, pushing them both towards ecstasy.

Cole felt Abby's heated breath on his cheek, then on his neck as she licked and nipped at the skin there. He reached down between them and tore the gauzy lace of her panties, ripping them clean off. If Abby even noticed, she didn't make a sound, just guided his cock along the wetness of her slit before she sunk down onto him. Cole breathed in a short gasp, still not used to the tightness of her, the way she felt around him. He hoped he never would be.

They were both still fully dressed, and there was something incredibly hot about that, Cole thought, but he wanted to feel the soft swell of her breasts between his teeth. So he lazily unbuttoned Abby's blouse, his half-hooded eyes following every slow, lust-filled movement she made as she rode him, fingers digging into his chest, gripping the fabric of his shirt. Once Abby's blouse was halfway unbuttoned, Cole slid the collar over her shoulders, letting it drape across the middle of her back. He pulled down the lacy cup of her bra and slid her nipple into his mouth. He bit down ever-so-gently, then laved at the delicate skin with his tongue to soften the sting. Abby gripped the short hair at the crown of his head between her fingers, pulling his head to the other breast so he could lavish it with attention. When she pulled him away to plant a kiss on his lips, he cupped her breasts in his hands, letting his thumb graze the valley between them as he gave them a gentle squeeze.

"Cole," she whispered, her movements kind of erratic as he kneaded the backs of her thighs, working out the knots.

"I can't wait to be married to you," he said, hiding a smile in the crook of her neck. "You'll be mine forever."

"I'm already yours," she replied, placing one hand over his as he gripped her waist, bringing the other one down to play with her clit, the way he knew she liked it. "Forever."

He felt her orgasm come in soft, cresting waves; it was longer than it was intense, and she squeezed around him, pulling him along with her as he spent himself inside of her. Cole's head fell back against the chair and Abby looked down at him with the soft, satisfied smile of a woman who didn't have a care in the world. Mission accomplished.

She pulled her shirt back up around her shoulders, and Cole felt her shiver, so he gathered her tightly to his chest and kissed the top of her head. He breathed deep, loving the smell of her shampoo. Sometimes, on the weekend mornings when she'd wake up early to head to the shop and he opened his eyes to find her side of the bed empty, he pulled her pillow into his chest and wrapped his arms around it, surrounding himself with the smell of her. She'd call him a sap if she ever found out he did that, but he *was* a sap. For her.

"Are you feeling better?" Cole asked with a bit of a laugh.

"Yes," she mewled, stretching her arms out over his shoulders like a satisfied cat.

Cole leaned back a bit, in order to get a better look at her beautiful face, get a read on her. In the time they'd been together, he'd learned how to read her better than anyone else. There wasn't anything she could hide from him, really, but sometimes he just needed to coax out whatever was bothering her.

"Are you sure you're not having any regrets? Second thoughts?"

"About marrying you?"

Cole shook his head, smiling as he pressed his lips to the inside of her arm. "No, about the wedding." It'd been the thing he'd worried about when she told him that she wanted something small. She didn't have any family to speak of, and she kept her circle of friends pared down to only a special few. She'd almost looked ashamed when she mentioned that if they had a traditional wedding, her side of the church would be empty. *No matter*, he told her then as he kissed the tips of her fingers. *We won't have sides*, he'd said. *Everyone will sit together, and they'll like it.*

Still, she insisted she wanted something small. Cole was okay with that; he'd never been one for society weddings, and he just wanted Abby to be happy. If standing on his parents' back porch overlooking the ocean was how she wanted to marry him, well…that's exactly what they were going to do. Unless…

"It's not too late if you've changed your mind," he continued, wrapping a strand of her hair around his finger. "If you want something more-"

Abby reached up and pressed her finger to his lips. "I want you. On Saturday morning, on your parents' porch, with the sound of the waves crashing behind us. I want you, and me, and our closest friends and your family on that porch with us. I want intimate and honest and *us*, Cole. That's what I want."

Cole took a deep breath and nodded. "And if you wanted to go even smaller-"

"Smaller would involve going to a Justice of the Peace or doing it at City Hall."

"Like I said," he repeated, a sly grin on his face. "If you wanted to go smaller..."

"That's not going to happen." Abby laughed as she shook her head. "I had a hard enough time convincing your mother to go the beach house route as it is. If I tried to go minuscule, she'd have a real problem. I mentioned City Hall in passing once, as a joke, and I think she actually had a case of the vapors."

Cole laughed, pulling her closer. "It's not her wedding, it's ours."

"But it's our life, and she's going to be a part of it. And I want her there. I want your father there. And your brother and Susie and Alexandra. I want Tristan there. Becca, too. Those are the only people who matter, okay?"

"Okay," Cole replied, bringing her left hand to his lips and placing a soft kiss above her engagement ring.

Abby took a deep breath and looked at Cole for a disconcertingly long time before she finally said something. The anticipation was nearly too much.

"There is something that's bothering me, although you knew that. It's just not what you thought it was. It's not the wedding."

"What is it then?" Cole asked, feeling the electricity in

his nerves fizzle out just a bit.

"I want to talk to you about Pete," she said, sounding a little shy.

A rush of dread and anger flowed through him, practically making him shake. "No, Abby."

"Just-"

"Your safety is non-negotiable."

Abby rolled her eyes, sliding off of Cole's lap. He leaned forward and buttoned his pants as Abby sat down on the ottoman across from him, her hands clasped and resting on her leg. She felt a hundred miles away from him, when he'd been inside of her just a minute ago.

"Is this about Josh?" she asked, cringing a little as she mentioned his name.

Cole took a deep, calming breath. Josh Hamilton was a person Cole would rather forget even existed, but that was impossible for so many reasons. After Abby had opened her shop, he began stopping by, buying a few candies here and there, doing his best to freak Abby out. It wasn't until his fourth visit that he actually spoke to her, issuing a very vague threat. She called Cole and told him right after it happened, and he'd had Pete stationed in the store by the time the sun went down that day.

Cole tracked Josh down that night, finding him at some seedy bar, feeling up a waitress. He offered Josh a quick reminder that if he went near Abby again, he'd ruin Josh's life. It wasn't just an idle threat, and to make sure Josh knew he was serious, Cole paid a visit to Josh's father, who knew just where to hit Josh where it hurt. If there was one thing that fueled an entitled brat's lifestyle more than his ego, it was his trust fund. When Josh's father threatened to cut him off, Josh stopped bothering Abby. But the threat of something happening to Abby wouldn't stop bothering Cole.

So Pete stayed.

"It's not about Josh," Cole replied, lying a little.

Abby knew. She always knew.

"Okay, it's not *just* about Josh."

"He threatened you, not me," she said, cheeks tinged pink. "So what's the point of having a bodyguard? You don't have one."

"Because, Abby." Cole leaned in, gathering her hands between his. "There are other people like Josh in this world. People *worse* than Josh. People who will want to get close to you because of who you are, who you married. People—like Josh—who know that the only way to hurt me is to hurt you. And I can't, I *won't* leave you vulnerable like that. Can you understand why this is important to me? Knowing you're safe?"

He silently pleaded with her to stop fighting him on this, to let him have this one thing; just the simple knowledge that she was safe when he was away from her.

"And if it would make me feel better to know that someone was with you, protecting you?"

He swallowed hard, looking down at his feet before he squeezed her hand and met her gaze again. "Then I would make that happen."

Abby nodded minutely. "No Pete at the wedding?"

Cole let out a small laugh. "No Pete at the wedding."

"And no Pete on the honeymoon?"

Cole gently tugged on Abby's hands, pulling her onto his lap again. She leaned in close to him, and he teased her earlobe between his teeth as he whispered in a low rumble, "I couldn't do all the things I want to do to you if Pete was around."

His words sent a shiver coursing through her, and a smile broke out across his face.

"We're getting married in a day and a half," Abby said, nuzzling into the crook of Cole's neck.

He nodded, pressing a kiss to her forehead. A day and a half. The longest thirty-six hours of his life.

CHAPTER
Three

*W*hen Cole maneuvered his Mercedes into the driveway of the Kerrigan family's summer home, Abby's heart was hammering in her chest so hard that she was certain Cole could feel it in her fingertips. Their hands were wrapped together, resting just below the gearshift, and as if he somehow knew she needed reassurance, he gave hers a gentle squeeze.

Abby had been here a handful of times; it was the place the family usually gathered outside of the city, when they weren't making the trek to Cole's parents' home in upstate New York. Situated right outside of Norwalk on a private stretch of beach, the house was stately and huge, imposing along the shoreline, breathtaking with its pristine white siding, black shutters and red door.

It was a breezy, sunny day; warm enough to be pleasant,

but not too hot. On the porch, Cole's mother, Olivia, and his father, Jack, were standing side-by-side, hands clasped together, looking like they just stepped out of a magazine. Cole's looks were all Jack; rugged handsomeness coupled with to-die-for bone structure. His eyes were Olivia's, clear and kind. Abby waved timidly from the passenger seat as the car came to a stop. Olivia made her so, so nervous.

Abby liked Olivia, and she knew that Olivia liked her. It probably didn't hurt that Abby was constantly plying Olivia with chocolate, making Olivia a hit at her bridge club, her book club, and her Junior League meetings. She wasn't foolish enough to believe that Cole's feelings hinged on Olivia's like or dislike of her, but she wanted their relationship to be easy and drama-free, and she never wanted to come between Cole and his mother.

Cole walked around to Abby's side of the car and opened the door for her. As he took her hand, she looked up into his eyes and when he smiled at her, all the nerves just melted away into nothing.

"How do they always know when we get here?" Abby asked quietly as she stood, smoothing out her skirt. "They're always standing on the front porch waiting, like a Norman Rockwell painting or something."

Cole grinned and slid his hand down her arm, leaving goosebumps in its wake. "Parental radar," he teased.

Olivia gracefully walked down the porch steps, Jack following in her wake.

"Abby," she said warmly as she reached out and clasped Abby's hands in hers and leaned in to kiss her cheek. Once

Olivia let go and focused her attention on her son, Abby gave Jack a quick hug. Abby thought it was strange the way the Kerrigans showed affection, like it was some kind of a chore. It was the direct opposite of the kind of relationship she remembered having with her mother. Luckily neither one of them passed that trait on to their son.

"Welcome," Jack said, in his always friendly but distant way. Jack Kerrigan was nice enough, but there seemed to be a wall built up between him and the outside world. The only person he really seemed to be at all affectionate with was his wife, and that was limited to rare hand holding, or the occasional hand on the small of her back. Even his granddaughter couldn't draw out much warmth from him. It was such a strange contrast, seeing the home life Cole had grown up in compared to the man he was today, practically radiating love for her in every look and every touch and he wasn't ever afraid to show it, even when he probably shouldn't.

Cole opened the trunk and started to pull out Abby's suitcase, when his father waved a dismissive hand. "Let Paul get that Cole," he said. "That's what we pay him for." Jack motioned toward the butler standing stiffly a few feet away from the car.

Cole hesitated for a moment, then stepped aside. Abby didn't like the grim set of Cole's lips, so she slid her hand down the inside of his arm, then twined her fingers with his. He always went to great lengths to not exactly *hide* his privilege, since that would be quite a feat, but to downplay it. He didn't have any servants, and he and Abby only had a housekeeper come once a week because they were both simply too busy to take the time to dust.

Olivia sighed and stepped forward. "Cole, you're staying in your old room. Abby, you'll be in the guest room a few doors down."

"Thank you," Abby replied.

Cole shot Abby a look, something that was a mixture of both amusement and disappointment, which made her smile. She'd known that Olivia was going to have them staying in separate rooms, and she was okay with that. Even if they weren't having a wedding in the traditional sense, Abby knew her future mother-in-law well enough to realize that she'd want to stick to some traditions. The bride and groom not seeing each other on the day of the wedding seemed to be the easiest one to adhere to in their situation.

After a bit of an awkward silence, Cole looked around the driveway before turning to his mother. "Are Scott and Sara here?"

Olivia nodded, offering her son a smile. "They're down on the beach."

"With Tyler and Alexandra?" he asked.

"Tyler has a touch of the flu, remember? He's with Sara's mother.

"Oh, that's right," Cole replied, with just a hint of sadness.

Olivia picked up on her son's mood and said the one thing that could've lifted him out of it. "Alexandra's down on the beach with Scott and Sara."

Even though Abby knew Cole was disappointed that his nephew couldn't be there, a warm rush flooded through

Abby as she watched Cole's lip quirk up at the mention of his niece. He'd always been very attentive to her, but now that she was walking and her little personality was starting to shine through, he wanted to be around her every chance that he got.

Abby turned her head and looked far down the beach, where the surf was breaking against the sand. She could see her future brother and sister-in-law on the horizon, a squirming Alexandra wearing a cute little hat, wrapped in Sara's arms.

Remembering the gift she was holding, Abby grinned at Olivia and placed the bag in Olivia's outstretched hands. "I brought these for you," Abby said.

Olivia smiled indulgently, knowing exactly what was inside. "Horrible for my hips, but *so* delicious. Thank you, dear."

Abby nodded. "I put a few extra peanut clusters that Cordelia likes in there. Hopefully you can sneak a glance or two at her cards while she's picking at them the next time you play bridge."

Olivia tossed her head back in a full-throated laugh that made Abby feel oddly proud, like she was one of the family already.

"Come." Olivia took Abby's hand and led her into the house, while Cole and his father trailed behind them. "Let me show you what we've done." She led Abby through the open, bright, sunlit rooms that looked like they came straight out of an interior design catalog. Cole had told her once that their home had been used in a few publications, and every time

Abby walked through this place, she was reminded of just how much wealth and prestige surrounded her. Sometimes it felt like a horrible burden, like a noose around her neck. Today was not one of those days.

Pushing through a grand set of French doors that led onto the back deck, Abby stepped out onto the wooden planks and took in the wedding decorations. There were a few white chairs with pink ribbons tied to the back, all in a neat row, positioned in front a white lattice altar that was covered with delicate pink flowers. The same flowers were strewn along the patio, long chains of stems and petals winding along the railing.

There wasn't a bride's side or a groom's side, there were just enough chairs to seat the people they loved most in this world, which is exactly what Abby wanted for her wedding. It had taken awhile to get Olivia on board with the idea, but once she had, she ran with it. It was going to be a small ceremony followed by an unfussy dinner of Cole and Abby's favorite things. Small, intimate, perfect.

"It's beautiful," Abby said, running her fingertips along the back of one of the chairs. "Isn't it beautiful?" She turned to Cole, who wasn't even looking at his mother's handiwork. His eyes were focused solely on her, filled with so much love and want that she felt like she might burst.

"It is beautiful," he replied, reaching out and running the backs of his fingers along her cheek. She grinned at him shyly, some part of her still unbelieving that this wonderful, seemingly unattainable man could be so in love with her. This was her *life*. So often it seemed too good to be true.

Reluctantly, Abby turned back toward Olivia. "I know you weren't really thrilled about the idea of us getting married like this, in such small ceremony. But this is...gorgeous. It's everything I wanted."

"Look," Olivia said as she took one of Abby's hands and led her over to sit in one of the chairs. "I won't pretend that I wasn't a bit surprised. Society weddings are almost expected around here, and that's the kind of thing that we're used to. But I understand, Abby. That kind of thing, it's not you. Truth be told, I like that about you. You love my son, and that's the most important thing. I wanted to see him get married to a wonderful woman; the manner in which he marries her doesn't concern me as much as what happens after that, do you understand? If there's anything that I've learned living the life that I do, it's that a wedding is just a day, a marriage is forever."

Abby blinked away the tears she felt stinging her eyes. "I didn't want to cause a rift between you and anyone who might be offended because they weren't invited."

Olivia waved her hand dismissively. "We have a gathering with the family in August. They'll all be here, and they'll be lovely. They'll offer you their best wishes without animosity. And if they don't, then you'll let me know."

Abby nodded, understanding. "Thank you," she replied, finally feeling at ease.

Abby and Olivia sat on the patio, looking out at the ocean, talking about how Abby's business was thriving, and how Olivia had been asked to sit on the board of a local non-profit. Abby always enjoyed these talks with Cole's mother; even though she lacked the kind of warmth that most mothers had toward their children, there was absolutely no doubt in Abby's mind that the woman cared about her. There wasn't anyone in the world who could fill the hole that Abby's mother had left in her heart when she died, but on days like today, Olivia wasn't a bad stand-in.

Abby wasn't sure how long the two of them had been sitting out there—just enjoying the breeze and each other's company—before Cole pushed open the patio door.

"Sorry to interrupt," he said, smiling. He always had this soft expression on his face whenever he saw Abby speaking with his mother; something about it warmed Abby's heart. "Becca's here."

Abby felt positively giddy at the sound of Becca's name; she hadn't seen her in what felt like forever. Abby looked at Olivia eagerly, silently asking the woman for permission to take her leave.

Olivia just smiled and said, "Go."

Abby stood and walked toward Cole, sliding her fingers down his arm as she walked past him. He grabbed her hand just as her fingers were slipping away, and pulled her to him. He slid his fingers through her hair, gently cradling her head in his hand, then he pressed a soft kiss to her lips. "Tomorrow," he whispered as he dropped his forehead to hers.

Abby offered him a love-struck grin, but she didn't even have the heart to be embarrassed about it, because he was looking at her the same way.

"She's in the foyer," Cole said as Abby made her way back into the house. She turned and smiled at him as he walked over and sat down in the chair right next to his mother.

Abby practically ran to the front of the house, and had to laugh when she saw Becca standing in the front hall, staring up at the ceiling like she was in the Sistine Chapel. When Becca saw her, she let out a high-pitched squeal, and the two of them giggled like giddy schoolgirls.

"It's such a pity I only get to stay here for one night," Becca said, taking in the lush decor of the beach house. "Can't you and Cole get married on Sunday? Just push it back a day, no one will ever know."

"I can't wait that long," Abby said, kind of breathless.

Becca playfully rolled her eyes at her friend, then took her hand. "Are you going to show me to my room or what?"

"Yeah, come on." Abby was familiar enough with the house to know exactly where Becca's room was. Up the stairs, down the hallway, third door on the right. When they entered the room, she heard Becca's sharp intake of breath. Everything in there was so bright and warm from the sun shining through the french doors that led out onto a private little balcony. The room was decorated in beachy greens and yellows, and much like the rest of the house (or the rest of the Kerrigan's real estate holdings, Abby admitted), it looked like something out of a catalog. One of the housekeepers had even laid a couple of mints on Becca's pillow.

Becca let her bag drop to the floor and she plopped on the bed, her legs flipping up in the air as Abby laughed. She rolled over onto her stomach and brushed a few curls off of her forehead as she propped her head up in her hands and grinned at Abby. "I'm going to love you being rich. I mean, I love *you*, rich or not. But I'm going to love the part where you're rich, because I get to stay in places like this for free."

Abby sat down next to her, smoothing down her skirt. "I'm not rich though. Cole is."

Becca flung her legs over the side of the bed and gave Abby the side-eye. It was an expression that Abby had grown to love the longer she knew her friend. It was Becca's way of letting you know she thought you were being ridiculous without subjecting you to some harsh words of tough love, as she liked to call it.

"You know once you say 'I do' tomorrow, he's going to pretty much sign everything away to you, right? That man is so deep in love he doesn't even realize how deep he is."

Abby had to laugh. Becca always had a way of making even the most serious subjects lighthearted. "You realize that even if he wanted to do something that stupid there would be a team of lawyers about a mile long just waiting to stop him, right? Besides, I don't even want it, I just-"

"If you say you just want to be married to him, I might vomit all over this designer toile," Becca said, the affection in her voice completely voiding the threat she just made. "So, who else is coming?"

"Just Cole's friend Tristan."

"Tristan Blackwell?" Becca said, sounding surprised even though Abby knew that she knew he was coming.

"Yes, that's the one." Abby had been trying to get the two of them in a room for the past few months, but Becca always avoided it. Given Becca's love of the tabloids, she had to be familiar with Cole's best friend. In fact, Abby was pretty sure his reputation was what was keeping Becca from wanting to meet him in the first place. Becca sighed, running a hand through her hair. "The Tristan Blackwell you keep trying to set me up with? Tristan Blackwell who has three girls on his arm on a *bad* night? That Tristan Blackwell?"

"I'm not trying to set you up with him. I just thought you'd like him. Platonically. You'd be good for him, I think."

"Riiiiiight," Becca said with a huff. "You just happened to think I'd be good for him right after I broke up with Roger."

Abby cringed at the bitterness in Becca's voice. Smiling, she mimicked the sign of the cross. "Don't say that name in here," she teased. "Anyway, Tristan is a person I think you'll like independently of the R-word."

"I've seen him in the tabs, Abby. That's doubtful. He seems like a shit."

"You've met Cole," Abby reminded her. "And he's pretty much the exact opposite of the kind of person the tabloids painted him as, isn't he? I mean, we're getting married tomorrow, who would've ever thought that would happen? Besides, Tristan's your type."

"Tall, blonde and built like a god is pretty much

everyone's type, Abby. Don't try to pull that on me."

"He's just a little lost. He could use someone like you in his life."

"Someone like me?" Becca replied, her left brow lifting in a skeptical arch.

Abby shrugged. "The kind of person who delivers the things you need to hear in a way that doesn't make it hurt so badly to hear it. I'm probably biased, but I think everyone could use someone like you. Or you, you know...whichever."

Becca's expression softened, and she let out a little sigh as she lightly bumped Abby's shoulder. "Just get married to your perfect man and leave the matchmaking out of it, okay?"

Abby nodded reluctantly, but decided to save her argument for another day. Maybe once Becca met Tristan she wouldn't have anything left to argue. "Okay."

"Promise?" Becca asked.

"I promise."

CHAPTER
Four

*C*ole was willing to admit that when Abby told him that she wanted a small wedding, he hadn't realized exactly how small she was talking. Not that he ever thought about his wedding all that much before he met her, but when and if the thought had ever crossed his mind, he assumed it would be held in the ballroom of some grand hotel, or at his parents' estate in New York. It would be announced in the *New York Times* and would be the kind of boring affair that he had attended countless times throughout his privileged existence.

Before he met Abby, Cole used to think that the idea of marriage just didn't appeal to him, and to some extent that might've been true; but the more he thought about it the more he realized that the promise of a big, public wedding was not something he'd looked forward to either. It wasn't until he was sitting on the deck of the pool behind the beach house with his brother Scott, his father, and his best friend that he realized that the small, private gathering Abby wanted was exactly what he wanted, too.

All four of them had beers in hand while the setting sun burned the sky a deep, rich orange, and the smell of charcoal from the grill wafted through the air. Scott held the grill tongs in his left hand, squeezing them together in strange intervals, like he was tapping out some kind of code.

Tristan was looking out at the surf, wearing that ever-present shit-eating grin of his. Cole and Tristan had met early in life, in the way that the children of most rich people meet: at prep school. They'd become fast friends, and Tristan had been a fixture in Cole's life ever since. They'd been in their fair share of tabloids together, cementing both of their playboy images. It wasn't something Cole was very proud of at this point in his life, but he wanted Tristan with him as he made the commitment that would take him to the next stage in his life, and part of him hoped—however futile that hope was—that Tristan would soon follow.

"You know," Scott said between sharp, metallic plinks, "I never did understand the point of having a pool when you're literally fifty feet from the ocean."

Tristan took a pull from his beer, then set it down on the arm of his chair. "There are some things you just can't do in salt water, my friend."

Cole grinned as his father rolled his eyes and let out a long-suffering sigh. "You're not allowed in my pool again."

They all laughed in unison as Cole leaned forward,

resting his elbows on his knees. "Aren't you all supposed to be giving me marriage advice, not arguing the finer points of saltwater vs. Chlorine?" Even though Cole wasn't sure he wanted marriage advice from his emotionally distant father, his marriage had lasted for over thirty years, so Cole figured his father had to be doing *something* right. Cole knew that some of Olivia and Jack's friends were on their third, fourth, *fifth* marriages. There had to be a reason his parents were still going strong after all this time.

"I'm gonna go ahead and bow out of this," Tristan said, grinning as he leaned back in his chair. "I'm the very last person who should be giving anyone relationship advice."

"Very true," Cole replied, clinking the neck of his bottle against Tristan's.

Cole thought maybe his father would speak up, but he didn't. Instead, surprisingly, it was his brother.

"Just keep her happy," Scott said, shrugging, like that was the most obvious answer in the world. "If she does whatever she can to keep you happy and you do the same, and you compromise over the things you're both unhappy about, then what else is there?"

Cole pondered that for a moment. Wasn't that what he had been doing? Putting Abby's happiness and well-being before his own? He already planned on doing exactly that for the rest of his life. It was then that he began to realize that he might not need as much advice as he thought he did.

It was then that Jack's phone rang, the shrill ringtone cutting through the calming crash of the surf behind them. Jack looked at the screen, then stood. "Sorry, I have to take this." He pressed a button and brought the phone to his ear, then did something he'd been doing for quite a long time. He walked away from his family.

Whenever the familiar bitterness Cole felt towards Jack welled up in his chest, Cole always did his best to tamp it down. It seemed wrong to be angry with his father for putting his business first, when that business had provided Cole and his brother with the kind of lives and privilege that other people could only dream of. He and Scott had never wanted for anything, except for a father.

As if his brother knew exactly what he was thinking, Scott stood, and hung the tongs on the side of the grill. "Another piece of advice," he said, tipping his beer in the direction their father had just walked off in. "Don't do that, okay? Don't let frivolous, material shit take you away from the things that really matter in life. Spend time with Abby, with your kids. Don't let anything else in life dictate how much time you spend with them." He walked over to where Cole was sitting, and patted him on the shoulder.

"Where are you going?" Tristan said, an exaggerated note of panic in his voice. "Those steaks I bought for dinner are things that really matter in life, and they need to spend some time on that grill, grill master."

The corners of Scott's mouth quirked up into a half smile. "I'll be back to show you how the master does it, Blackwell. First I'm going to go see my wife and daughter."

Tristan let out a small laugh as he nodded.

Cole sighed, realizing that if he needed someone to look up to as he entered this new phase in his life, it should be his brother. After all, Scott's always been the first person Cole turned to when he needed advice. Hell, he was the one who told him to get his shit together where Abby was concerned. Cole had only ever thought about his future family in abstract terms; he'd have a wife, a few kids. Then, when he started to think about the future, he saw Abby beside him. Lately he'd been able to picture their children; small and smart and beautiful. All Abby, and the good parts of him, too. And for the first time in Cole's life, that dream didn't seem too far off.

"Cold feet?" Tristan asked, clearly teasing him. That was kind of their thing. Only this time Cole wasn't in the mood to be teased; not about Abby, not about spending the rest of his life with her.

"I'm just thinking."

"That's never good."

Cole offered his friend a withering look. Just as he was about to open his mouth to say something he would most likely regret, Becca walked onto the patio. "Hey," she said, looking at Cole before her eyes drifted over to Tristan for a moment. "Your future wife is surrounded by scrapbooks and just fell down a Cole Kerrigan baby photo rabbit hole. You better pull her out now or kiss your wedding goodbye. She's on the verge of becoming a weepy mess, and I think only you can save her."

Cole heard Tristan snort as he stood. "Becca," Cole said, holding a hand out to Abby's friend, "this is Tristan Blackwell. We've been friends since...what was it, fourth grade?"

Tristan looked wounded. "Third."

"Tristan, this is Abby's best friend, Becca."

Tristan stood and reached for her hand. "Nice to meet you, Becca."

Becca smiled. "You too."

"Excuse me," Cole said as he stepped down off of the patio and walked towards the house. "You should tell her about that time you slipped a laxative into Mrs. Praeger's tea. She'd like that."

"A laxative?" he heard Becca say as he stepped into the house. "Do tell."

Cole leaned against the doorframe to Abby's room, watching her as she stared out the window at the surf breaking along the beach. She was curled up on the window seat, a blanket flung over her legs, the woven grey cotton spilling over onto the floor. She had one of his old scrapbooks in her hands, clutched tightly against her chest. Several others were next to her, in a neat stack on the floor. She was lost in thought, something she did quite often. She had such a brilliant mind, and sometimes everything caught up with her at once. This seemed to be one of those times.

Cole knew Abby well enough to understand that she needed her space when she got like this, but it was the sun glinting on her face, revealing the tears in her eyes that finally drew him to her. He walked very purposefully, not wanting to startle her. She probably already realized that he was in the room, but he wanted to be careful just in case. She turned to him as he approached, offering him a sad smile as he sat down. He reached over and slid his hand down her calf, just wanting some kind of contact with her, needing to touch her, hoping he could pull her from her thoughts.

Gently slipping his fingers around Abby's ankle and situating her leg across his lap, Cole began kneading the ball of Abby's foot, hoping that would relax her into telling him what was bothering her.

"We're getting married tomorrow," he said, very softly. "How can you possibly be sad? Are you having second thoughts?" He had difficulty speaking the last part of that sentence even when he was teasing her, but he made himself smile at her anyway.

She looked over at him, her eyes still swimming in unshed tears. "Yeah," she replied, her voice a little thick from crying. "I was just sitting here thinking, 'Abby, you've found this wonderful, thoughtful, loving man. What are you thinking actually *marrying* him?'"

"You forgot handsome," he said with a wink.

Abby reached over and slid her fingers between his. God, Cole loved the warmth of her. The softness. He thought about it sometimes when he was at work, missing her. Let his thoughts linger on the lushness of her skin, the way her hair smelled. The way her hand felt when it was wrapped around his.

"Handsome," she replied, tapping her chin. "How could I possibly forget handsome?"

"And rich."

"So rich," she teased, moving closer. She snaked her hand

along the ridge of his collarbone until her fingertips found the hair at the nape of his neck. Her fingers glided through it, tugging a little, and Cole closed his eyes, trying to commit this feeling to memory. "Look at me Cole." Abby's voice was so gentle that he probably would've done anything she asked of him just then.

Cole opened his eyes as she cupped his cheek, and he leaned into her touch.

"You know how much I love you, right?" she asked.

He wrapped his fingers around her wrist and brought the palm of her hand to his lips, placing a kiss there. "Of course I do. Now tell me why you're upset so I can fix it."

She sighed. "There's nothing to fix."

"Try me."

She took a deep breath. "You know how I feel about your family, don't you?" she asked, gripping his hand. "And I don't want to hurt you, okay? I really don't want that, but before we get married, I…I have to say this."

Cole swallowed against the lump in his throat, even though he was pretty sure he knew exactly where this was going.

"I hadn't seen any of these before," Abby said, opening the scrapbook in her hands to a page somewhere in the middle. "Your mom wanted me to pick out a few, for some kind of collage or something she wants to give us, I don't know."

Cole turned his head to get a better look. The page was full of pictures from Cole's freshman year in high school, when the soccer team for the prep school he'd attended won the state championship. He was in a ton of the pictures, laughing, smiling, lifting the trophy over his head. His parents were nowhere to be found that day; they had stayed at their penthouse in the city if he was remembering correctly, having committed themselves to attending a fundraiser that evening. Not that he thought they would've attended even if they hadn't had something else to do. His nanny, the woman who had practically raised him, the woman who wasn't biologically his mother but had mothered him in every conceivable way, was the one who had taken these pictures. She'd taken nearly all of the pictures in every one of these scrapbooks.

Abby didn't wait for Cole to respond before she continued. "All these pictures, Cole. All of them are of you and Scott and your nannies. Or of you and your friends. Your parents aren't in any of these. Not at your soccer games, your football games. They aren't in a single one of them."

Cole could hear the hitch in her voice; he knew she was upset. He was sad for her, for her realization that this was the way he'd grown up. He'd had a blessed childhood in every way but one: the people who brought him into this world weren't ever around to see it. Growing up, that was just the way Cole thought things were. As a matter of fact, it was more rare to see a parent show up to these games; it was always the hired help who did the dirty work, who raised the little ones until they were ready to go out into the world alone.

Abby closed the scrapbook and put it aside, then took both of Cole's hands between hers. "I know we've only ever talked about having kids in an abstract way, never really got into the nuts and bolts of how to make that work. Cole-"

"I know what you're worried about," he said softly, soothingly. He didn't want her to waste one second of her life worrying about something that was never, ever going to happen. "We are not going to be those kinds of parents, Abby."

She gave him a sad, resigned smile. "People don't set out to be like this, Cole. They have the best intentions, you know? They don't have children thinking that someone else is going to raise them. They don't plan to be at fundraisers and charity events while someone else watches their children grow up."

"Abby," Cole said with a soft sigh. He'd thought about having a family with her more times than he could count, but he'd never felt the *want* rise up like this before. Everything was so close now, he could practically reach out and take it. In a year or two, this hypothetical family they were talking about raising could be real. "Our children are not going to be raised by nannies." He looked deep into her eyes and squeezed her hand so she'd know how serious he was about this. "After knowing how it feels to look up into the stands and not see the two faces you were looking for, do you think there's a single thing that could keep me from a recital? From a soccer game?"

Abby laughed, her eyes shining with tears. "With my store, and the company...Cole, we'll have to make some sacrifices."

Cole shrugged, like it was the easiest thing in the world. "So we'll make them." He could see them now, little brown-haired girls with his eyes and Abby's smile, giggling in the back seat of the car as he drove them to the beach to spend the weekend playing in the sand. He couldn't help the smile that spread across his face.

Abby smiled back. "I don't just want kids, Cole," she said, pulling him to her. "I want a family. Promise me that's what we'll have."

Cole leaned in and pressed a soft kiss to her lips as he threaded his fingers through her hair and held her close. "I promise."

CHAPTER
Five

*J*ust before dinner, when the kitchen staff was setting places at the picnic table on the back deck, Becca followed Abby inside the house to the guest bathroom right off the foyer.

"You better?" Becca asked as Abby washed her hands, working the soapy lather into giant bubbles. It was the first chance they'd had to talk about Abby's little crying jag earlier while she was looking at the Kerrigan family scrapbooks; the one that sent Becca out looking for Cole and sending him to her room.

"I'm better," Abby said, nodding as she dried her hands on the pristine white towel that hung from the towel rack. "It was just a minor freakout."

Becca sighed, then pulled Abby in for a hug. "I love you, so I mean this in the best possible way, okay? But are you dense?"

Abby couldn't help herself, she had to laugh. "What do you mean?"

Becca took Abby's hand in hers and walked her through the house, coming to a stop at the giant bay window in the sitting room that overlooked the beach. Scott was standing not too far from the house, holding his daughter in his arms. Cole was right behind them, making funny faces at Alex. She was squealing laughing, so loud that Abby could hear it through the window, and she got this far-off look in her eyes, imagining him making their own children laugh like that someday. Three shrieks of laughter later, Scott was handing Alex over to Cole, and she immediately began pawing at Cole's face, tiny hands all over his cheeks as he playfully nipped at her fingers.

"Look at him holding that baby, Abs," Becca said, smiling. "Do you think there's a single thing in this world that could ever keep a man like that away from his own children? There isn't a business meeting or a fundraiser that would stop him from being there for them."

"I know," Abby said quietly. "I just-"

"You don't see how much he's changed, do you?"

Utterly confused, Abby's brows scrunched together.

Becca rolled her eyes, a little exasperated. "The way he looks at you, Abby. Hell, even the way he talks. He used to be so goddamned uptight, don't you remember? He used to stand all stiff and like, recite words like he was reading them off of a teleprompter." Becca straightened her posture and schooled her features into a stone-faced mask. "Abby," Becca said, her voice all formal and tight as she imitated Cole. "I assure you that if I did cause offense, that was certainly not my intention. I'd like to offer you my utmost apologies."

"He didn't sound like that," Abby said, laughing, even though she knew that he…yeah, he did sound like that sometimes.

"Yes he did and you know it. Now he's just all light and stuff, and that's because of you, okay? So if you're worried about the kind of life you're going to have with him or if you think he's going to somehow shirk his responsibilities once you two have a family, then you don't know him like I think you do. And that would mean that I don't know you like I think I do, because the you I know would never marry a man who would do that."

Abby smiled through the tears in her eyes, because Becca was right, just like usual. "I just needed to hear him say it, you know?"

Becca grinned at her best friend and tucked her under her arm. "Yeah," she sighed. "I know."

"Well?" Scott asked, looking at Tristan with wide eyes, waiting for Tristan's review of his grilling techniques.

"It's not the best I've ever had," he said, tapping his fingers along the arm of the deck chair he was sitting in. "But it's close." Tristan leaned back into his chair, the light from the fire in the pit to the left of them casting long shadows over his face. Becca wasted no time rolling her eyes at him, a sight which made Abby smile.

"Have you ever even cooked a steak?" she asked, kind of teasing, kind of not. "Or cooked anything for that matter? Like, do you even know what a microwave is?"

Tristan smiled a huge, genuine smile. "You mean those big shiny boxes with doors and numbered buttons on them? You can cook *food* in those?"

"I saw him make popcorn once," Cole said, as Abby settled back against his chest, relishing in the warmth of him. They were sharing a chair, and Abby was perched on Cole's thigh, his arm wrapped around her shoulder as he held her tight. "It was one of those foil things, I think? It…did not end well."

"Didn't end well how?" Becca asked, leaning forward, resting her elbows on her knees. "Was there bloodshed? Tears? Mass destruction?"

"All of the above," Scott said, laughing.

Sara joined in, cradling a sleepy Alex to her chest. "It was at the apartment we were sharing in college. Cole and Tristan came to the city from New Haven for a quick visit during mid-terms. They were drunk and hungry and too damn lazy to turn on the stove," she said, glaring at Tristan. "Held the popcorn thingy right into the fireplace, which made it catch on fire, popping out little fiery kernels onto the carpet, which set off the fire alarms and the sprinklers."

Tristan and Cole gave each other a conspiratorial glance, both trying so hard not to laugh. Sara swatted at Tristan. "You destroyed my favorite Picasso!"

Abby looked over at Becca, who mouthed 'Picasso?' with wide eyes. Becca clearly wasn't used to being around people that had so much money they just name-dropped artists like Picasso in casual conversation. Truthfully, Abby wasn't sure if she'd ever get used to it either.

"I said I was sorry. I replaced it!" Tristan yelled through laughter.

"This is why all of our property is insured to the hilt," Olivia said, glancing over at the house. Abby's eyes followed hers, and she could make out Cole's father standing in the kitchen, phone pressed to his ear. It seemed to be a constant fixture there these days.

Just then, Alex stirred in Sara's arms, starting to get fussy.

"I'll take her," Cole said with a smile.

Sara stood and bounced her daughter on her hip as she walked over to where Cole and Abby were sitting. "You want to see your Uncle Cole?"

The second Sara laid her daughter on Cole's chest, she stopped crying.

"My son, the baby whisperer," Olivia said, almost reverently. "I wish I had someone like you around when you were a baby." She reached for her wine glass, and brought it to her lips.

Cole's hand was rubbing soothing circle's on baby Alex's back, his eyes meeting Abby's, as if he wanted to offer her some kind of reaffirmation that he was serious about what he'd said to her earlier. If she'd had any doubt that he was sincere then, that doubt would've been long gone in this moment; the way he was looking at her made a warmth spread out all the way to her toes. She reached over and pushed a strand of hair off of Alex's forehead, then cupped Cole's cheek and gently pressed her lips against his.

"So," Sara said, watching Cole and Abby with her daughter. "Where are the two of you going on your honeymoon?"

Abby exhaled, feeling a familiar frustrating knot coil in her stomach. It always seemed to reappear whenever this subject was brought up. "I don't know," she admitted, trying to sound like that fact didn't irritate her as much as it did. "Cole won't tell me."

"Why does that not surprise me," Olivia replied, laughing.

"What exactly are you trying to imply, Mother?" Cole asked, feigning offense.

"I'm implying that you, my dear, come from a long line of Kerrigan men who like to surprise their women."

"Scott did the same thing to me," Sara said, smiling at her husband before giving him a peck on the cheek.

"He was going to take you to Iowa," Tristan said to Sara. "I talked him out of it; you're welcome. I did the same thing for you, by the way," he said, winking at Abby. She couldn't help but laugh at him.

"Where did you wind up going?" Becca asked.

"Venice." Sara looked over at Scott, grinning at him as he gently squeezed her knee. "We had a private villa right on the water. There was this wraparound balcony; it was beautiful."

Cole leaned in until his lips brushed against the shell of Abby's ear, making her shiver. "We're not going to Venice," he whispered. She could feel his smile, which made her smile too.

"I know," Abby replied. Even though she didn't know where they were going, she did know that wherever it was? She wasn't going to be disappointed.

CHAPTER
Six

*C*ole was up late, way past the time when everyone had retired to their rooms for the evening. He'd spent the past hour tossing and turning, not the least bit tired and completely unable to will his body to calm down the the point where he would be able to get even a little bit of sleep. He felt wound-up, on edge in a way that he knew would result in a restless night. His heart was pounding, heavy with anticipation. Resigned to the fact that he'd probably be up for the rest of the night, Cole threw the covers off the bed and swung his feet around until they were resting on the floor.

He figured that making sure he had everything in order for tomorrow might quell his nerves a bit, so he stood and walked over to his closet and pulled out his slacks, checking to make sure it was wrinkle-free and presentable. He opened the lid to his laptop, going through email after email to make sure that he'd made all the reservations he'd needed to for their trip to Paris. Cole smiled when he thought of Abby stepping out of their limo and looking up in wonder at the Eiffel Tower. He pictured the look of delight he'd see on her face when they shared a fresh-baked baguette while they walked along the Champs-Élysées. He wondered how she'd react when he told her that he'd called in a few favors and had arranged for her to spend the afternoon working with a world-renowned French chocolatier.

He wanted to give her the world, but he'd start with Paris.

After he had checked the flight plan and made sure that his plane would be ready for takeoff late Sunday morning, he turned to his dresser and picked up the small white box that sat atop it, a gift—made special for sentimental reasons only—which he planned on somehow giving to her before the ceremony tomorrow.

After double-checking and triple-checking every single thing, Cole was still restless, sitting on the edge of his bed, the balls of his feet tapping impatiently against the cool hardwood floor. He knew why he couldn't sleep, and there was most likely nothing he could do to ease the ache tonight.

He couldn't sleep without Abby at this point. After having her beside him in bed for so long, he struggled. Even on business trips he had to steal one of her pillowcases so he could have something that smelled like her nearby. When he'd told her that, she smiled; she thought it was cute. There wasn't anything cute about it in his opinion. It was simply necessary.

He wanted Abby. He couldn't sleep without her, couldn't

function without her.

They'd only said goodnight to each other an hour ago, and he'd kissed her then, like it was the most important thing he could do tonight, like it was the most important thing he'd ever do. But it wasn't enough.

It wasn't quite midnight yet, he still had a few minutes.

So, tradition be damned. Cole walked out into the hallway and opened the door to Abby's room.

Then he stepped inside.

CHAPTER
Seven

*A*bby couldn't sleep.

She was a bundle of nerves tonight, and the one person who could calm her down was the one person she wasn't supposed to see until morning, when he was standing at the latticework altar next to a judge and with a ring in his pocket, waiting to marry her. She'd checked and rechecked her bags, making sure she had everything Cole told her she'd need for their trip, even though she had no idea where exactly it was they were going. She carefully put out her makeup on the vanity table in the far corner of the room, spacing out her brushes meticulously.

A few minutes ago she'd walked the hallway, stopping at Cole's door before thinking better of knocking on it. If she went in there, she wouldn't want to leave, and they'd both promised his mother that even though they were having a small, untraditional wedding, they'd stick to one tradition and not see each other after midnight. She didn't want to break the first promise she'd ever made to Olivia Kerrigan. No good could come of it.

So, she'd gone to Becca's door instead, knocking and knocking to no answer. Thinking that she was probably somewhere with Tristan put a smile on her face, but it didn't ease her jumbled-up nerves.

She missed Cole terribly, which was ridiculous considering she'd seen him an hour ago and he was only a few doors down. She'd see him again in the morning, and every morning thereafter for the rest of their lives. What was a few hours without him? It should be nothing, but right now it felt like everything. She wanted to laugh at herself; just this afternoon she'd promised Becca that she and Cole wouldn't become one of those married couples who couldn't stand to be separated for even the smallest amount of time. They weren't even married yet and already it seemed like they were one of those couples.

It was strange, this anxiety Abby felt with Cole not being there beside her. She should be a little used to it by now. They spent plenty of time apart these days, what with both of their businesses thriving, but tonight seemed different, since everyone in this house came here specifically to watch her and Cole pledge to spend the rest of their lives together. It felt odd that they were in separate rooms.

Abby got up to splash her face and maybe wash her hands, hoping that the warm water might soothe her frazzled nerves. She stood at the sink and turned on the faucet, running her fingers under the water, waiting for it to heat up. Seconds later, Cole stepped into the bathroom. Abby wasn't even surprised to see him there, somewhere deep inside, she'd even hoped he'd come.

"I couldn't sleep," he said, taking a step forward, until he was standing behind her.

When Abby looked up, she could see his reflection next to hers in the mirror. She offered him a soft smile, one that let him know that she understood exactly what he was going through. It always seemed that whatever one of them felt, the other felt too.

Cole placed his hands on her hips, pulling her close to him, then he placed a soft kiss on her shoulder. He slid his lips across the nape of her neck, then moved on to the other shoulder, making goosebumps break out across her skin.

"I missed you," she said, feeling him smile.

He slid his knees between her legs, letting her know that he wanted her to open up to him. She was pretty grateful at that moment that she was wearing nothing but a pair of undies and a short pink camisole. His hand slipped below the silk, cupping her breast as his thumb slipped across her nipple.

"It's almost midnight," Abby whispered, even though at this point she really didn't care what time it was. All she could focus on was his hands on her skin and how much she wanted to be with him like this, always. "You're not supposed to see me before the wedding."

Cole grinned wickedly, sending shivers down Abby's spine. She knew that look; in fact, she did whatever she could to make him wear that look as often as possible. "Do you have any idea what I can do to you in ten minutes?"

Abby slid her fingers down Cole's forearm, which was draped across her chest as his hand continued to work her nipple, and glanced at his watch.

"Eight minutes," she breathed.

"Even better."

"Being quick at this is never a good thing."

Cole inhaled through his nose, a sure sign that he was accepting that challenge. "Never say never," he said, his lips brushing the shell of Abby's ear. He gently pulled her earlobe through his teeth before he spoke again. "Speed occasionally has its benefits."

He pinched her nipple, knowing just how to get her going, and she arched into him, grinding her ass against him, feeling his hardness pressed and throbbing against her back. His other hand snaked its way down her belly and across her hip, sliding beneath the delicate lace of her panties until he was cupping her. Cole's fingers slid and teased, slipping against the wetness between her legs, flicking and rubbing, knowing all the spots that drove her crazy.

Abby reached back and fumbled with the waistband of Cole's boxers—the angle was absolutely terrible for what she was trying to accomplish—just wanting, no, *needing* to touch him. He tutted at her, shaking his head as he took her hand and pressed it against the cool marble vanity, twining their fingers together so that she couldn't (and wouldn't) move again. She sighed, because he was always doing this, always denying himself to focus on her. It drove her crazy in more ways than one.

Cole's fingers were still working, still teasing her clit, driving her higher and higher. Her breaths were ragged and she was ready to fall apart, practically begging for it. Cole withdrew his hand and pushed down his boxers just as Abby was getting ready to come. She started to protest but she didn't have to wait long, because soon she felt the tip of his cock lined up against her, right where she wanted him the most, and she tried to push herself back into him, just needing him inside her already. She hated waiting, and he always seemed to want to make her do just that.

Cole pushed her hair over her right shoulder, his chin coming to rest in the crook of her neck. She loved the feel of his stubble against her delicate skin, and his mouth was *right there*. She could feel every breath he took, and every exhale made her entire body buzz.

"Look at me," he said, and she met his gaze in the mirror. She couldn't take her eyes off of him, the way his soft, pink lips pressed against her ear, the way his hand possessively splayed across her breast. She could hardly breathe for wanting him so badly. Apparently, he had the same idea.

"Do you have any idea how much I want you?" Cole whispered, a low rumble right in her ear.

If the hardness he'd settled between Abby's legs was any indication, then yes, she had a pretty good idea. She nodded, letting the corner of her lip quirk up into a half-smile, and he laughed, a rumble she could feel against her shoulder blades.

"Just the *thought* of a night without you sent me in here with the need to touch you. I can't bear not being with you."

"You don't have to bear it," she said, reaching back and threading her fingers through the soft hair at the crown of his head. "I'm always with you."

Cole held her tight, completely flush against him. "Promise me," he asked, his voice like honey over rough sand and soft, so soft.

She brought their twined fingers up to her mouth, then pressed a kiss to his thumb. "I promise."

With those two little words, he pushed inside of her, making her gasp.

The sex was frantic and hurried, more about lust and desire and need than intimacy and tenderness. They were both chasing release, satisfied by the simple act of being close, as close as two people could possibly be. They took pleasure where and while they could, Abby's hands braced against the vanity, palms splayed to give her some leverage as she tried desperately to keep herself upright. Cole kept pounding into her, building this growing current inside her as he pressed one hand low across her belly, thrusting toward it, reaching this place that she didn't even know existed. But Cole found it; he always seemed to find the places that made her feel so, so good.

Stars danced behind Abby's eyelids and she had to focus on her breathing as she felt her climax overtake her in quick, tight waves, making her squeeze against him. Cole rubbed her clit, fucking her through her orgasm, trying to prolong it, nearly making Abby's knees give out. She knew he was close so she spread her legs a little wider, gripping his forearms which were wrapped around her waist, clinging to her like she was a life raft on the open sea. His tendons constricted beneath her palms—he was trying so hard to stay in control—but soon Abby bucked back against him, knowing he wouldn't be able to withstand the sudden change in movement. It was then that he finally let go, head sagging, forehead against her neck, sighing her name as he spilled into her.

When they had both come down and their breathing had steadied, Cole turned Abby and held her close, kissing her with a reverence that she found difficult to reconcile with the way he'd just fucked her, all needy and possessive, right here against the counter. She looked positively debauched: hair tousled, camisole all rumpled from where Cole had gripped it between his fingers. The sight of her must've done something to him, because he kissed her again, long and slow and deep, his tongue gliding against hers as he held her so tight. It was a kiss that was the direct opposite of what they'd just done. This kiss was slow, unhurried. Perfect.

When Cole pulled away from Abby, he nuzzled the crook of her neck, sliding her hair between his fingers. "I'll see you in the morning," he whispered.

"I'll be the one in the white dress."

"White, huh?" he teased.

Abby laughed, gently swatting Cole's ass as he walked away from her.

He closed her bedroom door right as the grandfather clock in the hallway struck midnight.

Abby stood in front of the mirror in the bathroom the next morning, looking at her reflection. Her minimal makeup was set and ready to go as Becca stood behind her, twining her hair around the barrel of a scalding-hot curling iron.

"Never thought I'd be attempting to do beach waves while I was at an actual beach, which is stupid, I admit."

Abby laughed, looking down at her pale pink nails and the gorgeous engagement ring on her finger. Today Cole would slip another ring on that finger. Today she'd *marry* him; she still couldn't believe it. Tomorrow she'd be jetting off to some unknown destination, the first day of her new life that probably wouldn't be all that different from her old one, apart from the fact that she'd be starting it with a new last name.

Abby *Kerrigan.*

She looked down at the counter and smiled, a light blush creeping up her cheeks.

"I don't even want to know what happened in here last night that keeps making you look like that," Becca said, peering over Abby's shoulder as she curled another strand of hair.

"Oh, like you're one to talk. I went looking for you last night and you were nowhere to be found." Abby shot her friend a skeptical look.

"I didn't have sex with him, if that's what you think."

"I don't think anything," Abby replied, grinning. "But I told you that you'd like him."

Becca shrugged in that familiar way of hers that let Abby know that she didn't want to tell her that she was right.

"All done," Becca sighed, patting Abby on the shoulder.

Abby walked out of the bathroom and into her bedroom, towel wrapped around her body as she looked in the full-length mirror. Her hair was long and wavy, makeup light, lips pink and glossy. She felt understated and comfortable and *beautiful*. Unfussy. She looked and felt exactly the way she wanted to on this day.

"I should put on my dress," she said, turning to look at Becca.

Becca walked over to the closet and pulled the dress off of its hanger. It was a light, airy thing, so lovely. Abby found it while she was looking through a vintage shop in the city. It was made of silk cotton and embroidered lace. It was kind of flouncy and flowing, reaching just below her knees, with a mother of pearl waist that made such a simple dress look so elegant.

Becca helped Abby slip it over her head, careful to avoid flattening her hair. Once she had it on, Abby stepped back and looked in the mirror.

"You're so gorgeous," Becca said, her voice barely a whisper. There were tears in her eyes, and Abby found it difficult to fight the ones that were welling up in her own. She was marrying Cole; she had absolutely nothing to be sad about. The thing is, she was trying so desperately to avoid thinking about how she'd give anything to have the one person who was missing here with her.

Her mother.

Becca, of course, knew exactly what she was thinking. "She would've loved this, you know. This whole thing," she said, sliding her fingers along the pearls that lined Abby's waist. "This is exactly what she would've wanted for you; everything she didn't have. She would've loved Cole."

Abby pressed her lips together for a moment before she could speak again. "I know."

"Speaking of Cole," Becca said, walking over to the dresser. "He asked me to give you something. In retrospect, it probably would've been smart for me to have done it before you put your makeup on. He wanted to give it to you himself, but I didn't trust him not to push the door open to get a look at you. I know how you two are; you can't keep your hands off each other. So I told him I'd do it so I didn't have to break his fingers if he tried something."

Abby laughed, butterflies fluttering in her stomach. "Okay."

Becca handed her a small white box. Underneath it was a picture, and Abby gasped when she saw it. It was one of the few she had of her and her mother, all worn around the edges from years of holding it tight. The sight of this picture always made her sad, but not today. Today, she was nothing but happy. It felt nice to look at this picture with a new set of eyes, under different circumstances, on the best day. The two of them stood in the middle of the kitchen of the apartment they lived in when Abby was six. They were laughing, bright pink frosting smeared all over their faces. They had been making strawberry cupcakes; her mother's special recipe.

Hands shaking, Abby opened the box.

Inside was a strawberry cupcake, just like the ones her mother used to make.

"He made a whole batch of them last night," Becca said, unable to hide the note of affection in her voice. "He wanted to give you a whole box of them, but he's picky, you know? This is the only one that turned out perfectly. He was real fussy about the shape; spent fifteen minutes frosting the damn thing. He wanted it to be just right."

Abby took a deep breath and smiled, wondering exactly how she'd gotten to be so lucky. To find a man like Cole, to have him treat her like a queen. She'd only told him about these cupcakes once, in passing, when he'd asked her about the picture. It was a two minute memory that she shared with him, and somehow he knew this would be the right moment to bring it to light again.

Abby saw a little white paper peeking out from beneath the cupcake. Gently, she pulled it out.

Written on fancy white card stock in Cole's handwriting was a simple, "I love you."

There were no platitudes, no 'I'm sorry's, no 'I know how much you want her here.' Just three simple words, the most perfect thing he could've written on that card. He loved her, and that was enough to get her through anything.

"You couldn't have found a more wonderful man," Becca said.

Abby swallowed the lump in her throat, and smiled through her tears. She couldn't wait to tie herself to Cole forever. It had always seemed like such a long time, but when she thinks about it in terms of her future with him, it seems like the blink of an eye; not nearly long enough.

"I know," Abby replied.

No one could love her more than Cole, no one could love her better. No one could make her happier. Those were the most calming thoughts you could have about a person before you committed yourself to them for the rest of your life.

Becca picked up a compact and touched up Abby's powder, then gave her a watery smile as she offered her a hand, then pulled her up off the bed.

"Come on," she said, leading Abby to the door. "Let's go get you married."

CHAPTER
Eight

*C*ole stood on the porch looking out at the ocean, letting the calming sea air wash over him. He was more anxious than nervous, just wanting to get this part of the day over with so he could slip his ring on Abby's finger and start the rest of his life with her by his side. He knew that was a fairly ridiculous way to look at things; this was his *wedding* after all. But the thing is, he had already committed himself to her in every single way that mattered to him, all he needed to do now was make it legal. As the gaggle of lawyers kept on retainer could tell you, Cole never had any patience for making things legal, and he certainly never saw the romance in it.

The romantic thing was when he'd proposed to her, when she'd said yes. When he'd purchased a home for them to build their life together in. In his mind, the romantic part of this day would come much later, when he and his bride were far away from the prying eyes of his beloved friends and family.

He just wanted to see Abby, wanted to touch her, wanted to kiss her. He looked down at his watch, counting down the minutes until he'd see her walking out onto the porch, making her way toward him. He sighed, wishing the minute hand of his watch would move a little faster. Five minutes. Five minutes until he'd see her. In twenty she'd be his wife. His *wife*. Just thinking the word made a carefree, unbridled smile bloom across his face. He knew he probably looked like an idiot, but he didn't care; he'd be an idiot for Abby, hell…he probably always had been.

"Now that's the smile of a man in love," Judge Michaels said as he fiddled with the button on the cuff of his shirt. Once he was situated, he reached out and wrapped his large, calloused hand around Cole's, giving him a firm handshake.

"Judge," Cole said with a smile. "Thank you for coming."

"Thank you for asking me," he replied. "You know, there was a time in your life when I never would've seen this day coming."

Cole winced a bit at that admission. Judge Michaels was an old friend of his father's, and he'd managed to get Cole out of a few scrapes when he was younger. Back then he'd often find himself in front of the judge for legal proceedings that were entirely different from the one he was presiding over today. It was never anything too major, just public intoxication and a few other misdemeanors, but those incidents were parts of his life before Abby that he didn't really like thinking of, even though he was still a teenager when they happened. They reeked of misspent youth and a certain kind of indignity that he didn't like associated with thoughts of her.

"You and me both, sir," Cole admitted with a smile.

"Judge, excuse me," Scott said, nodding at the older man. Scott patted his brother on the back and ushered him off to the side, just to the right of the small altar. "You all right?" The corner of Scott's mouth quirked up a bit as he asked the question.

"Just anxious," Cole said, rubbing his hands together. He wanted to feel the weight of Abby's ring on his finger. "I just want to be married to her already."

Scott laughed. "Believe me, I understand the feeling. And just so you know, I took Dad's cell phone. Told him he could have it back at the end of the night."

Cole laughed. "Thanks."

"Hey," Tristan said, approaching the brothers and wrapping Cole in a tight hug. "Scott's going to vouch for me on this one; I didn't decorate your car with condoms like I said I would."

"Car's condom-free," Scott affirmed.

"Scott?" Sara said, calling him over to her. Before he turned away, he gave Cole a smile. "Guess I'll see you on the other side."

"I'm proud of you, man," Tristan said. "Who would've thought?"

"You know, you're the second person today who's said that. Who knows how many have thought it," Cole said, pinching the bridge of his nose.

Tristan grinned. "It's a good thing. You know, you and I didn't really have the best examples growing up, we really didn't have anyone to show us how to make a relationship work. I can't seem to do it, that's for sure. But you met Abby, and she changed you. She changed you in ways I don't even think you can see."

Cole nodded, knowing his friend was right. He knew for sure that Abby had loosened him up, taught him to enjoy life in a way he hadn't been able to—or hadn't let himself be able to—before. It was one of the countless things he owed her for. And he was going to make sure he spent the rest of his life showing her just how grateful he was for everything she'd done for him.

"I know she did."

Tristan looked at Cole for a moment, silence blanketing between them before Tristan finally spoke. "Let's get together more often when you come back, okay?"

"I'll make sure Abby invites Becca," Cole replied, grinning.

"It's not Becca," Tristan said quickly, seeming to want to say more before he thought better of it. "Well, it's not *just* Becca."

"Okay."

"Tristan, honey," Olivia said, her voice dripping with cheer. "Go take your seat, we're about to start."

Tristan shook Cole's hand. "Good luck," he said, and Cole wasn't sure if he was wishing him luck for the ceremony or wishing him luck for the talk he was about to have with his mother.

Olivia reached up and straightened his tie, and if Cole

didn't know any better he could've sworn that he saw tears in her eyes. His mother was someone who simply did not get emotional.

"She looks beautiful," Olivia said as she reached out and straightened Cole's tie. "And you look so handsome. You're both going to be so happy together. So very happy."

Cole took Olivia's hands in his, then leaned down and kissed her cheek. "Thanks, Mother."

Olivia began to walk away, turning around only to say one more thing. "Oh, Scott took your father's phone, just so you know."

Cole laughed. He looked over at Jack, who was already seated. His father had offered him a quick hug a few minutes before he stepped outside, but that was pretty much it; he just took his seat and waited for the proceedings to begin.

And begin they did.

Everyone was seated, and Cole stood next to the judge. And then Abby was standing in the doorway leading out to the patio, wearing a gauzy dress that made her look like an angel. The flash of color from the flowers she held made her seem more vibrant than ever. And when Cole looked at her, his heart thundered in his chest. He always thought he'd be overwhelmingly nervous in this moment, but he wasn't, not at all. He just wanted her next to him.

When his eyes met hers, she smiled that smile that was brighter than sunshine, and there was no music, no grand entrance. She just walked over to him and handed her bouquet to Becca, then took his hands in hers.

It was like they were the only two people in the world.

Just the way it should be.

CHAPTER
Nine

The very second Abby saw Cole standing at the altar, all she wanted to do was kiss him and tell him just how much she loved him. She didn't even see the adoring eyes of her family; both the family she'd made in Becca and the family she was marrying into. Her gaze was locked on Cole's, and she couldn't stop smiling. When she finally reached him—a trip of only a few steps that seemed like miles—she wrapped her arms around his neck and pressed her lips to his. If he was surprised by it, he didn't let it show. In fact, he almost seemed to be expecting it.

When they parted, Abby cupped his face with her hand, her eyes searching his.

"Thank you," she whispered, and his forehead fell to hers. He understood everything she wasn't saying in that moment: Thank you for the cupcake. Thank you for including my mother. Thank you for being in my life. Thank you for loving me.

The judge cleared his throat, and everyone laughed. "Maybe we should wait for that until after the ceremony," he said. But all that did was make her want to do it again.

"Well get on with it then," Cole said before he snuck one more kiss.

Cole held Abby's hands and gazed at her lovingly as he promised to love her forever, 'til death do they part, and Abby, she did the same. They slid rings onto each other's fingers and finally, finally they were husband and wife. And nothing in Abby's life had ever felt as right as that moment did, when Cole cupped her face in his hands and kissed her lips, all soft and sweet, sealing the promises that they'd made to each other that morning.

Of course Abby would always remember what Cole was wearing (tan pants with a white shirt and blue tie that matched the flowers she carried), and she'd remember what they ate for dinner that night (filet mignon with roasted asparagus and fingerling potatoes), but she'd remember the little things, too. Like the way he looked at her when she was laughing, or how he kept his hand on her thigh during dinner because he just had to touch her, or the way he took her hand and led her away from the table while everyone was still eating just so he could dance with her while no music was playing. She'd remember their walk down to the pier, and how they just sat together in the quiet as they dangled their feet over the edge. She'd remember the way Becca kissed her cheek as she wished her well, and the way Olivia and Jack welcomed her to the family while she and Cole were standing in the driveway, right before he led her to the car.

"Where are we going?" Abby asked, once Cole was in the car beside her. He grinned, a sly thing, and clasped her hand in his. He leaned down and pressed a kiss against her ring before he started the engine.

They pulled out onto the long, winding road that ran alongside the shoreline, seeing nothing but hazy purples and oranges in the sky as the sun slowly sunk down below the horizon.

"Cole," Abby laughed. "Where are we going?"

"It's a surprise," he said.

CHAPTER
Ten

*A*ttempting to be at least a little inconspicuous as he watched Abby from the driver's seat, Cole carefully tried to gauge her reaction as they drove down the secluded road in the residential area on the far side of town, about fifteen minutes away from his parents' home. If she had any idea at all where they were headed, she didn't let on. She just closed her eyes and let the wind from the open window blow through her hair.

It wasn't until Cole turned down the long, nondescript driveway that Abby's breathing picked up. He tried unsuccessfully to hide his smile as the gravel crackled under the tires and the house came into view. She recognized exactly where they were now; she gripped the armrest and pushed herself up in the seat, as if somehow that would bring her closer, make it easier for her to see. He pressed on the accelerator just a tad, feeling the excitement build as he got ready to give her the biggest present he'd ever given her.

"Cole," she said, her voice shaking. She looked over at him with wide eyes, her cute, perfect little mouth shaped into an 'o.' Honestly, this was the exact reaction he was hoping for when he first started planning this night a few weeks ago. When they'd left his parents' house, she thought they were headed to the airport, ready to hop on the plane. But tonight? He had something much, much better planned.

He pulled the car into the circular driveway, coming to a stop right in front of the steps that led up to the wraparound porch, and Abby seemed like she just couldn't believe her eyes. She'd been looking at this house in the real estate section of the Times for months now, and he'd found links to the realtor's site in the browser history on their computer. It had been all he could do to keep this from her in the weeks since he'd purchased it. He'd seen the disappointment on her face when it disappeared from the listing sites, but he didn't say a word.

It was a beautiful piece of real estate, he had to admit. His wife had excellent taste. It was somewhat similar to the house that belonged to his parents: classic and large, very New England. White siding and black shutters. Three stories and more windows than they could probably ever open. Beautiful beach views, and room to stretch out. He would've married her here, but giving her this at the same time they were trying to plan a wedding would probably have been too much of a shock to her system.

"Stay here," Cole said as he climbed out of the car, quickly walking around to her side and opening the door. He took her hand and helped her out, completely unable to take his eyes off the expression on her face.

"What did you do?" she whispered, even though he knew that she was smart enough to realize exactly what it was he had done.

Cole could feel Abby trembling as he took her hand, and right then he just wanted to kiss her. So he slid the pad of his thumb along her bottom lip and pressed his lips to hers in a kiss that was soft and slow and warm, everything he wanted this night to be.

He led her up the porch steps and opened the door, then quickly lifted her up, laughing at the surprised shriek that escaped her lips, and carried her over the threshold.

"Welcome to your new home, Mrs. Kerrigan," Cole said, smiling at the sound of his name. Her name. *Their* name, he supposed. Abby just stood there next to him and took it all in. The freshly painted walls, the cavernous ceilings, the pristine wood floors. Everything in this house was a blank canvas that she could cover with all the different shades of her. "Come here, let me show you my favorite part." He pulled her towards the back of the house, where there were bay windows and French doors everywhere and a wraparound porch, complete with the swing she said she wanted.

They stood there, looking out at the ocean; a small stretch of beach that belonged just to them.

"Why did you do this?" Abby asked. There wasn't any censure in her tone, just genuine curiosity. Cole imagined that it must've been difficult for her to accept things like this, given the way she grew up. That was one of the many reasons he wanted to shower her with everything he possibly could, why he wanted to offer her every single good thing in life.

Cole looked into Abby's clear, deep eyes and smiled. "I did it because we lead busy, hectic lives and it's nice to get out of the city on weekends. We need room to move, fresh air to breathe. I did it because we need a place that's far away from work and other obligations. I did it because I have good memories of the beach house when I was I kid. So many great things happened there, and I want our children to have the same kinds of memories that I do. I want them to have a place where they can bring their friends," he said as he reached over and brushed a tendril of hair behind her ear. "A place where they can get married, when they're ready."

Abby wrapped her fingers around his tie, pulling him down to her until their lips crashed together. "I love you," she whispered against his lips, over and over, and he could taste the salt of her tears. He knew she wasn't just thanking him for the house, she was thanking him for the memories that they would make in it.

Abby's kisses were desperate, and something in them reminded him of the night before, in her bathroom, when all he could think about was touching her, kissing her, being inside her. Cole slid his hands around Abby's waist and they came down, cupping her ass as he lifted her up. She wrapped her legs around his waist and he carried her up the steps, carefully taking them one at a time, because Abby was licking and nipping at the skin on his neck and he didn't trust his knees. Luckily their bedroom was at the top of the stairs, and it was a straight shot right down the hallway. Their bedroom was the only room he'd put any furniture in. Just a bed, a nightstand and a lamp. Enough for tonight.

Abby seemed surprised when Cole laid her on the bed, like she hadn't realized it was there. Her back arched up, her hair fanning out across the crisp white sheets. God, she was so beautiful. Cole leaned down over her, and she pawed at his tie, desperately slipping the knot down and pulling the silk over his head, tossing it to the side. She'd changed out of her wedding dress and into another dress, one he just slipped right over her shoulders and threw onto the floor. Cole righted himself, working the buttons of his shirt, and Abby reached for the clasp of her bra, a pretty, lacy little thing.

"Leave it on," Cole said, his voice so raspy that he almost didn't recognize it.

He could see her swallow, bare lust in her eyes, and she pressed her palms against his chest. There wasn't enough power there to move him, but he stood, because he would always, always do whatever it was that she wanted. She stood along with him, pushing up onto her tiptoes to unbutton the rest of his shirt, gently pushing it off of his shoulders and into a puddle on the floor. She pressed into him, his erection straining against her belly.

"Abby," he whispered, a bit of a warning, a bit of a prayer. She kissed her way across his chest, tongue licking a trail over his abs and around his nipples. He buried his hands in her hair, just wanting to touch her.

Abby unbuttoned and unzipped Cole's pants, pushing them down along with his boxers, leaving them in a messy pile right next to his shirt. She gripped his cock, making him hiss, making his fingers twist in her hair. Gripping his hips beneath her fingers, pressing into his skin, she pushed him back onto the bed.

In seconds Abby was on her knees before Cole, fitting herself between his legs. Her fingernails traced lazy patterns up the insides of his calves, around the swell of his thighs, across the planes of his hips, drawing goosebumps from his skin. She leaned forward, anchoring herself on the bed with her hands splayed on either side of him, then licked a stripe from the base of his cock to the tip, making him groan as she swirled her perfect tongue across the moisture that beaded along the slit.

"Please," Cole gasped. "Please."

Abby gave him a wicked grin, but she wasn't a cruel woman, so she slowly, so *slowly* sucked his cock into her mouth, until he was surrounded by her. He leaned back on his elbows, almost helpless from the pleasure of it all. Her tongue swirled as her hand pumped up and down in tandem with her hot, tight mouth. She worked some kind of pattern—he couldn't figure out exactly what it was—but he'd hit the back of her throat, then she'd tease him a little more, never repeating the same motion twice. He wanted nothing more but to watch her, because he loved the way she looked at him like this, loved the sight of her perfect pink lips wrapped around him. But it was all too much; all the love he felt for her and the physical pleasure of the act just swirled together into a wave of emotion that made it impossible for Cole to keep his eyes open. So he closed his eyes and listened to the waves breaking on the sand as his wife gave him the most satisfying, intense blow job of his life.

Abby kept Cole going for a while, bringing him right to the brink with a hum or a lick, then backing off and giving him a chance to build back up to it again. But he wanted to be inside her when he came, so when he thought he just couldn't take it anymore, he gently tugged on her hair, pulling her back enough so that her lips were on offer for the taking. He kissed her, long and deep, as he pulled her up and onto his lap.

Abby wrapped her arms around him, pressing her breasts to his chest, rubbing against him so that the warmth between her thighs and the friction from her lace panties against the underside of his cock was all he could think about. All he wanted in this world was to taste her, so he reached down between them and hooked his thumbs on the lacy waistband, and ripped them clean off. Abby reached over to turn on the lamp, leaving her breasts on offer, and Cole took that chance to nip at her breasts through her bra.

"I want to watch," Abby said as she flipped the lamp switch, but she sighed when the bulb popped on and then promptly fizzled out.

Cole flipped her over onto her back and crawled up onto the bed. He lifted her left leg towards his shoulder, kissing his way across her ankle.

"I don't need the light. Do you think there's a single inch of you that I don't know by taste?" he said, licking a path down the inside of her thigh, drawing a soft gasp from her lips. "By touch?" He slid his thumb down the length of her slit, circling around her clit until she was writhing against him. Not wanting to give her what she needed just yet, Cole leaned over her, relishing in the scrape of her nails against his scalp and the way her fingers tugged at his hair. He pulled one cup of her bra down, taking her left breast into his mouth, biting and then laving over the sting with his tongue. He sucked at her nipple, making her squirm before moving on to the other one. He kissed across her chest and lower, circling her belly button with his tongue.

"Please," Abby said, gasping. That seemed to be the word of the night, and Cole didn't have the heart to refuse her. So he laved her with the flat of his tongue, making her cry out as he slipped two fingers inside of her, twisting them up in that way that made her toes curl. He worked her clit, tongue circling, sucking, driving her crazy until her breathing was so, so fast. He loved seeing her like this; wet from him and completely at his mercy. With a quick flick of his tongue she was falling apart and he licked her through it, trying to prolong the pleasure. He wanted her to feel good tonight. He always wanted her to feel so *good*.

Cole leaned over Abby, threading their fingers together and holding their hands above her head. He kissed her, long and slow and a little unfocused, because he could barely think about her mouth when he could feel the slick wetness where he was lined up between her legs.

"I need you, can you just…" Abby breathed, unable to complete the thought. She pushed herself up on the balls of her feet, trying to get some friction.

"Yeah," Cole said, voice tight. "I want…*fuck*." When

Abby brought herself down, the head of his cock slipped inside her, and he buried his head in the crook of her neck as she moved further down, pulling him all the way in. It was almost too much for him, being surrounded by her, looking into her eyes when they were together like this. She looked at him like he was her whole world, and she was his. She was definitely his.

Cole moved slowly, rocking into her, wanting so badly to melt against her, just mold her to his body so that a part of her would always be with him. He needed more, more… more of her, more of his skin against her skin. They weren't touching nearly enough; just the thought of a single inch of her skin not touching his was…abhorrent to him. Cole could feel his orgasm blossoming deep, all the way down in his spine, starting to make him feel weak, and he didn't trust his arms to hold him up any longer.

Cole slid his arm around the small of Abby's back and pulled them both up so that she was resting all of her weight on him as he kneeled, weight resting on his calves. The momentum offered Abby leverage to move, and she took it.

"Hold onto me," Cole said, reaching for her arms and gently slipping them over his shoulders. "Tight, okay? I just want to feel you everywhere."

She did as he asked, pressing every available inch of her body against him, leaving marks on his skin with her fingernails. She used their position to her advantage, pushing herself up while she rocked against him, desperately chasing pleasure. They were together in every way, breathing in the same rhythm, foreheads pressed together. Their noses brushed, their breaths mingled. They weren't kissing, but their lips touched as they just breathed and moved and held onto each other for dear life.

When Abby's orgasm hit her, she squeezed around Cole, muscles fluttering until he couldn't take it anymore and he pulled her to him, trapping her in his arms to the point where she could hardly move save for short, quick strokes of her hips that were just enough to push him over the edge, crying out her name, grasping for anything he could hold onto as he came inside of her.

They stayed like that for a long while, clinging to each other, together and happy and touching. Everywhere.

Exhausted, they eventually fell back onto the bed. Cole stretched out, pulling Abby to him to spoon her. They tangled their legs together and he held her close, wrapping his hand around hers, clasping their fingers together until their wedding rings were pressed into each others' skin.

They laid like that together, quiet, until Cole pushed Abby's hair off of her neck so that he could plant kisses there. Kisses led to soft sighs, which led to soft words, which led to soft touches, over and over again throughout the night. After all, they didn't really need the sleep.

Tomorrow, they'd have Paris.

Tonight? They had each other, and the promise of the rest of their lives.

About the Author

Cassie Cross is a Maryland native and a romantic at heart, who lives outside of Baltimore with her two dogs and a closet full of shoes. Cassie's fondness for swoon-worthy men and strong women are the inspiration for most of her stories, and when she's not busy writing a book, you'll probably find her eating takeout and indulging in her love of 80's sitcoms.

Cassie loves hearing from her readers, so please follow her on Twitter (@ CrossWrites) or leave a review for this book on the site you purchased it from. Thank you!

17407652R00200

Printed in Poland
by Amazon Fulfillment
Poland Sp. z o.o., Wrocław